P9-DNN-355

BY DEBORAH ELLIS

FICTION

LOOKING FOR X

THE BREADWINNER

PARVANA'S JOURNEY

MUD CITY

THE BREADWINNER TRILOGY

A COMPANY OF FOOLS

THE HEAVEN SHOP

I AM A TAXI

SACRED LEAF

JACKAL IN THE GARDEN:
AN ENCOUNTER WITH BIHZAD

JAKEMAN

BIFOCAL (CO-WRITTEN WITH ERIC WALTERS)

LUNCH WITH LENIN AND OTHER STORIES

NO SAFE PLACE

TRUE BLUE

NO ORDINARY DAY

MY NAME IS PARVANA

NONFICTION

THREE WISHES: ISRAELI AND
PALESTINIAN CHILDREN SPEAK

OUR STORIES, OUR SONGS:
AFRICAN CHILDREN TALK ABOUT AIDS

OFF TO WAR: VOICES OF SOLDIERS' CHILDREN

CHILDREN OF WAR: VOICES OF IRAQI REFUGEES

KIDS OF KABUL: LIVING BRAVELY THROUGH
A NEVER-ENDING WAR

LOOKS LIKE DAYLIGHT: VOICES OF INDIGENOUS KIDS

THE BREADWINNER TRILOGY

THE BREADWINNER
PARVANA'S JOURNEY
MUD CITY

THE BREADWINNER TRILOGY

DEBORAH ELLIS

GROUNDWOOD BOOKS
HOUSE OF ANANSI PRESS
TORONTO   BERKELEY

(*The Breadwinner* first published in 2000; *Parvana's Journey*, 2002;
Mud City, 2003)
Published in Canada and the USA in 2009 by Groundwood Books
Sixth printing 2014

Groundwood Books / House of Anansi Press
110 Spadina Avenue, Suite 801 Toronto, Ontario M5V 2K4
or c/o Publishers Group West
1700 Fourth Street, Berkeley, CA 94710

We acknowledge for their financial support of our publishing program the Canada Council for the Arts, the Government of Canada through the Canada Book Fund (CBF) and the Ontario Arts Council.

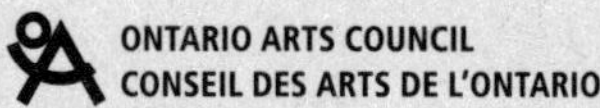

Library and Archives Canada Cataloguing in Publication
Ellis, Deborah
The breadwinner trilogy / Deborah Ellis.
Contents: The breadwinner – Parvana's journey – Mud city.
ISBN 978-0-88899-959-7
1. Girls–Afghanistan–Juvenile fiction. 2. Women–Afghanistan–Juvenile fiction.
I. Title. II. Title: The breadwinner. III. Title: Parvana's journey.
IV. Title: Mud city.
PS8559.L5494B74 2009 jC813'.54 C2009-902745-3

Cover photo by Laurent Rappa
Cover design by Alysia Shewchuk
Text design by Michael Solomon
Printed and bound in Canada

MIX
Paper from
responsible sources
FSC® C004071

FOREWORD

Dear Readers:

I am thrilled at the release of this new edition of the Breadwinner trilogy. It brings back memories of all the women and children I met in the refugee camps in Pakistan – their courage, their pain, and their hopes for a better future.

A decade has passed since the first book came out. During this time, new wars have started, old ones have continued, and refugee camps have emptied out, only to fill up again somewhere else. The Afghan people cannot be blamed for their situation. Outsiders bear an enormous responsibility for all of this.

And ten years from now?

Thank you to all who have shared their stories with me. Thank you to all who have opened one of my books and looked inside. And thank you most of all to those who continue to survive, against all odds, and who remind us that we are capable of better decisions.

Deborah Ellis
2009

AFGHANISTAN

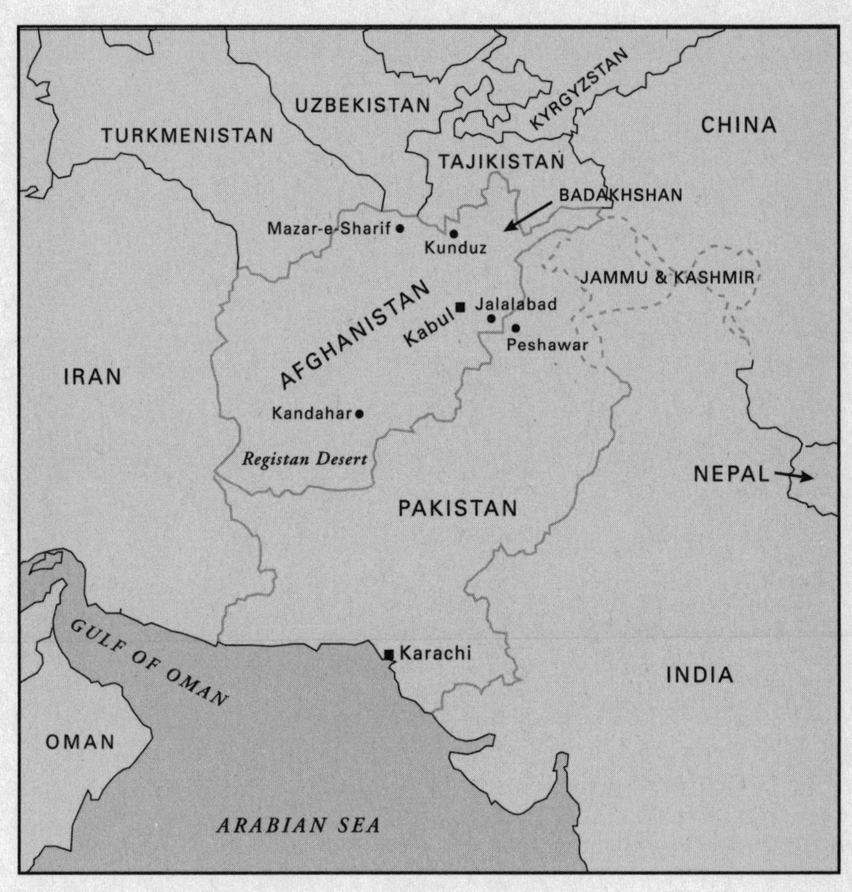

UZBEKISTAN
KYRGYZSTAN
CHINA
TURKMENISTAN
TAJIKISTAN
BADAKHSHAN
Mazar-e-Sharif
Kunduz
JAMMU & KASHMIR
AFGHANISTAN
Jalalabad
Kabul
Peshawar
IRAN
Kandahar
Registan Desert
NEPAL
PAKISTAN
GULF OF OMAN
Karachi
INDIA
OMAN
ARABIAN SEA

THE BREADWINNER

To the children of war

ONE

"I can read that letter as well as Father can," Parvana whispered into the folds of her chador. "Well, almost."

She didn't dare say those words out loud. The man sitting beside her father would not want to hear her voice. Nor would anyone else in the Kabul market. Parvana was there only to help her father walk to the market and back home again after work. She sat well back on the blanket, her head and most of her face covered by her chador.

She wasn't really supposed to be outside at all. The Taliban had ordered all the girls and women in Afghanistan to stay inside their homes. They even forbade girls to go to school. Parvana had had to leave her sixth grade class, and her sister Nooria was not allowed to go to her high school. Their mother had been kicked out of her job as a writer for a Kabul radio station. For more than a year now, they had all been stuck inside one room, along with five-year-old Maryam and two-year-old Ali.

Parvana did get out for a few hours most days to

help her father walk. She was always glad to go outside, even though it meant sitting for hours on a blanket spread over the hard ground of the marketplace. At least it was something to do. She had even got used to holding her tongue and hiding her face.

She was small for her eleven years. As a small girl, she could usually get away with being outside without being questioned.

"I need this girl to help me walk," her father would tell any Talib who asked, pointing to his leg. He had lost the lower part of his leg when the high school he was teaching in was bombed. His insides had been hurt somehow, too. He was often tired.

"I have no son at home, except for an infant," he would explain. Parvana would slump down further on the blanket and try to make herself look smaller. She was afraid to look up at the soldiers. She had seen what they did, especially to women, the way they would whip and beat someone they thought should be punished.

Sitting in the marketplace day after day, she had seen a lot. When the Taliban were around, what she wanted most of all was to be invisible.

Now the customer asked her father to read his letter again. "Read it slowly, so that I can remember it for my family."

Parvana would have liked to get a letter. Mail delivery had recently started again in Afghanistan, after years of being disrupted by war. Many of her friends had fled the country with their families. She thought they were in Pakistan, but she wasn't sure, so she couldn't write to them. Her own family had moved so often because of the bombing that her friends no longer knew where she was. "Afghans cover the earth like stars cover the sky," her father often said.

Her father finished reading the man's letter a second time. The customer thanked him and paid. "I will look for you when it is time to write a reply."

Most people in Afghanistan could not read or write. Parvana was one of the lucky ones. Both of her parents had been to university, and they believed in education for everyone, even girls.

Customers came and went as the afternoon wore on. Most spoke Dari, the same language Parvana spoke best. When a customer spoke Pashtu, she could recognize most of it, but not all. Her parents could speak English, too. Her father had gone to university in England. That was a long time ago.

The market was a very busy place. Men shopped for their families, and peddlers hawked their goods and services. Some, like the tea shop, had their own stalls. With such a big urn and so many trays of cups, it had to stay in one place. Tea boys ran back and forth into the labyrinth of the marketplace, carrying tea to customers who couldn't leave their own shops, then running back again with the empty cups.

"I could do that," Parvana whispered. She'd like

to be able to run around in the market, to know its winding streets as well as she knew the four walls of her home.

Her father turned to look at her. “I'd rather see you running around a school yard.” He turned around again to call out to the passing men. “Anything written! Anything read! Pashtu and Dari! Wonderful items for sale!”

Parvana frowned. It wasn't her fault she wasn't in school! She would rather be there, too, instead of sitting on this uncomfortable blanket, her back and bottom getting sore. She missed her friends, her blue-and-white school uniform, and doing new things each day.

History was her favorite subject, especially Afghan history. Everybody had come to Afghanistan. The Persians came four thousand years ago. Alexander the Great came, too, followed by the Greeks, Arabs, Turks, British, and finally the Soviets. One of the conquerors, Tamerlane from Samarkand, cut off the heads of his enemies and stacked them in huge piles, like melons at a fruit stand. All these people had come to Parvana's beautiful country to try to take it over, and the Afghans had kicked them all out again!

But now the country was ruled by the Taliban militia. They were Afghans, and they had very definite ideas about how things should be run. When they first took over the capital city of Kabul and forbade girls to go to school, Parvana wasn't terribly unhappy. She had a test coming up in arithmetic that she hadn't prepared for, and she was in trouble for talking in class again. The teacher was going to send a note to her mother, but the Taliban took over first.

"What are you crying for?" she had asked Nooria, who couldn't stop sobbing. "I think a holiday is very nice." Parvana was sure the Taliban would let them go back to school in a few days. By then her teacher would have forgotten all about sending a tattletale note to her mother.

"You're just stupid!" Nooria screamed at her. "Leave me alone!"

One of the difficulties of living with your whole family in one room was that it was impossible to really leave anyone alone. Wherever Nooria went, there was Parvana. And wherever Parvana went, there was Nooria.

Both of Parvana's parents had come from old respected Afghan families. With their education, they had earned high salaries. They had had a big house with a courtyard, a couple of servants, a television set, a refrigerator, a car. Nooria had had her own room. Parvana had shared a room with her little sister, Maryam. Maryam chattered a lot, but she thought Parvana was wonderful. It had certainly been wonderful to get away from Nooria sometimes.

That house had been destroyed by a bomb. The family had moved several times since then. Each time, they moved to a smaller place. Every time their house was bombed, they lost more of their things. With each bomb, they got poorer. Now they lived together in one small room.

There had been a war going on in Afghanistan for more than twenty years, twice as long as Parvana had been alive.

At first it was the Soviets who rolled their big tanks into the country and flew war planes that dropped bombs on villages and the countryside.

Parvana was born one month before the Soviets started going back to their own country.

"You were such an ugly baby, the Soviets couldn't stand to be in the same country with you," Nooria was fond of telling her. "They fled back across the border in horror, as fast as their tanks could carry them."

After the Soviets left, the people who had been shooting at the Soviets decided they wanted to keep shooting at something, so they shot at each other. Many bombs fell on Kabul during that time. Many people died.

Bombs had been part of Parvana's whole life. Every day, every night, rockets would fall out of the sky, and someone's house would explode.

When the bombs fell, people ran. First they ran one way, then they ran another, trying to find a place ruins, and it was hard for her to imagine it another way. It hurt her to hear stories of old Kabul before the bombing. She didn't want to think about everything the bombs had taken away, including her father's health and their beautiful home. It made her angry, and since she could do nothing with her anger, it made her sad.

They left the busy part of the market and turned down a side street to their building. Parvana carefully guided her father around the pot holes and broken places in the road.

"How do women in burqas manage to walk along these streets?" Parvana asked her father. "How do they see where they are going?"

"They fall down a lot," her father replied. He was right. Parvana had seen them fall.

She looked at her favorite mountain. It rose up majestically at the end of her street.

"What's the name of that mountain?" she had asked her father soon after they moved to their new neighborhood.

"That's Mount Parvana."

"It is not," Nooria had said scornfully.

"You shouldn't lie to the child," Mother had said. The whole family had been out walking together, in the time before the Taliban. Mother and Nooria just wore light scarves around their hair. Their faces soaked up the Kabul sunshine.

"Mountains are named by people," Father said.

"I am a person, and I name that mountain Mount Parvana."

Her mother gave in, laughing. Father laughed, too, and Parvana and baby Maryam, who didn't even know why she was laughing. Even grumpy Nooria joined in. The sound of the family's laughter scampered up Mount Parvana and back down into the street.

Now Parvana and her father slowly made their way up the steps of their building. They lived on the third floor of an apartment building. It had been hit in a rocket attack, and half of it was rubble.

The stairs were on the outside of the building, zigzagging back and forth on their way up. They had been damaged by the bomb, and didn't quite meet in places. Only some parts of the staircase had a railing. "Never rely on the railing," Father told Parvana over and over. Going up was easier for Father than going down, but it still took a long time.

Finally they reached the door of their home and went inside.

TWO

Mother and Nooria were cleaning again. Father kissed Ali and Maryam, went to the bathroom to wash the dust off his feet, face and hands, then stretched out on a toshak for a rest.

Parvana put down her bundles and started to take off her chador.

"We need water," Nooria said.

"Can't I sit down for awhile first?" Parvana asked her mother.

"You will rest better when your work is done. Now go. The water tank is almost empty."

Parvana groaned. If the tank was almost empty, she'd have to make five trips to the water tap. Six, because her mother hated to see an empty water bucket.

"If you had fetched it yesterday, when Mother asked you, you wouldn't have so much to haul today," Nooria said as Parvana passed by her to get to the water bucket. Nooria smiled her superior big-sister smile and flipped her hair back over her shoulders. Parvana wanted to kick her.

Nooria had beautiful hair, long and thick. Parvana's hair was thin and stringy. She wanted hair like her sister's, and Nooria knew this.

Parvana grumbled all the way down the steps and down the block to the neighborhood tap. The trip home, with a full bucket, was worse, especially the three flights of stairs. Being angry at Nooria gave her the energy to do it, so Parvana kept grumbling.

"Nooria never goes for water, nor does Mother. Maryam doesn't, either. She doesn't have to do anything!"

Parvana knew she was mumbling nonsense, but she kept it up anyway. Maryam was only five, and she couldn't carry an empty bucket downstairs, let alone a full bucket upstairs. Mother and Nooria had to wear burqas whenever they went outside, and they couldn't carry a pail of water up those uneven broken stairs if they were wearing burqas. Plus, it was dangerous for women to go outside without a man.

Parvana knew she had to fetch the water because there was nobody else in the family who could do it. Sometimes this made her resentful. Sometimes it made her proud. One thing she knew—it didn't matter how she felt. Good mood or bad, the water had to be fetched, and she had to fetch it.

Finally the tank was full, the water bucket was full, and Parvana could slip off her sandals, hang up her chador and relax. She sat on the floor beside Maryam and watched her little sister draw a picture.

"You're very talented, Maryam. One day you will sell your drawings for tons and tons of money. We will be very rich and live in a palace, and you will wear blue silk dresses."

"Green silk," Maryam said.

"Green silk," Parvana agreed.

"Instead of just sitting there, you could help us over here." Mother and Nooria were cleaning out the cupboard again.

"You cleaned out the cupboard three days ago!"

"Are you going to help us or not?"

Not, Parvana thought, but she got to her feet. Mother and Nooria were always cleaning something. Since they couldn't work or go to school, they didn't have much else to do. "The Taliban have said we must stay inside, but that doesn't mean we have to live in filth," Mother was fond of saying.

Parvana hated all that cleaning. It used up the water she had to haul. The only thing worse was for Nooria to wash her hair.

Parvana looked around their tiny room. All of the furniture she remembered from their other houses had been destroyed by bombs or stolen by looters. All they had now was a tall wooden cupboard, which had been in the room when they rented it. It held the few belongings they had been able to save. Two toshaks were set against the walls, and that was all the furniture they had. They used to have beautiful Afghan carpets. Parvana remembered tracing the intricate patterns of them with her fingers when she was younger. Now there was just cheap matting over the cement floor.

Parvana could cross their main room with ten regular steps one way and twelve regular steps the other way. It was usually her job to sweep the mat with their tiny whisk broom. She knew every inch of it.

At the end of the room was the lavatory. It was a very small room with a platform toilet – not the modern Western toilet they used to have! The little propane cookstove was kept in there because a tiny vent, high in the wall, kept fresh air coming into the room. The water tank was there, too – a metal drum that held five pails of water – and the wash basin was next to that.

Other people lived in the part of the building that was still standing. Parvana saw them as she went to fetch water or went out with her father to the marketplace. "We must keep our distance," Father told her. "The Taliban encourage neighbor to spy on neighbor. It is safer to keep to ourselves."

It may have been safer, Parvana often thought, but it was also lonely. Maybe there was another girl her age, right close by, but she'd never find out. Father had his books, Maryam played with Ali, Nooria had Mother, but Parvana didn't have anybody.

Mother and Nooria had wiped down the cupboard shelves. Now they were putting things back.

"Here is a pile of things for your father to sell in the market. Put them by the door," Mother directed her.

The vibrant red cloth caught Parvana's eye. "My good shalwar kameez! We can't sell that!"

"I decide what we're going to sell, not you. There's no longer any use for it, unless you're planning to go to parties you haven't bothered to tell me about."

Parvana knew there was no point arguing. Ever since she had been forced out of her job, Mother's temper grew shorter every day.

Parvana put the outfit with the other items by the door. She ran her fingers over the intricate embroidery. It had been an Eid present from her aunt in Mazar-e-Sharif, a city in the north of Afghanistan. She hoped her aunt would be angry at her mother for selling it.

"Why don't we sell Nooria's good clothes? She's not going anywhere."

"She'll need them when she gets married."

Nooria made a superior sort of face at Parvana. As an extra insult, she tossed her head to make her long hair swing.

"I pity whoever marries you," Parvana said. "He will be getting a stuck-up snob for a wife."

"That's enough," Mother said.

Parvana fumed. Mother always took Nooria's side. Parvana hated Nooria, and she'd hate her mother, too, if she wasn't her mother.

Her anger melted when she saw her mother pick up the parcel of Hossain's clothes and put it away on the top shelf of the cupboard. Her mother always looked sad when she touched Hossain's clothes.

Nooria hadn't always been the oldest. Hossain had been the oldest child. He had been killed by a land mine when he was fourteen years old. Mother and Father never talked about him. To remember him was too painful. Nooria had told Parvana about him during one of the rare times they were talking to each other.

Hossain had laughed a lot, and was always trying to get Nooria to play games with him, even though she was a girl. "Don't be such a princess," he'd say. "A little football will do you good!" Sometimes, Nooria said, she'd give in and play, and Hossain would always kick the ball to her in a way that she could stop it and kick it back.

"He used to pick you up and play with you a lot," Nooria told Parvana. "He actually seemed to like you. Imagine that!"

From Nooria's stories, Hossain sounded like someone Parvana would have liked, too.

Seeing the pain in her mother's face, Parvana put her anger away and quietly helped get supper ready.

The family ate Afghan-style, sitting around a plastic cloth spread out on the floor. Food cheered everyone up, and the family lingered after the meal was over.

At some point, Parvana knew, a secret signal would pass between her mother and Nooria, and the two of them would rise at the same instant to begin clearing up. Parvana had no idea how they did it. She would watch for a sign to go between the two of them, but she could never see one.

Ali was dozing on Mother's lap, a piece of nan in his little fist. Every now and then he would realize he was falling asleep and would rouse himself, as if he hated the thought of missing something. He'd try to get up, but Mother held him quite firmly. After wiggling for a moment, he'd give up and doze off again.

Father, looking rested after his nap, had changed into his good white shalwar kameez. His long beard was neatly combed. Parvana thought he looked very handsome.

When the Taliban first came and ordered all men to grow beards, Parvana had a hard time getting used to her father's face. He had never worn a beard before. Father had a hard time getting used to it, too. It itched a lot at first.

Now he was telling stories from history. He had been a history teacher before his school was bombed. Parvana had grown up with his stories, which made her a very good student in history class.

"It was 1880, and the British were trying to take over our country. Did we want the British to take over?" he asked Maryam.

"No!" Maryam answered.

"We certainly did not. Everybody comes to Afghanistan to try to take over, but we Afghans kick them all out. We are the most welcoming, hospitable people on earth. A guest to us is a king. You girls remember that. When a guest comes to your house, he must have the best of everything."

"Or she," Parvana said.

Father grinned at her. "Or she. We Afghans do everything we can to make our guest comfortable. But if someone comes into our home or our country and acts like our enemy, then we will defend our home."

"Father, get on with the story," Parvana urged. She had heard it before, many times, but she wanted to hear it again.

Father grinned again. "We must teach this child some patience," he said to Mother. Parvana didn't need to look at her mother to know she was probably thinking they needed to teach her a whole lot more than that.

"All right," he relented. "On with the story. It was 1880. In the dust around the city of Kandahar, the Afghans were fighting the British. It was a terrible battle. Many were dead. The British were winning, and the Afghans were ready to give up. Their spirits were low, they had no strength to keep fighting. Surrender and capture were starting to look good to them. At least they could rest and maybe save their lives.

"Suddenly a tiny girl, younger than Nooria, burst out from one of the village houses. She ran to the front of the battle and turned to face the Afghan troops. She ripped the veil off her head, and with the hot sun streaming down on her face and her bare head, she called to the troops.

"'We can win this battle!' she cried. 'Don't give up hope! Pick yourselves up! Let's go!' Waving her veil in the air like a battle flag, she led the troops into a final rush at the British. The British had no chance. The Afghans won the battle.

"The lesson here, my daughters," he looked from one to the other, "is that Afghanistan has always been the home of the bravest women in the world. You are all brave women. You are all inheritors of the courage of Malali."

"We can win this battle!" Maryam cried out, waving her arm around as if she were holding a flag. Mother moved the tea pot out of harm's way.

"How can we be brave?" Nooria asked. "We can't even go outside. How can we lead men into battle? I've seen enough war. I don't want to see any more."

"There are many types of battles," Father said quietly.

"Including the battle with the supper dishes," Mother said.

Parvana made such a face that Father started to laugh. Maryam tried to imitate it, which made

Mother and Nooria laugh. Ali woke up, saw everybody laughing, and he started to laugh, too.

The whole family was laughing when four Taliban soldiers burst through the door.

Ali was the first to react. The slam of the door against the wall shocked him, and he screamed.

Mother leapt to her feet, and in an instant Ali and Maryam were in a corner of the room, shrieking behind her legs.

Nooria covered herself completely with her chador and scrunched herself into a small ball. Young women were sometimes stolen by soldiers. They were snatched from their homes, and their families never saw them again.

Parvana couldn't move. She sat as if frozen at the edge of the supper cloth. The soldiers were giants, their piled-high turbans making them look even taller.

Two of the soldiers grabbed her father. The other two began searching the apartment, kicking the remains of dinner all over the mat.

"Leave him alone!" Mother screamed. "He has done nothing wrong!"

"Why did you go to England for your education?" the soldiers yelled at Father. "Afghanistan doesn't need your foreign ideas!" They yanked him toward the door.

"Afghanistan needs more illiterate thugs like you," Father said. One of the soldiers hit him in the face. Blood from his nose dripped onto his white shalwar kameez.

Mother sprang at the soldiers, pounding them with her fists. She grabbed Father's arm and tried to pull him out of their grasp.

One of the soldiers raised his rifle and whacked her on the head. She collapsed on the floor. The soldier hit her a few more times. Maryam and Ali screamed with every blow to their mother's back.

Seeing her mother on the ground finally propelled Parvana into action. When the soldiers dragged her father outside, she flung her arms around his waist. As the soldiers pried her loose, she heard her father say, "Take care of the others, my Malali." Then he was gone.

Parvana watched helplessly as two soldiers dragged him down the steps, his beautiful shalwar kameez ripping on the rough cement. Then they turned a corner, and she could see them no more.

Inside the room, the other two soldiers were ripping open the toshaks with knives and tossing things out of the cupboard.

Father's books! At the bottom of the cupboard was a secret compartment her father had built to hide the few books that had not been destroyed in one of the bombings. Some were English books about history and literature. They were kept hidden because the Taliban burned books they didn't like.

They couldn't be allowed to find Father's books!

The soldiers had started at the top of the cupboard and were working their way down. Clothes, blankets, pots – everything landed on the floor.

Closer and closer they came to the bottom shelf, the one with the false wall. Parvana watched in horror as the soldiers bent down to yank the things out of the bottom shelf.

"Get out of my house!" she yelled. She threw herself at the soldiers with such force that they both fell to the ground. She swung at them with her fists until she was knocked aside. She heard rather than felt the thwack of their sticks on her back. She kept her head hidden in her arms until the beating stopped and the soldiers went away.

Mother got off the floor and had her hands full with Ali. Nooria was still curled up in a terrified ball. It was Maryam who came over to help Parvana.

At the first touch of her sister's hands, Parvana flinched, thinking it was the soldiers. Maryam kept stroking her hair until Parvana realized who it was. She sat up, aching all over. She and Maryam clung to each other, trembling.

She had no idea how long the family stayed like that. They remained in their spots long after Ali stopped screaming and collapsed into sleep.

THREE

Mother gently placed the sleeping Ali on an uncluttered spot on the floor. Maryam had fallen asleep, too, and was carried over to sleep beside her brother.

"Let's clean up," Mother said. Slowly, they put the room back together. Parvana's back and legs ached. Mother moved slowly, too, all hunched over.

Mother and Nooria replaced things in the cupboard. Parvana got the whisk broom down from its nail in the lavatory and swept up the spilled rice. She wiped up the spilled tea with a cloth. The ripped toshaks could be repaired, but that would wait until tomorrow.

When the room looked somewhat normal again, the family, minus Father, spread quilts and blankets on the floor and went to bed.

Parvana couldn't sleep. She could hear her mother and Nooria tossing and turning as well. She imagined every single noise to be either Father or the Taliban coming back. Each sound made Parvana hopeful and fearful at the same time.

She missed her father's snoring. He had a soft, pleasant snore. During the heavy bombing of Kabul, they changed homes many times to try to find a safe place. Parvana would wake up in the middle of the night and not remember where she was. As soon as she heard her father's snoring, she knew she was safe.

Tonight, there was no snoring.

Where was her father? Did he have a soft place to sleep? Was he cold? Was he hungry? Was he scared?

Parvana had never been inside a prison, but she had other relatives who had been arrested. One of her aunts had been arrested with hundreds of other schoolgirls for protesting the Soviet occupation of her country. All the Afghan governments put their enemies in jail.

"You can't be truly Afghan if you don't know someone who's been in prison," her mother sometimes said.

No one had told her what prison was like. "You're too young to know these things," the grown-ups would tell her. She had to imagine it.

It would be cold, Parvana decided, and dark.

"Mother, turn on the lamp!" She sat bolt upright with a sudden thought.

"Parvana, hush! You'll wake Ali."

"Light the lamp," Parvana whispered. "If they let Father go, he'll need a light in the window to guide him home."

"How could he walk? He left his walking stick here. Parvana, go to sleep. You are not helping the situation."

Parvana lay down again, but she didn't sleep.

The only window in the room was a small one, high up on one wall. The Taliban had ordered all windows painted over with black paint so that no one could see the women inside. "We won't do it," Father had said. "The window is so high and so small, no one can possibly see in." So far, they had gotten away with leaving it unpainted.

For short periods, on clear days, the sun would come through the window in a thin stream. Ali and Maryam would sit in that ray of sunshine. Mother and Nooria would join them there and, for a few moments, the sun would warm the flesh on their arms and faces. Then the planet would continue its spin, and the sunbeam would be gone again.

Parvana kept her eyes on the spot where she thought the window was. The night was so dark, she could not distinguish between the window and the wall. She kept watch all night, until the dawn finally pushed the darkness away, and morning peeked in through the window.

At first light, Mother, Nooria and Parvana stopped pretending they were asleep. Quietly, so they didn't wake the young ones, they got up and dressed.

For breakfast they chewed on leftover nan.

Nooria started to heat water for tea on the little gas stove in the bathroom, but Mother stopped her. "There is boiled water left from last night. We'll just drink that. We don't have time to wait for tea. Parvana and I are going to get your father out of jail." She said it the way she might say, "Parvana and I are going to the market to get peaches."

The nan fell from Parvana's lips onto the plastic cloth. She didn't argue, though.

Maybe I'll get to finally see what the inside of a jail looks like, she thought.

The prison was a long way from their home. Buses were not permitted to carry women who did not have a man with them. They would have to walk the whole way. What if Father was being held somewhere else? What if they were stopped by the Taliban in the street? Mother wasn't supposed to be out of her home without a man, or without a note from her husband.

"Nooria, write Mother a note."

"Don't bother, Nooria. I will not walk around my own city with a note pinned to my burqa as if I were a kindergarten child. I have a university degree!"

"Write the note anyway," Parvana whispered to Nooria, when Mother was in the washroom. "I'll carry it in my sleeve."

Nooria agreed. Her penmanship was more grown-up than Parvana's. She quickly wrote, "I give permission for my wife to be outside." She signed it with Father's name.

"I don't think it will do much good," Nooria whispered, as she handed Parvana the note. "Most of the Taliban don't know how to read."

Parvana didn't answer. She quickly folded the note into a small square and tucked it into the wide hem of her sleeve.

Nooria suddenly did something very unusual. She gave her sister a hug. "Come back," she whispered.

Parvana didn't want to go, but she knew that sitting at home waiting for them to return would be even harder.

"Hurry up, Parvana," her mother said. "Your father is waiting."

Parvana slipped her feet into her sandals and wound her chador around her head. She followed Mother out the door.

Helping Mother down the broken stairs was a little like helping Father, as the billowing burqa made it hard for her to see where she was going.

Mother hesitated at the bottom of the stairs. Parvana thought she might be having second thoughts. After that moment, though, her mother pulled herself up to her full height, straightened her back and plunged into the Kabul street.

Parvana rushed after her. She had to run to keep up with her mother's long, quick steps, but she didn't dare fall behind. There were a few other women in the street and they all wore the regulation burqa, which made them all look alike. If Parvana lost track of her mother, she was afraid she'd never find her again.

Now and then, her mother stopped beside a man and a woman, or a small group of men, or even a peddler boy, and held out a photograph of Father. She didn't say anything, just showed them the photo.

Parvana held her breath every time her mother did this. Photographs were illegal. Any one of these people could turn Parvana and her mother over to the militia.

But everyone looked at the photo, then shook their heads. Many people had been arrested. Many people had disappeared. They knew what Mother was asking without her having to say anything.

Pul-i-Charkhi Prison was a long walk from Parvana's home. By the time the huge fortress came into view, her legs were sore, her feet ached and, worst of all, she was scared all over.

The prison was dark and ugly, and it made Parvana feel even smaller.

Malali wouldn't be afraid, Parvana knew. Malali would form an army and lead it in a storming of the prison. Malali would lick her lips at such a challenge. Her knees wouldn't be shaking as Parvana's were.

If Parvana's mother was scared, she didn't show it. She marched straight up to the prison gates and said to the guard, "I'm here for my husband."

The guards ignored her.

"I'm here for my husband!" Mother said again.

She took out Father's photograph and held it in front of the face of one of the guards. "He was arrested last night. He has committed no crime, and I want him released!"

More guards began to gather. Parvana gave a little tug on her mother's burqa. Her mother ignored her.

"I'm here for my husband!" she kept saying, louder and louder. Parvana tugged harder on the loose cloth of the burqa.

"Hold steady, my little Malali," she heard her father say in her mind. Suddenly, she felt very calm.

"I'm here for my father!" she called out.

Her mother looked down at her through the screen over her eyes. She reached down and took Parvana's hand. "I'm here for my husband!" she called again.

Over and over, Parvana and her mother kept yelling out their mission. More and more men came to stare at them.

"Be quiet!" ordered one of the guards. "You should not be here! Go from this place! Go back to your home!"

One of the soldiers snatched the photo of Parvana's father and tore it into pieces. Another started hitting her mother with a stick.

"Release my husband!" her mother kept saying.

Another soldier joined in the beating. He hit Parvana, too.

Although he did not hit her very hard, Parvana fell to the ground, her body covering the pieces of her father's photograph. In a flash, she tucked the pieces out of sight, under her chador.

Her mother was also on the ground, the soldiers' sticks hitting her across her back.

Parvana leapt to her feet. "Stop! Stop it! We'll go now! We'll go!" She grabbed the arm of one of her mother's attackers. He shook her off as if she were a fly.

"Who are you to tell me what to do?" But he did lower his stick.

"Get out of here!" he spat at Parvana and her mother.

Parvana knelt down, took her mother's arm and helped her to her feet. Slowly, with her mother leaning on her for support, they hobbled away from the prison.

FOUR

It was very late by the time Parvana and her mother returned home from the prison. Parvana was so tired she had to lean against Mother to make it up the stairs, the way Father used to lean against her. She had stopped thinking of anything but the pain that seemed to be in every part of her body, from the top of her head to the bottom of her feet.

Her feet burned and stung with every step. When she took off her sandals, she could see why. Her feet, unused to walking such long distances, were covered with blisters. Most of the blisters had broken, and her feet were bloody and raw.

Nooria and Maryam's eyes widened when they saw the mess of Parvana's feet. They grew wider still when they saw their mother's feet. They were even more torn up and bloody than Parvana's.

Parvana realized that Mother hadn't been out of the house since the Taliban had taken over Kabul a year and a half before. She could have gone out. She had a burqa, and Father would have gone with her any time she wanted. Many husbands were happy to make their wives stay home, but not Father.

"Fatana, you are a writer," he often said. "You must come out into the city and see what is happening. Otherwise, how will you know what to write about it?"

"Who would read what I write? Am I allowed to publish? No. Then what is the point of writing, and what is the point of looking? Besides, it will not be for long. The Afghan people are smart and strong. They will kick these Taliban out. When that happens, when we have a decent government in Afghanistan, then I will go out again. Until then, I will stay here."

"It takes work to make a decent government," Father said. "You are a writer. You must do your work."

"If we had left Afghanistan when we had the chance, I could be doing my work!"

"We are Afghans. This is our home. If all the educated people leave, who will rebuild the country?"

It was an argument Parvana's parents had often. When the whole family lived in one room, there were no secrets.

Mother's feet were so bad from the long walk that she could barely make it into the room. Parvana had been so preoccupied with her own pain and exhaustion, she hadn't given any thought to what her mother had been going through.

Nooria tried to help, but Mother just waved her

away. She threw her burqa down on the floor. Her face was stained with tears and sweat. She collapsed onto the toshak where Father had taken his nap just yesterday.

Mother cried for a long, long time. Nooria sponged off the part of her face that wasn't buried in the pillow. She washed the dust from the wounds in her mother's feet.

Mother acted as if Nooria wasn't there at all. Finally, Nooria spread a light blanket over her. It was a long time before the sobs stopped, and Mother fell asleep.

While Nooria tried to look after Mother, Maryam looked after Parvana. Biting her tongue in concentration, she carried a basin of water over to where Parvana was sitting. She didn't spill a drop. She wiped Parvana's face with a cloth she wasn't quite able to wring out. Drips from the cloth ran down Parvana's neck. The water felt good. She soaked her feet in the basin, and that felt good, too.

She sat with her feet in the basin while Nooria got supper.

"They wouldn't tell us anything about Father," Parvana told her sister. "What are we going to do? How are we going to find him?"

Nooria started to say something, but Parvana didn't catch what it was. She began to feel heavy, her eyes started to close, and the next thing she knew, it was morning.

Parvana could hear the morning meal being prepared.

I should get up and help, she thought, but she couldn't bring herself to move.

All night long she had drifted in and out of dreams about the soldiers. They were screaming at her and hitting her. In her dream, she shouted at them to release her father, but no sound came from her lips. She had even shouted, "I am Malali! I am Malali!" but the soldiers paid no attention.

The worst part of her dream was seeing Mother beaten. It was as if Parvana was watching it happen from far, far away, and couldn't get to her to help her up.

Parvana suddenly sat up, then relaxed again when she saw her mother on the toshak on the other side of the room. It was all right. Mother was here.

"I'll help you to the washroom," Nooria offered.

"I don't need any help," Parvana said. However, when she tried to stand, the pain in her feet was very bad. It was easier to accept Nooria's offer and lean on her across the room to the washroom.

"Everybody leans on everybody in this family," Parvana said.

"Is that right?" Nooria asked. "And who do I lean on?"

That was such a Nooria-like comment that Parvana immediately felt a bit better. Nooria being grumpy meant things were getting back to normal.

She felt better still after she'd washed her face and tidied her hair. There was cold rice and hot tea waiting when she had finished.

"Mother, would you like some breakfast?" Nooria gently shook their mother. Mother moaned a little and shrugged Nooria away.

Except for trips to the washroom, and a couple of cups of tea, which Nooria kept in a thermos by the toshak, Mother spent the day lying down. She kept her face to the wall and didn't speak to any of them.

The next day, Parvana was tired of sleeping. Her feet were still sore, but she played with Ali and Maryam. The little ones, especially Ali, couldn't understand why Mother wasn't paying attention to them.

"Mother's sleeping," Parvana kept saying.

"When will she wake up?" Maryam asked.

Parvana didn't answer.

Ali kept waddling over to the door and pointing up at it.

"I think he's asking where Father is," Nooria said. "Come on, Ali, let's find your ball."

Parvana remembered the pieces of photograph and got them out. Her father's face was like a jigsaw puzzle. She spread the pieces out on the mat in front of her. Maryam joined her and helped her put them in order.

One piece was missing. All of Father's face was there except for a part of his chin. "When we get some tape, we'll tape it together," Parvana said. Maryam nodded. She gathered up the little pieces into a tidy pile and handed them to Parvana. Parvana tucked them away in a corner of the cupboard.

The third day barely creeped along. Parvana even considered doing some housework, just to pass the time, but she was worried she might disturb her mother. At one point, all four children sat against the wall and watched their mother sleep.

"She has to get up soon," Nooria said.

"She can't just lie there forever."

Parvana was tired of sitting. She had lived in that room for a year and a half, but there had always been chores to do and trips to the market with Father.

Mother was still in the same place. They were taking care not to disturb her. All the same, Parvana thought if she had to spend much more time whispering and keeping the young ones quiet, she would scream.

It would help if she could read, but the only books they had were Father's secret books. She didn't dare take them out of their hiding place. What if the Taliban burst in on them again? They'd take the books, and maybe punish the whole family for having them.

Parvana noticed a change in Ali. "Is he sick?" she asked Nooria.

"He misses Mother." Ali sat in Nooria's lap. He didn't crawl around any more when he was put on the floor. He spent most of the time curled in a ball with his thumb in his mouth.

He didn't even cry very much any more. It was nice to have a break from his noise, but Parvana didn't like to see him like this.

The room began to smell, too. "We have to save water," Nooria said, so washing and cleaning didn't get done. Ali's dirty diapers were piled in a heap in the washroom. The little window didn't open very far. No breeze could get into the room to blow the stink away.

On the fourth day, the food ran out.

"We're out of food," Nooria told Parvana.

"Don't tell me. Tell Mother. She's the grown-up. She has to get us some."

"I don't want to bother her."

"Then I'll tell her." Parvana went over to Mother's toshak and gently shook her.

"We're out of food." There was no response. "Mother, there's no food left." Mother pulled away. Parvana started to shake her again.

"Leave her alone!" Nooria yanked her away. "Can't you see she's depressed?"

"We're all depressed," Parvana replied. "We're also hungry." She wanted to shout, but didn't want to frighten the little ones. She could glare, though, and she and Nooria glared at each other for hours.

No one ate that day.

"We're out of food," Nooria said again to Parvana the next day.

"I'm not going out there."

"You have to go. There's no one else who can go."

"My feet are still sore."

"Your feet will survive, but we won't if you don't get us food. Now, move!"

Parvana looked at Mother, still lying on the toshak. She looked at Ali, worn out from being hungry and needing his parents. She looked at Maryam, whose cheeks were already beginning to look hollow, and who hadn't been in the sunshine in such a long time. Finally, she looked at her big sister, Nooria.

Nooria looked terrified. If Parvana didn't obey her, she would have to go for food herself.

Now I've got her, Parvana thought. I can make her as miserable as she makes me. But she was surprised to find that this thought gave her no pleasure. Maybe she was too tired and too hungry. Instead of turning her back, she took the money from her sister's hand.

"What should I buy?" she asked.

FIVE

It was strange to be in the marketplace without Father. Parvana almost expected to see him in their usual place, sitting on the blanket, reading and writing his customer's letters.

Women were not allowed to go into the shops. Men were supposed to do all the shopping, but if women did it, they had to stand outside and call in for what they needed. Parvana had seen shopkeepers beaten for serving women inside their shops.

Parvana wasn't sure if she would be considered a woman. On the one hand, if she behaved like one and stood outside the shop and called in her order, she could get in trouble for not wearing a burqa. On the other hand, if she went into a shop, she could get in trouble for not acting like a woman!

She put off her decision by buying the nan first. The baker's stall opened onto the street.

Parvana pulled her chador more tightly around her face so that only her eyes were showing. She held up ten fingers – ten loaves of nan. A pile of nan was already baked, but she had to wait a little while for four more loaves to be flipped out of the oven. The attendant wrapped the bread in a piece of newspaper and handed it to Parvana. She paid without looking up.

The bread was still warm. It smelled so good! The wonderful smell reminded Parvana how hungry she was. She could have swallowed a whole loaf in one gulp.

The fruit and vegetable stand was next. Before she had time to make a selection, a voice behind her shouted, "What are you doing on the street dressed like that?"

Parvana whirled around to see a Talib glaring at her, anger in his eyes and a stick in his hand.

"You must be covered up! Who is your father? Who is your husband? They will be punished for letting you walk the street like that!" The soldier raised his arm and brought his stick down on Parvana's shoulder.

Parvana didn't even feel it. Punish her father, would they?

"Stop hitting me!" she yelled.

The Talib was so surprised, he held still for a moment. Parvana saw him pause, and she started to run. She knocked over a pile of turnips at the vegetable stand, and they went rolling all over the street.

Clutching the still-warm nan to her chest, Parvana kept running, her sandals slapping against the pavement. She didn't care if people were staring at her. All she wanted was to get as far away from the soldier as she could, as fast as her legs could carry her.

She was so anxious to get home, she ran right into a woman carrying a child.

"Is that Parvana?"

Parvana tried to get away, but the woman had a firm grip on her arm.

"It is Parvana! What kind of a way is that to carry bread?"

The voice behind the burqa was familiar, but Parvana couldn't remember who it belonged to.

"Speak up, girl! Don't stand there with your mouth open as though you were a fish in the market! Speak up!"

"Mrs. Weera?"

"Oh, that's right, my face is covered. I keep forgetting. Now, why are you running, and why are you crushing that perfectly good bread?"

Parvana started to cry. "The Taliban...one of the soldiers...he was chasing me."

"Dry your tears. Under such a circumstance, running was a very sensible thing to do. I always thought you had the makings of a sensible girl, and you've just proven me right. Good for you! You've outrun the Taliban. Where are you going with all that bread?"

"Home. I'm almost there."

"We'll go together. I've been meaning to call on your mother for some time. We need a magazine, and your mother is just the person to get it going for us."

"Mother doesn't write any more, and I don't think she'll want company."

"Nonsense. Let's go."

Mrs. Weera had been in the Afghan Women's Union with Mother. She was so sure Mother wouldn't mind her dropping in that Parvana obediently led the way.

"And stop squeezing that bread! It's not going to suddenly jump out of your arms!"

When they were almost at the top step, Parvana turned to Mrs. Weera. "About Mother. She's not been well."

"Then it's a good thing I'm stopping by to take care of her!"

Parvana gave up. They reached the apartment door and went inside.

Nooria saw only Parvana at first. She took the nan from her. "Is this all you bought? Where's the rice? Where's the tea? How are we supposed to manage with just this?"

"Don't be too hard on her. She was chased out of the market before she could complete her shopping." Mrs. Weera stepped into the room and took off her burqa.

"Mrs. Weera!" Nooria exclaimed. Relief washed

over her face. Here was someone who could take charge, who could take some of the responsibility off her shoulders.

Mrs. Weera placed the child she'd been carrying down on the mat beside Ali. The two toddlers eyed each other warily.

Mrs. Weera was a tall woman. Her hair was white, but her body was strong. She had been a physical education teacher before the Taliban made her leave her job.

"What in the world is going on here?" she asked. In a few quick strides she was in the bathroom, searching out the source of the stench. "Why aren't those diapers washed?"

"We're out of water," Nooria explained. "We've been afraid to go out."

"You're not afraid, are you, Parvana?" She didn't wait for her answer. "Fetch the bucket, girl. Do your bit for the team. Here we go!" Mrs. Weera still talked like she was out on the hockey field, urging everyone to do their best.

"Where's Fatana?" she asked, as Parvana fetched the water bucket. Nooria motioned to the figure on the toshak, buried under a blanket. Mother moaned and tried to huddle down even further.

"She's sleeping," Nooria said.

"How long has she been like this?"

"Four days."

"Where's your father?"

"Arrested."

"Ah, I see." She caught sight of Parvana holding the empty bucket. "Are you waiting for it to rain inside so your bucket will fill itself? Off you go!"

Parvana went.

She made seven trips. Mrs. Weera met her outside the apartment at the top of the steps and took the first two full buckets from her, emptied them inside and brought back the empty bucket. "We're getting your mother cleaned up, and she doesn't need another pair of eyes on her."

After that, Parvana carried the water inside to the water tank as usual. Mrs. Weera had gotten Mother up and washed. Mother didn't seem to notice Parvana.

She kept hauling water. Her arms were sore, and the blisters on her feet started to bleed again, but she didn't think about that. She fetched water because her family needed it, because her father would have expected her to. Now that Mrs. Weera was there and her mother was up, things were going to get easier, and she would do her part.

Out the door, down the steps, down the street to the tap, then back again, stopping now and then to rest and change carrying arms.

After the seventh trip, Mrs. Weera stopped her.

"You've filled the tank and the wash basin, and there's a full bucket to spare. That's enough for now."

Parvana was dizzy from doing all that exercise with no food and nothing to drink. She wanted some water right away.

"What are you doing?" Nooria asked as Parvana filled a cup from the tank. "You know it has to be boiled first!"

Unboiled water made you sick, but Parvana was so thirsty that she didn't care. She wanted to drink, and raised the cup to her lips.

Nooria snatched it from her hands. "You are the stupidest girl! All we need now is for you to get sick! How could anyone so stupid end up as my sister!"

"That's no way to keep up team spirit," Mrs. Weera said. "Nooria, why don't you get the little ones washed for dinner. Use cold water. We'll let this first batch of boiled water be for drinking."

Parvana went out into the larger room and sat down. Mother was sitting up. She had put on clean clothes. Her hair was brushed and tied back. She looked more like Mother, although she still seemed very tired.

It felt like an eternity before Mrs. Weera handed Parvana a cup of plain boiled water.

"Be careful. It's very hot."

As soon as she could, she drank the water, got another cupful, and drank that, too.

Mrs. Weera and her granddaughter stayed the night. As Parvana drifted off to sleep, she heard her, Nooria and Mother talking quietly together. Mrs.

Weera told them about Parvana's brush with the Taliban.

The last thing she heard before she fell asleep was Mrs. Weera saying, "I guess we'll have to think of something else."

SIX

They were going to turn her into a boy.

"As a boy, you'll be able to move in and out of the market, buy what we need, and no one will stop you," Mother said.

"It's a perfect solution," Mrs. Weera said.

"You'll be our cousin from Jalalabad," Nooria said, "come to stay with us while our father is away."

Parvana stared at the three of them. It was as though they were speaking a foreign language, and she didn't have a clue what they were saying.

"If anybody asks about you, we'll say that you have gone to stay with an aunt in Kunduz," Mother said.

"But no one will ask about you."

At these words, Parvana turned her head sharply to glare at her sister. If ever there was a time to say something mean, this was it, but she couldn't think of anything. After all, what Nooria said was true. None of her friends had seen her since the Taliban closed the schools. Her relatives were scattered to different parts of the country, even to different countries. There was no one to ask about her.

"You'll wear Hossain's clothes." Mother's voice caught, and for a moment it seemed as though she would cry, but she got control of herself again. "They will be a bit big for you, but we can make some adjustments if we have to." She glanced over at Mrs. Weera. "Those clothes have been idle long enough. It's time they were put to use."

Parvana guessed Mrs. Weera and her mother had been talking long and hard while she was asleep. She was glad of that. Her mother already looked better. But that didn't mean she was ready to give in.

"It won't work," she said. "I won't look like a boy. I have long hair."

Nooria opened the cupboard door, took out the sewing kit and slowly opened it up. It looked to Parvana as if Nooria was having too much fun as she lifted out the scissors and snapped them open and shut a few times.

"You're not cutting my hair!" Parvana's hands flew up to her head.

"How else will you look like a boy?" Mother asked.

"Cut Nooria's hair! She's the oldest! It's her responsibility to look after me, not my responsibility to look after her!"

"No one would believe me to be a boy," Nooria said calmly, looking down at her body. Nooria being calm just made Parvana madder.

"I'll look like that soon," Parvana said.

"You wish."

"We'll deal with that when the time comes," Mother said quickly, heading off the fight she knew was coming. "Until then, we have no choice. Someone has to be able to go outside, and you are the one most likely to look like a boy."

Parvana thought about it. Her fingers reached up her back to see how long her hair had grown.

"It has to be your decision," Mrs. Weera said. "We can force you to cut off your hair, but you're still the one who has to go outside and act the part. We know this is a big thing we're asking, but I think you can do it. How about it?"

Parvana realized Mrs. Weera was right. They could hold her down and cut off her hair, but for anything more, they needed her cooperation. In the end, it really was her decision.

Somehow, knowing that made it easier to agree.

"All right," she said. "I'll do it."

"Well done," said Mrs. Weera. "That's the spirit."

Nooria snapped the scissors again. "I'll cut your hair," she said.

"I'll cut it," Mother said, taking the scissors away. "Let's do it now, Parvana. Thinking about it won't make it any easier."

Parvana and her mother went into the washroom where the cement floor would make it easier to clean up the cut-off hair. Mother took Hossain's clothes in with them.

"Do you want to watch?" Mother asked, nodding toward the mirror.

Parvana shook her head, then changed her mind. If this was the last she would see of her hair, then she wanted to see it for as long as she could.

Mother worked quickly. First she cut off a huge chunk in a straight line at her neck. She held it up for Parvana to see.

"I have a lovely piece of ribbon packed away," she said. "We'll tie this up with it, and you can keep it."

Parvana looked at the hair in her mother's hand. While it was on her head, it had seemed important. It didn't seem important any more.

"No, thanks," said Parvana. "Throw it away."

Her mother's lips tightened. "If you're going to sulk about it," she said, and she tossed the hair down to the floor.

As more and more hair fell away, Parvana began to feel like a different person. Her whole face showed. What was left of her hair was short and shaggy. It curled in a soft fringe around her ears. There were no long parts to fall into her eyes, to become tangled on a windy day, to take forever to dry when she got caught in the rain.

Her forehead seemed bigger. Her eyes seemed bigger, too, maybe because she was opening them so wide to be able to see everything. Her ears seemed to stick out from her head.

They look a little funny, Parvana thought, but a nice sort of funny.

I have a nice face, she decided.

Mother rubbed her hands brusquely over Parvana's head to rub away any stray hairs.

"Change your clothes," she said. Then she left the washroom.

All alone, Parvana's hand crept up to the top of her head. Touching her hair gingerly at first, she soon rubbed the palm of her hand all over her head. Her new hair felt both bristly and soft. It tickled the skin on her hand.

I like it, she thought, and she smiled.

She took off her own clothes and put on her brother's. Hossain's shalwar kameez was pale green, both the loose shirt and the baggy trousers. The shirt hung down very low, and the trousers were too long, but by rolling them up at the waist, they were all right.

There was a pocket sewn into the left side of the shirt, near the chest. It was just big enough to hold money and maybe a few candies, if she ever had candies again. There was another pocket on the front. It was nice to have pockets. Her girl clothes didn't have any.

"Parvana, haven't you changed yet?"

Parvana stopped looking at herself in the mirror and joined her family.

The first face she saw was Maryam's. Her little

sister looked as if she couldn't quite figure out who had walked into the room.

"It's me, Maryam," Parvana said.

"Parvana!" Maryam laughed as she recognized her.

"Hossain," her mother whispered.

"You look less ugly as a boy than you do as a girl," Nooria said quickly. If Mother started remembering Hossain, she'd just start crying again.

"You look fine," said Mrs. Weera.

"Put this on." Mother handed Parvana a cap. Parvana put it on her head. It was a white cap with beautiful embroidery all over it. Maybe she'd never wear her special red shalwar kameez again, but she had a new cap to take its place.

"Here's some money," her mother said. "Buy what you were not able to buy yesterday." She placed a pattu around Parvana's shoulder. It was her father's. "Hurry back."

Parvana tucked the money into her new pocket. She slipped her feet into her sandals, then reached for her chador.

"You won't be needing that," Nooria said.

Parvana had forgotten. Suddenly she was scared. Everyone would see her face! They would know she wasn't a boy!

She turned around to plead with her mother. "Don't make me do this!"

"You see?" Nooria said in her nastiest voice. "I told you she was too scared."

"It's easy to call someone else scared when you're safe inside your home all the time!" Parvana shot back. She spun around and went outside, slamming the door behind her.

Out on the street, she kept waiting for people to point at her and call her a fake. No one did. No one paid any attention to her at all. The more she was ignored, the more confident she felt.

When she had gone into the market with her father, she had kept silent and covered up her face as much as possible. She had tried her best to be invisible. Now, with her face open to the sunshine, she was invisible in another way. She was just one more boy on the street. She was nothing worth paying attention to.

When she came to the shop that sold tea, rice and other groceries, she hesitated for a slight moment, then walked boldly through the door. I'm a boy, she kept saying to herself. It gave her courage.

"What do you want?" the grocer asked.

"Some...some tea," Parvana stammered out.

"How much? What kind?" The grocer was gruff, but it was ordinary bad-mood gruff, not gruff out of anger that there was a girl in his shop.

Parvana pointed to the brand of tea they usually had at home. "Is that the cheapest?"

"This one is the cheapest." He showed her another one.

"I'll take the cheapest one. I also need five pounds of rice."

"Don't tell me. You want the cheapest kind. Big spender."

Parvana left the shop with rice and tea, feeling very proud of herself. "I can do this!" she whispered.

Onions were cheap at the vegetable stand. She bought a few.

"Look what I got!" Parvana exclaimed, as she burst through the door of her home. "I did it! I did the shopping, and nobody bothered me."

"Parvana!" Maryam ran to her and gave her a hug. Parvana hugged her back as best she could with her arms full of groceries.

Mother was back on the toshak, facing the wall, her back to the room. Ali sat beside her, patting her and saying, "Ma-ma-ma," trying to get her attention.

Nooria took the groceries from Parvana and handed her the water bucket.

"As long as you've got your sandals on," she said.

"What's wrong with Mother now?"

"Shhh! Not so loud! Do you want her to hear you? She got upset after seeing you in Hossain's clothes. Can you blame her? Also, Mrs. Weera went home, and that's made her sad. Now, please go and get water."

"I got water yesterday!"

"I had a lot of cleaning to do. Ali was almost out of diapers. Would you rather wash diapers than fetch the water?"

Parvana fetched the water.

"Keep those clothes on," Nooria said when Parvana returned. "I've been thinking about this. If you're going to be a boy outside, you should be a boy inside, too. What if someone comes by?"

That made sense to Parvana. "What about Mother? Won't it upset her to see me in Hossain's clothes all the time?"

"She'll have to get used to it."

For the first time, Parvana noticed the tired lines on Nooria's face. She looked much older than seventeen.

"I'll help you with supper," she offered.

"You? Help? All you'd do is get in my way."

Parvana fumed. It was impossible to be nice to Nooria!

Mother got up for supper and made an effort to be cheerful. She complimented Parvana on her shopping success, but seemed to have a hard time looking at her.

Later that night, when they were all stretched out for sleep, Ali fussed a little.

"Go to sleep, Hossain," Parvana heard her mother say. "Go to sleep, my son."

SEVEN

The next morning, after breakfast, Parvana was back on the street.

"Take your father's writing things and his blanket, and go to the market," Mother told her. "Maybe you can earn some money. You've been watching your father all this time. Just do what he did."

Parvana liked the idea. Yesterday's shopping had gone well. If she could earn money, she might never have to do housework again. The boy disguise had worked once. Why shouldn't it work again?

As she walked to the marketplace, her head felt light without the weight of her hair or chador. She could feel the sun on her face, and a light breeze floating down from the mountain made the air fresh and fine.

Her father's shoulder bag was slung across her chest. It bumped against her legs. Inside were Father's pens and writing paper, and a few items she would try to sell, including her fancy shalwar kameez. Under her arm, Parvana carried the blanket she would sit on.

She chose the same spot where she had gone with her father. It was next to a wall. On the other side of the wall was a house. The wall hid most of it from view. There was a window above the wall, but it had been painted black, in obedience to the Taliban decree.

"If we're at the same place every day, people will get to know we are here, and they will remember us when they need something read or written," Father used to say. Parvana liked that he said "we," as if she was part of his business. The spot was close to home, too. There were busier places in the market, but they took longer to get to, and Parvana wasn't sure she knew the way.

"If anyone asks who you are, say you are Father's nephew Kaseem," Mother said. They had gone over and over the story until Parvana knew it cold. "Say Father is ill, and you have come to stay with the family until he is well again."

It was safer to say Father was ill than to tell people he'd been arrested. No one wanted to look like an enemy of the government.

"Will anyone hire me to read for them?" Parvana asked. "I'm only eleven."

"You still have more education than most people in Afghanistan," Mother said. "However, if they don't hire you, we'll think of something else."

Parvana spread her blanket on the hard clay of the market, arranged her goods for sale to one side, as Father had done, and spread her pens and writing paper out in front of her. Then she sat down and waited for customers.

The first hour went by with no one stopping. Men would walk by, look down at her and keep walking. She wished she had her chador to hide behind. She was certain that at any moment someone would stop, point at her and yell, "Girl!" The word would ring out through the market like a curse, and everyone would stop what they were doing. Staying put that first hour was one of the hardest things she had ever done.

She was looking the other way when someone stopped. She felt the shadow before she saw it, as the man moved between her and the sun. Turning her head, she saw the dark turban that was the uniform of the Taliban. A rifle was slung across his chest as casually as her father's shoulder bag had been slung across hers.

Parvana began to tremble.

"You are a letter reader?" he asked in Pashtu.

Parvana tried to answer, but she couldn't find her voice. Instead, she nodded.

"Speak up, boy! A letter reader who has no voice is no good to me."

Parvana took a deep breath. "I am a letter reader," she said in Pashtu, in a voice that she hoped was loud enough. "I can read and write in Dari and Pashtu." If this was a customer, she hoped her Pashtu would be good enough.

The Talib kept looking down at her. Then he put his hand inside his vest. Keeping his eyes on Parvana, he drew something out of his vest pocket.

Parvana was about to squish her eyes shut and wait to be shot when she saw that the Talib had taken out a letter.

He sat down beside her on the blanket.

"Read this," he said.

Parvana took the envelope from him. The stamp was from Germany. She read the outside. "This is addressed to Fatima Azima."

"That was my wife," the Talib said.

The letter was very old. Parvana took it out of the envelope and unfolded it. The creases were embedded in the paper.

"Dear Niece," Parvana read. "I am sorry I am not able to be with you at the time of your wedding, but I hope this letter will get to you in time. It is good to be in Germany, away from all the fighting. In my mind, though, I never really leave Afghanistan. My thoughts are always turned to our country, to the family and friends I will probably never see again.

"On this day of your marriage, I send you my very best wishes for your future. Your father, my brother, is a good man, and he will have chosen a good man to be your husband. You may find it hard at first, to be away from your family, but you will have a new family. Soon you will begin to feel you belong there. I hope you will be happy, that you will be blessed with many children, and that you will live to see your son have sons.

"Once you leave Pakistan and return to Afghanistan with your new husband, I will likely lose track of you. Please keep my letter with you, and do not forget me, for I will not forget you.

"Your loving aunt, Sohila."

Parvana stopped reading. The Talib was silent beside her. "Would you like me to read it again?"

He shook his head and held out his hand for the letter. Parvana folded it and gave it back to him. His hands trembled as he put the letter back in the envelope. She saw a tear fall from his eye. It rolled down his cheek until it landed in his beard.

"My wife is dead," he said. "This was among her belongings. I wanted to know what it said." He sat quietly for a few minutes, holding the letter.

"Would you like me to write a reply?" Parvana asked, as she had heard her father do.

The Talib sighed, then shook his head. "How much do I owe you?"

"Pay whatever you like," Parvana said. Her father had also said that.

The Talib took some money out of his pocket and gave it to her. Without another word, he got up off the blanket and went away.

Parvana took a deep breath and let it out slowly. Up until then, she had seen Talibs only as men who beat women and arrested her father. Could they have feelings of sorrow, like other human beings?

Parvana found it all very confusing. Soon she had another customer, someone who wanted to buy something rather than have something read. All day long, though, her thoughts kept floating back to the Talib who missed his wife.

She had only one other customer before she went home for lunch. A man who had been walking back and forth in front of her blanket finally stopped to talk to her.

"How much do you want for that?" he asked, pointing at her beautiful shalwar kameez.

Mother hadn't told her what price to ask. Parvana tried to remember how her mother used to bargain with vendors in the market when she was able to do the shopping. She would argue the vendor down from whatever price he named first. "They expect you to bargain," she explained, "so they begin with a price so high only a fool would pay it."

Parvana thought quickly. She pictured her aunt in Mazar working hard to do all the embroidery on the dress and around the cuffs of the trousers. She thought of how pretty she'd felt when she wore it, and how much she hated giving it up.

She named a price. The customer shook his head and made a counter-offer, a much lower price. Parvana pointed out the detailed designs of the needlework, then named a price slightly lower than her first one. The customer hesitated, but didn't leave. After a few more prices back and forth, they agreed on an amount.

It was good to make a sale, to have more money to stuff away in the little pocket in the side of her shirt. It felt so good that she almost felt no regret as she watched the vibrant red cloth flutter in the breeze as it was carried away into the crowded labyrinth of the market, never to be seen again.

Parvana stayed on the blanket for another couple of hours, until she realized she had to go to the bathroom. There was nowhere for her to go in the market, so she had to pack up and go home. She went through many of the same motions she went through when she was with her father – packing up the supplies in the shoulder bag, shaking the dust out of the blanket. It made her miss Father.

"Father, come back to us!" she whispered, looking up at the sky. The sun was shining. How could the sun be shining when her father was in jail?

Something caught her eye, a flicker of movement. She thought it came from the blacked-out window, but how could it? Parvana decided she was imagining things. She folded up the blanket and tucked it under her arm. She felt the money she'd earned, tucked safely in her pocket.

Feeling very proud of herself, she ran all the way home.

EIGHT

Mrs. Weera was back. "I'll be moving in this afternoon, Parvana," she said. "You can help me."

Parvana wanted to get back to her blanket, but helping Mrs. Weera would be another change in routine, so that was fine with her. Besides, as long as Mrs. Weera was around, Mother seemed like her old self.

"Mrs. Weera and I are going to work together," Mother announced. "We're going to start a magazine."

"So we'll all have our jobs to do. Nooria will look after the little ones, your mother and I will work on our project, and you will go out to work," Mrs. Weera declared, as though she were assigning positions on the hockey field. "We'll all pull together."

Parvana showed them the money she'd earned.

"Wonderful!" Mother said. "I knew you could do it."

"Father would have made much more," Nooria said, then bit her lip, as if she were attempting to bite back her words.

Parvana was in too good a mood to be bothered.

After tea and nan for lunch, Parvana headed out with Mrs. Weera to get her belongings. Mrs. Weera wore the burqa, of course, but she had such a distinctive way of walking that Parvana was sure she could pick her out of a whole marketplace of women wearing burqas. She walked as though she were rounding up children who were dawdling after class. She walked swiftly, head up and shoulders back. Just to be safe, though, Parvana stayed close to her.

"The Taliban don't usually bother women out alone with small children," Mrs. Weera was saying, "although you can't be certain of that. Fortunately, I can probably outrun any of these soldiers. Outfight them, too, if they tangle with me. I've handled many a teenage boy in my teaching years. There wasn't one I couldn't reduce to tears with a good lecture!"

"I saw a Talib cry this morning," Parvana said, but her words were lost in the whoosh of air as they moved quickly through the streets.

Mrs. Weera had been living with her grandchild in a room even smaller than Parvana's. It was in the basement of a ruined building.

"We are the last of the Weeras," she said. "The bombs took some, the war took others, and pneumonia took the rest."

Parvana didn't know what to say. Mrs. Weera did not sound as though she was looking for sympathy.

"We have the loan of a karachi for the afternoon," Mrs. Weera said. "The owner needs it back this evening to go to work. But we'll manage it all splendidly in one trip, won't we?"

Mrs. Weera had lost a lot of things, too, in bombing raids. "What the bombs didn't get, the bandits did. Makes it easier to move, though, doesn't it?"

Parvana loaded a few quilts and cooking things onto the karachi. Mrs. Weera had everything packed and ready.

"Here's something they didn't get." She took a medal on a bright ribbon out of a box. "I won this in an athletics competition. It means I was the fastest woman runner in all of Afghanistan!"

The sun caught the gleaming gold on the medal. "I have other medals, too," Mrs. Weera said. "Some have been lost, but some I still have." She sighed a little, then caught herself. "Enough recess! Back to work!"

By the end of the afternoon, Mrs. Weera had been moved in and the karachi had been returned. Parvana was too wound up from the day's activities to sit still.

"I'll get some water," she offered.

"You, offering to do something?" Nooria asked. "Are you feeling well?"

Parvana ignored her. "Mother, can I take Maryam to the tap with me?"

"Yes, yes, yes!" Maryam jumped up and down. "I want to go with Parvana!"

Mother hesitated.

"Let her go," Mrs. Weera advised. "Parvana's a boy now. Maryam will be safe."

Mother relented, but first she spoke to Maryam. "What do you call Parvana when you're outside?"

"Kaseem."

"Good. And who is Kaseem?"

"My cousin."

"Very good. Remember that, and do what Parvana says. Stay right with her, do you promise?"

Maryam promised. She ran to put on her sandals. "They're too tight!" She started to cry.

"She hasn't been outside in over a year," Mother explained to Mrs. Weera. "Of course, her feet have grown."

"Bring them to me and dry your tears," Mrs. Weera told Maryam. The sandals were plastic, all in one piece. "These will do for Ali soon, so I won't cut them. For today, we'll wrap your feet in cloth. Parvana will buy you proper sandals tomorrow. She should be out in the sunshine every day," she said to Mother. "But never mind. Now that I'm here, we'll soon have this family whipped into shape!" She tied several layers of cloth around the child's feet.

"The skin will be tender if she hasn't been outside in such a long time," she told Parvana. "Mind how you go."

"I'm not sure about this," Mother began, but Parvana and her sister hurried out before she could stop them.

Fetching water took a very long time. Maryam had seen nothing but the four walls of their room for almost a year and a half. Everything outside the door was new to her. Her muscles were not used to the most basic exercise. Parvana had to help her up and down the steps as carefully as she'd had to help Father.

"This is the tap," she said to her sister, as soon as they arrived. Parvana had walked a little ahead, to smooth a pathway free of stones. She turned on the tap so that water gushed out. Maryam laughed. She stuck a hand in the flow, then snatched it back as the cool water touched her skin. She looked at Parvana, eyes wide open. Parvana helped her to do it again. This time, she let the water flow over her.

"Don't swallow any," Parvana warned, then showed her how to splash her face with water. Maryam copied her, getting more water on her clothes than on her face, but at least she had a good time.

One trip was enough for Maryam that first time. The next day, Parvana took Maryam's sandals to the market and used them as a guide to get a bigger pair. She found some used ones that a man was selling along the street. Every day after that, Maryam went to the water tap with Parvana, and bit by bit she started to get stronger.

The days began to fall into a pattern. Parvana went out to the market early every morning, returned home for lunch, then went back to the market in the afternoon.

"I could stay out there if there was a latrine I could use in the market," she said.

"I would want you to come home at mid-day anyway," Mother said. "I want to know that you are all right."

One day, after she had been working for a week, Parvana had an idea. "Mother, I'm seen as a boy, right?"

"That's the idea," Mother said.

"Then I could be your escort," Parvana said. "I could be Nooria's escort, too, and you could both get outside sometimes." Parvana was excited about this. If Nooria got some exercise, maybe she wouldn't be so grumpy. Of course, she wouldn't get much fresh air under the burqa, but at least it would be a change.

"Excellent idea," Mrs. Weera said.

"I don't want you as my escort," Nooria said, but Mother stopped her from saying any more.

"Nooria, Ali should go outside. Parvana is able to manage fine with Maryam, but Ali squirms so much. You will have to hold onto him."

"You should get out sometimes, too, Fatana," Mrs. Weera said to Mother. Mother didn't answer.

For Ali's sake, Nooria went along with the idea. Every day after lunch, Parvana, Nooria, Ali and Maryam went outside for an hour. Ali had been only a few months old when the Taliban came. All he really knew was the little room they had been shut up in for a year and a half. Nooria had not been outside, either, in all that time.

They would walk around the neighborhood until their legs got tired, then they would sit in the sunshine. When there was no one around, Parvana would keep watch, and Nooria would flip up her burqa to let the sun pour down on her face.

"I'd forgotten how good this feels," she said.

When there was no line-up at the water tap, Nooria would wash the little ones right there and save Parvana having to carry that water. Sometimes Mrs. Weera was with them with her grandchild, and all three children were washed at the same time.

Business had good days and bad days. Sometimes Parvana would sit for hours without a customer. She made less money than her father had, but the family was eating, even though most days they ate just nan and tea. The children seemed livelier than they had in a long time. The daily sun and fresh air were doing them a lot of good, although Nooria said they were harder to look after now in the room. They had more energy and always wanted to go outside, which they couldn't do when Parvana was out at work.

At the end of each day, Parvana handed over all the money she'd made. Sometimes Mother asked her to buy nan or something else on the way home. Sometimes, the times Parvana liked best, Mother would come with her to the market to shop for the family – Mrs. Weera's arguments had finally worn her down. Parvana liked having her mother all to herself, even though they didn't talk about anything other than how much cooking oil to buy, or whether they could afford soap that week.

Parvana loved being in the market. She loved watching people move along the streets, loved hearing snatches of conversation that reached her ears, loved reading the letters people brought her.

She still missed her father, but as the weeks went by, she began to get used to him being gone. It helped that she was so busy now. The family didn't talk about him, but she heard Mother and Nooria crying sometimes. Once, Maryam had a nightmare and woke up calling for Father. It took Mother a long time to get her back to sleep.

Then, one afternoon, Parvana saw her father in the market!

He was walking away from her, but Parvana was sure it was him.

"Father!" she called out, springing off her blanket and rushing after him. "Father, I'm here!"

She ran into the crowd, pushing people out of her way, until she finally reached her father and threw her arms around him.

"Father, you're safe! They let you out of prison!"

"Who are you, boy?"

Parvana looked up into a strange face. She backed away.

"I thought you were my father," she said, tears falling down her face.

The man put his hand on her shoulder. "You seem like a fine boy. I'm sorry I am not your father." He paused, then said in a lower voice, "Your father is in prison?" Parvana nodded. "People are released from prison sometimes. Don't give up hope." The man went on his way into the market, and Parvana went back to her blanket.

One afternoon, Parvana was about to shake out her blanket before going home when she noticed a spot of color on the gray wool. She bent down to pick it up.

It was a small square of embroidered cloth, no more than two inches long and an inch wide. Parvana had never seen it before. As she wondered where it had come from, her eyes went up to the blacked-out window where she thought she had seen a flicker of movement a few weeks before. There was no movement now.

The wind must have carried the little piece of embroidery to her blanket, although it hadn't been a very windy day.

She couldn't blame the wind a few days later, though, when she found a beaded bracelet on her blanket after work. She looked up at the window.

It was open. It swung out over the wall of the house.

Parvana walked closer to get a better look. In the narrow open space, Parvana saw a woman's face.

The woman gave Parvana a quick smile, then pulled the window shut.

A few days later, Parvana was sitting watching the tea boys run back and forth between the customers and the tea shop. One of the boys almost collided with a donkey. Parvana was laughing and looking the other way when a tea boy tripped on something near her and spilled a tray of empty tea cups all over her blanket.

The boy sprawled in the dust in front of Parvana. She helped him gather the cups that had rolled away. She handed him the tray and saw his face for the first time. She let out a gasp and slapped a hand across her mouth.

The tea boy was a girl from her class.

NINE

"Shauzia?" Parvana whispered.

"Call me Shafiq. And what do I call you?"

"Kaseem. What are you doing here?"

"The same as you, silly. Look, I have to get back to the tea shop. Will you be here for a while?" Parvana nodded. "Good, I'll come back."

Shauzia picked up her tea things and ran back to the shop. Parvana sat there stunned, watching her old classmate blend in with the other tea boys. It was only by looking at them very carefully that Parvana could distinguish her friend from the others. Then, realizing it wasn't a good idea to stare in case someone asked what she was looking at, Parvana looked away. Shauzia melted back into the market.

Shauzia and Parvana had not been very close in school. They had different friends. Parvana thought Shauzia had been better at spelling, but she couldn't remember for certain.

So there were other girls like her in Kabul! She tried to remember who was in Shauzia's family, but didn't think she knew. Her mind was not on the last two customers of the day, and she was glad when she finally saw Shauzia jogging over to her blanket.

"Where do you live?" Shauzia asked. Parvana pointed. "Let's pack up and walk while we talk. Here, I brought you these." She handed Parvana a small twist of paper holding several dried apricots, something she had not eaten in ages. She counted them. There was one for everyone in her household, and an extra one for her to eat now. She bit into it, and a wonderful sweetness flooded her mouth.

"Thanks!" She put the rest of the apricots in her pocket with the day's wages and began to pack up. There was no little gift left on the blanket today. Parvana didn't mind. Seeing Shauzia was quite enough excitement for one day!

"How long have you been doing this?" Shauzia asked as they walked out of the market.

"Almost a month. How about you?"

"Six months. My brother went to Iran to find work nearly a year ago, and we haven't heard from him since. My father died of a bad heart. So I went to work."

"My father was arrested."

"Have you had any news?"

"No. We went to the prison, but they wouldn't tell us anything. We haven't heard anything at all."

"You probably won't. Most people who are

arrested are never heard from again. They just disappear. I have an uncle who disappeared."

Parvana grabbed Shauzia's arm and forced her to stop walking. "My father's coming back," she said. "He is coming back!"

Shauzia nodded. "All right. Your father is different. How's business?"

Parvana let go of Shauzia's arm and started walking again. It was easier to talk about business than about her father. "Some days are good, some days are bad. Do you make much money as a tea boy?"

"Not much. There are a lot of us, so they don't have to pay well. Hey, maybe if we work together, we can come up with a better way to make money."

Parvana thought of the gifts left on the blanket. "I'd like to keep reading letters, at least for part of the day, but maybe there's something we could do for the rest of the day."

"I'd like to sell things off a tray. That way I could move with the crowd. But first I need enough money to buy the tray and the things to sell, and we never have extra money."

"We don't, either. Could we really make a lot of money that way?" Often there was not enough money for kerosene, so they could not light the lamps at night. It made the nights very long.

"From what the other boys tell me, I'd make more than I'm making now, but what's the use of talking about it? Do you miss school?"

The girls talked about their old classmates until they turned down Parvana's street, the one with Mount Parvana at the end of it. It was almost like the old days, when Parvana and her friends would walk home from school together, complaining about teachers and homework assignments.

"I live up here," Parvana said, gesturing up the flight of stairs on the outside of her building. "You must come up and say hello to everyone."

Shauzia looked at the sky to try to judge how late it was. "Yes, I'll say hello, but after that I'll have to run. When your mother tries to get me to stay for tea, you must back me up and tell her I can't."

Parvana promised, and up the stairs they went.

Everyone was surprised when she walked in with Shauzia! Everyone embraced her as if she was an old friend, even though Parvana didn't think they had ever met before. "I'll let you leave without eating this time," Mother said, "but now that you know where we are, you must bring your whole family by for a meal."

"There's only my mother and me and my two little sisters left," Shauzia said. "My mother doesn't go out. She's sick all the time. We're living with my father's parents and one of his sisters. Everybody fights all the time. I'm lucky to be able to get away from them and go to work."

"Well, you're welcome here any time," Mother said.

"Are you keeping up with your studies?" Mrs. Weera asked.

"My father's parents don't believe in girls being educated, and since we're living in their house, my mother says we have to do what they say."

"Do they mind you dressing like a boy and going out to work?"

Shauzia shrugged. "They eat the food I buy. How could they mind?"

"I've been thinking of starting up a little school here," Mrs. Weera said to Parvana's surprise. "A secret school, for a small number of girls, a few hours a week. You must attend. Parvana will let you know when."

"What about the Taliban?"

"The Taliban will not be invited." Mrs. Weera smiled at her own little joke.

"What will you teach?"

"Field hockey," Parvana replied. "Mrs. Weera was a physical education teacher."

The idea of holding a secret field hockey school in their apartment was so ridiculous that everyone started to laugh. Shauzia was still laughing when she left for home a few minutes later.

There was much to talk about that night at supper.

"We must pay her mother a visit," Mother said. "I'd like to get her story for our magazine."

"How are you going to publish it?" Parvana asked.

Mrs. Weera answered that. “We will smuggle the stories out to Pakistan, where it will be printed. Then we'll smuggle it back in, a few at a time.”

“Who will do the smuggling?” Parvana asked, half afraid they were going to make her do it. After all, if they could turn her into a boy, they could have other ideas for her as well.

“Other women in our organization,” Mother answered. “We've had visitors while you've been in the market. Some of our members have husbands who support our work and will help us.”

Nooria had ideas for the school. She had been planning to go to teacher's college when she finished high school, before the Taliban changed her plans. Father had given her and Parvana lessons for awhile when the schools first closed, but his health was not good, and the practice fell away.

“I could teach arithmetic and history,” Nooria said. “Mrs. Weera could teach health and science, and Mother could teach reading and writing.”

Parvana didn't like the idea of learning from Nooria. As a teacher, she'd be even bossier than she was as a big sister! Still, she couldn't remember the last time she'd seen Nooria excited about something, so she kept quiet.

Almost every day, Parvana and Shauzia would see each other in the market. Parvana waited for her friend to come to her. She was still too shy to run among the pack of tea boys, looking for

Shauzia. They talked about some day having enough money to buy trays and things to sell from them, but so far neither could come up with a way to make it happen.

One afternoon, when she was between customers, something landed on Parvana's head. She quickly snatched it off. After checking to make sure no one was watching, she took a look at the latest present from the Window Woman. It was a lovely white handkerchief with red embroidery around the edges.

Parvana was about to look up and smile her thanks at the window, in case the Window Woman was watching, when Shauzia ran up to the blanket.

"What do you have there?"

Parvana jumped and stuffed the handkerchief in her pocket. "Nothing. How was your day?"

"The usual, but I've got some news. A couple of tea boys heard of a way to make money. Lots of money."

"How?"

"You're not going to like it. Actually, neither do I, but it will pay better than what we've been doing."

"What is it?"

Shauzia told her. Parvana's mouth dropped open. Shauzia was right. She didn't like it.

TEN

Bones. They were going to dig up bones.

"I'm not sure this is a good idea," Parvana said to Shauzia the next morning. She had her blanket and her father's writing things with her. She hadn't been able to tell her mother about going bone-digging, so she didn't have a reason to leave her usual work things behind.

"I'm glad you brought the blanket. We can use it to haul away the bones." Shauzia ignored Parvana's objections. "Come on. We'd better hurry or we'll get left behind."

Getting left behind did not sound so terrible to Parvana, but with a quick look across the market to the painted-in window with her secret friend, she obediently fell in behind Shauzia as they ran to catch up with the group.

The sky was dark with clouds. They walked for almost an hour, down streets Parvana didn't recognize, until they came to one of the areas of Kabul most heavily destroyed by rockets. There wasn't a single intact building in the whole area, just piles of bricks, dust and rubble.

Bombs had fallen on the cemetery, too. The explosions had shaken up the graves in the ground. Here and there, white bones of the long-dead stuck up out of the rusty-brown earth. Flocks of large black and gray crows cawed and pecked at the ground around the ruined graves of the newer section of the graveyard. The slight breeze carried a rotting stench to where Parvana and Shauzia were standing, on the edge of the cemetery's older section. They watched the boys fan out across the graveyard and start digging.

Parvana noticed a man setting up a large weigh scale next to the partially destroyed wall of a building. "Who's that?"

"That's the bone broker. He buys the bones from us."

"What does he do with them?"

"He sells them to someone else."

"Why would anyone want to buy bones?"

"What do we care, as long as we get paid." Shauzia handed Parvana one of the rough boards she'd brought along to use as a shovel. "Come on, let's get busy."

They walked over to the nearest grave. "What if...what if there's still a body there?" Parvana began. "I mean, what if it's not bones yet?"

"We'll find one with a bone sticking out of it."

They walked around for a moment, looking. It didn't take long.

"Spread out the blanket," Shauzia directed. "We'll pile the bones onto it, then make a bundle out of it."

Parvana spread the blanket, wishing she were back in the market, sitting under the window where her secret friend lived.

The two girls looked at each other, each hoping the other would make the first move.

"We're here to make money, right?" Shauzia said. Parvana nodded. "Then let's make money." She grabbed hold of the bone that was sticking out of the ground and pulled. It came out of the dirt as if it were a carrot being pulled up from a garden. Shauzia tossed it on the blanket.

Not willing to let Shauzia get the better of her, Parvana took up her board and started scraping away the soil. The bombs had done much of the work for them. Many bones were barely covered by dirt and were easy to get at.

"Do you think they'd mind us doing this?" Parvana asked.

"Who?"

"The people who are buried here. Do you think they'd mind us digging them up?"

Shauzia leaned on her board. "Depends on the type of people they were. If they were nasty, stingy people, they wouldn't like it. If they were kind and generous people, they wouldn't mind."

"Would you mind?"

Shauzia looked at her, opened her mouth to speak, then closed it again and returned to her digging. Parvana didn't ask her again.

A few minutes later, Parvana unearthed a skull. "Hey, look at this!" She used the board to loosen the ground around it, then dug the rest of it up with her fingers so she wouldn't break it. She held it up to Shauzia as though it were a trophy.

"It's grinning."

"Of course it's grinning. He's glad to be out in the sunshine after being in the dark ground for so long. Aren't you glad, Mr. Skull?" She made the skull nod. "See? I told you."

"Prop him up on the gravestone. He'll be our mascot."

Parvana placed him carefully on the broken headstone. "He'll be like our boss, watching us to make sure we do it right."

They cleaned out the first grave and moved on to the next, taking Mr. Skull with them. He was joined in a little while by another skull. By the time their blanket was full of bones, there were five skulls perched in a row, grinning down at the girls.

"I have to go to the bathroom," Parvana said. "What am I going to do?"

"I have to go, too." Shauzia looked around. "There's a doorway over there," she said, pointing toward a nearby ruined building. "You go first. I'll keep watch."

"Over me?"

"Over our bones."

"I should go right out here?"

"No one is paying attention to you. It's either that or hold it."

Parvana nodded and put down her board shovel. She'd been holding it for awhile already.

Checking to make sure no one was looking, she headed over to the sheltered doorway.

"Hey, Kaseem."

Parvana looked back at her friend.

"Watch out for land mines," Shauzia said. Then she grinned. Parvana grinned back. Shauzia was probably joking, but she kept her eyes open anyway.

"Kabul has more land mines than flowers," her father used to say. "Land mines are as common as rocks and can blow you up without warning. Remember your brother."

Parvana remembered the time someone from the United Nations had come to her class with a chart showing the different kinds of land mines. She tried to remember what they looked like. All she could remember was that some were disguised as toys – special mines to blow up children.

Parvana peered into the darkness of the doorway. Sometimes armies would plant mines in buildings as they left an area. Could someone have planted a land mine there? Would she blow up if she stepped inside?

She knew she was faced with three choices. One choice was to not go to the bathroom until she got home. That was not possible – she really couldn't hold it much longer. Another choice was to go to the bathroom outside the doorway, where people might see her and figure out she was a girl. The third was to step into the darkness, go to the bathroom in private, and hope she didn't explode.

She picked the third choice. Taking a deep breath and uttering a quick prayer, she stepped through the doorway. She did not explode.

"No land mines?" Shauzia asked when Parvana returned.

"I kicked them out of the way," Parvana joked, but she was still shaking.

When Shauzia came back from her trip to the doorway, they made a bundle of the bones in the blanket, with the skulls thrown in, and carried it together over to the bone broker and his scales. He had to fill the bucket on the scales three times to accommodate all their bones. He added up the weight, named an amount, and counted up the money.

Parvana and Shauzia didn't say anything until they were well away from the bone broker's stall. They were afraid he might have made a mistake and given them too much.

"This is as much as I made in three days last week," Parvana said.

"I told you we'd make money!" Shauzia said as she handed half the cash to Parvana. "Shall we quit for the day or keep digging?"

"Keep digging, of course." Mother expected her for lunch, but she'd think of something to tell her.

In the middle of the afternoon, there was a small break in the clouds. A stream of bright sunlight hit the graveyard.

Parvana gave Shauzia a nudge, and they looked out over the mounds of dug-up graves, at the boys, sweaty and smudged with dirt, at the piles of bones beside them, gleaming white in the sudden sunshine.

"We have to remember this," Parvana said. "When things get better and we grow up, we have to remember that there was a day when we were kids when we stood in a graveyard and dug up bones to sell so that our families could eat."

"Will anyone believe us?"

"No. But we will know it happened."

"When we're rich old ladies, we'll drink tea together and talk about this day."

The girls leaned on their board shovels, watching the other children work. Then the sun went back in, and they got back to work themselves. They filled their blanket again before stopping for the day.

"If we turn all this money over to our families, they'll find things to spend it on, and we'll never get our trays," Shauzia said. "I think we should keep something back, not turn it all over to them."

"Are you going to tell your family what you were doing today?"

"No," Shauzia said.

"Neither will I," Parvana said. "I'm just going to turn over my regular amount, maybe a little bit more. I'll tell them some day, but not just now."

They parted, arranging to meet again early the next morning for another day of bone digging.

Before going home, Parvana went to the water tap. Her clothes were dirty. She washed them off as best she could while they were still on her. She took the money out of her pocket and divided it in two. Some she put back in her pocket to give to her mother. The rest she hid in the bottom of her shoulder bag, next to her father's writing paper.

Finally, she stuck her whole head under the tap, hoping the cold water would wash the images of what she had done all day out of her head. But every time she closed her eyes, she saw Mr. Skull and his companions lined up on the gravestones, grinning at her.

ELEVEN

"You're all wet," Maryam said as soon as Parvana walked through the door.

"Are you all right?" Mother rushed up to her. "Where were you? Why didn't you come home for lunch?"

"I was working," Parvana said. She tried to twist away, but her mother held her firmly by the shoulders.

"Where were you?" Mother repeated. "We've been sitting here terrified that you had been arrested!"

All that she had seen and done that day came rushing into Parvana's mind. She threw her arms around her mother's neck and cried. Mother held her until she was calm again and could talk.

"Now, tell me where you were today."

Parvana found she could not bear to say it to her mother's face, so she pressed herself up against the wall and told her.

"I was digging up graves."

"You were doing what?" Nooria asked.

Parvana left the wall and sat down on the toshak. She told them all about her day.

"Did you see real bones?" Maryam asked. Mrs. Weera told her to hush.

"So this is what we've become in Afghanistan," Mother said. "We dig up the bones of our ancestors in order to feed our families!"

"Bones are used for all sorts of things," Mrs. Weera replied. "Chicken feed, cooking oil, soap and buttons. I've heard of animal bones being used this way, not human bones, but I suppose human beings are also animals."

"Was it worth it?" Nooria asked. "How much money did you make?"

Parvana took the money out of her pocket, then dug the rest of the money out of the shoulder bag. She put it all on the floor for everyone to see.

"All that for digging up graves," Mrs. Weera breathed.

"Tomorrow you'll go back to reading letters. No more of this digging!" Mother declared. "We don't need money that badly!"

"No," Parvana said to her mother.

"I beg your pardon?"

"I don't want to quit yet. Shauzia and I want to buy trays, and things to sell from the trays. I can follow the crowd that way, instead of waiting for the crowd to come to me. I can make more money."

"We are managing fine on what you earn reading letters."

"No, Mother, we're not," Nooria said.

Mother spun around to scold Nooria for talking back, but Nooria kept talking. "We have nothing left to sell. What Parvana earns keeps us in nan, rice and tea, but there's nothing extra. We need money for rent, for propane, for fuel for the lamps. If she can make money this way, and she's willing to do it, then I think she should be allowed."

It was Parvana's turn to be stunned. Nooria taking her side? Such a thing had never happened before.

"I'm glad your father isn't here to hear you talk to me with such disrespect!"

"That's just it," Mrs. Weera said gently. "Their father isn't here. These are unusual times. They call for ordinary people to do unusual things, just to get by."

In the end, Mother relented. "You must tell me everything that happens," she told Parvana. "We will put it in the magazine, so that everyone will know."

From then on, she sent Parvana off to work with a little packet of nan for her lunch, "since you won't be back at mid-day." Although Parvana got very hungry during the day, she couldn't bear to eat in the middle of the field of bones. She gave her nan to one of Kabul's many beggars, so that someone would get some use out of it.

At the end of two weeks, they had enough money to buy the trays, with straps to go around their necks to carry them.

"We should sell things that don't weigh much," Shauzia said. They decided on cigarettes, which they could buy in big cartons and sell by the pack. They also sold chewing gum, by the pack and sometimes by the stick. Boxes of matches filled up the empty spaces on the trays.

"My tea boy days are over!" Shauzia said gleefully.

"I'm just happy to be out of the graveyard," Parvana said. She was learning to walk and balance the tray at the same time. She didn't want all her lovely goods to fall into the dirt.

The first morning back at her letter-reading post was almost over before she felt something drop on her head again.

Her aim is getting good, Parvana thought. Two direct hits in a row.

This time, the gift was a single red wooden bead. Parvana rolled it around her fingers and wondered about the woman who had sent it.

Her graveyard stint over, she was back to going outside with Nooria and the little ones in the middle of the day. A change had come over Nooria. She hadn't said anything nasty to Parvana in ages.

Or maybe it's me who's changed, Parvana thought. Arguing with Nooria simply didn't make sense any more.

In the afternoon, she would meet up with Shauzia, and the two of them would wander around Kabul looking for customers. They did not earn as much as they did in the graveyard, but they did all right. Parvana was getting to know Kabul.

"There's a crowd," Shauzia said one Friday afternoon, pointing at the sports stadium. Thousands of people were headed into the stands.

"Wonderful!" exclaimed Parvana. "People will want to smoke and chew gum while they watch a soccer game. We'll sell out. Let's go!"

They ran over to the stadium entrance as fast as they could without bouncing their cigarettes onto the ground. Several Taliban soldiers were urging people inside, yelling at them to hurry. They pushed and shoved people through the stadium gates, swinging their sticks to get the slow ones to move faster.

"Let's avoid those guys," Shauzia suggested. She and Parvana dodged around some groups of men and slipped into the stadium.

The stadium stands were almost full. The two girls were a little intimidated by so many people and stayed next to each other as they went up into the bleachers to sell their wares.

"It's awfully quiet for a soccer game," Shauzia said.

"The game hasn't started yet. Maybe the cheering will start when the players come on the field." Parvana had seen sports events on television, and people in the stands always cheered.

No one was cheering. The men did not look at all happy to be there.

"This is very strange," Parvana whispered into Shauzia's ear.

"Look out!" A large group of Taliban soldiers walked onto the field close to them. The girls ducked down low so they could see the field but the Taliban couldn't see them.

"Let's get out of here," Shauzia said. "No one's buying anything from us, and I don't know why, but I'm getting scared."

"As soon as the game starts, we'll go," Parvana said. "If we try to leave now, people will look at us."

More men moved onto the field, but they weren't soccer players. Several men were brought in with their hands tied behind their backs. A heavy-looking table was carried out by two of the soldiers.

"I think those men are prisoners," Shauzia whispered.

"What are prisoners doing at a soccer game?" Parvana whispered back. Shauzia shrugged.

One of the men was untied, then bent over the table. Several soldiers held him down, his arms stretched out across the table-top.

Parvana didn't have a clue what was going on. Where were the soccer players?

All of a sudden one of the soldiers took out a sword, raised it above his head and brought it down on the man's arm. Blood flew in every direction. The man cried out in pain.

Next to Parvana, Shauzia started screaming. Parvana clamped her hand over Shauzia's mouth and pulled her down to the floor of the stadium stands. The rest of the stadium was quiet. There was still no cheering.

"Keep your heads down, boys," a kind voice above Parvana said. "There will be time enough when you are old to see such things."

The cigarettes and gum had fallen off their trays, but the men around them gathered up the spilled items and returned them to the girls.

Parvana and Shauzia stayed huddled among people's feet, listening to the sword thwack down on six more arms.

"These men are thieves," the soldiers called out to the crowd. "See how we punish thieves? We cut off one of their hands! See what we do!"

Parvana and Shauzia did not look. They kept their heads down until the man with the kind voice said, "It's over for another week. Come, now, raise yourselves up." He and several other men surrounded Parvana and Shauzia, escorting them out of the stadium.

Just before she left, Parvana caught a glimpse of a young Talib man, too young to have a beard.

He was holding up a rope strung with four severed hands, like beads on a necklace. He was laughing and showing off his booty to the crowd. Parvana hoped Shauzia hadn't seen.

"Go home, boys," the kind man told them. "Go home and remember better things."

TWELVE

Parvana stayed home for a few days. She went out to get water, and she and Nooria took the little ones out into the sunshine, but beyond that, she wanted to be with her family.

"I need a break," she told her mother. "I don't want to see anything ugly for a little while."

Mother and Mrs. Weera had heard about the events at the stadium from other women's group members. Some had husbands or brothers who had been there. "This goes on every Friday," Mother said. "What century are we living in?"

"Will Father be taken there?" Parvana wanted to ask, but she didn't. Her mother wouldn't know.

During her days at home, Parvana coached Maryam on her counting, tried to learn mending from Nooria and listened to Mrs. Weera's stories. They weren't as good as her father's stories. Mostly they were descriptions of field hockey games or other athletic events. Still, they were entertaining, and Mrs. Weera was so enthusiastic about them that she made other people enthusiastic, too.

No one said anything to Parvana when the bread ran out, but she got up and went to work that day anyway. Some things just had to be taken care of.

"I'm glad you're back," Shauzia said when she saw Parvana in the market. "I missed you. Where were you?"

"I didn't feel like working," Parvana replied. "I wanted some quiet days."

"I wouldn't mind some of those, but it's noisier in my home than it is out here."

"Is your family still arguing?"

Shauzia nodded. "My father's parents never really liked my mother anyway. Now they depend on her. It makes them grumpy. Mother's grumpy because we have to live with them since there's no place else to go. So everybody is grumpy. If they're not actually arguing, they sit and glare at each other."

Parvana thought about how it felt in her home sometimes, with everyone going around with tight lips and unshed tears in their eyes. It sounded even worse in Shauzia's house.

"Can I tell you a secret?" Shauzia asked. She led Parvana over to a low wall, and they sat down.

"Of course you can tell me. I won't tell anybody."

"I'm saving money, a little bit each day. I'm getting out of here."

"Where? When?"

Shauzia kicked at the wall in a rhythm, but

Parvana stopped her. She'd seen the Taliban hit a child for banging on an old board like it was a drum. The Taliban hated music.

"I'll stay until next spring," Shauzia said. "I'll have a lot of money saved by then, and it's better not to travel in the winter."

"Do you think we'll still have to be boys in the spring? That's a long time from now."

"I want to still be a boy then," Shauzia insisted. "If I turn back into a girl, I'll be stuck at home. I couldn't stand that."

"Where will you go?"

"France. I'll get on a boat and go to France."

"Why France?" she asked.

Shauzia's face brightened. "In every picture I've seen of France, the sun is shining, people are smiling, and flowers are blooming. France people must have bad days, too, but I don't think their bad days can be very bad, not bad like here. In one picture I saw a whole field of purple flowers. That's where I want to go. I want to walk into that field and sit down in the middle of it, and not think about anything."

Parvana struggled to remember her map of the world. "I'm not sure you can get to France by boat."

"Sure I can. I've got it all figured out. I'll tell a group of nomads that I'm an orphan, and I'll travel with them into Pakistan. My father told me they go back and forth with the seasons, looking for grass for their sheep. In Pakistan, I head down to the

Arabian Sea, get on a boat, and go to France!" She spoke as if nothing could be more simple. "The first boat I get on might not go directly to France, but at least I'll get away from here. Everything will be easy once I get away from here."

"You'll go by yourself!" Parvana couldn't imagine undertaking such a journey on her own.

"Who will notice one little orphan boy?" Shauzia replied. "No one will pay any attention to me. I just hope I haven't left it too late."

"What do you mean?"

"I'm starting to grow." Her voice dropped almost to a whisper. "My shape is changing. If it changes too much, I'll turn back into a girl, and then I'll be stuck here. You don't think I'll grow too fast, do you? Maybe I should leave before the spring. I don't want things to pop out of me all of a sudden."

Parvana did not want Shauzia to leave, but she tried to be honest with her friend. "I can't remember how it happened with Nooria. Mostly, I watched her hair grow. But I don't think growing happens all of a sudden. I'd say you have time."

Shauzia started to kick the building again. Then she stood up so she wouldn't be tempted. "That's what I'm counting on."

"You'll leave your family? How will they eat?"

"I can't help that!" Shauzia's voice rose and caught, as she tried not to cry. "I just have to get out of here. I know that makes me a bad person, but what else can I do? I'll die if I have to stay here!"

Parvana remembered arguments between her father and mother – her mother insisting they leave Afghanistan, her father insisting they stay. For the first time, Parvana wondered why her mother didn't just leave. In an instant, she answered her own question. She couldn't sneak away with four children to take care of.

"I just want to be an ordinary kid again," Parvana said. "I want to sit in a classroom and go home and eat food that someone else has worked for. I want my father to be around. I just want a normal, boring life."

"I don't think I could ever sit in a classroom again," Shauzia said. "Not after all this." She adjusted her tray of cigarettes. "You'll keep my secret?"

Parvana nodded.

"Do you want to come with me?" Shauzia asked. "We could look after each other."

"I don't know." She could leave Afghanistan, but could she leave her family? She didn't think so.

"I have a secret, too," she said. She reached into her pocket and pulled out the little gifts she'd received from the woman at the window. She told Shauzia where they had come from.

"Wow," Shauzia said. "That's a real mystery. I wonder who she could be. Maybe she's a princess!"

"Maybe we can save her!" Parvana said. She saw herself climbing up the wall, smashing the painted-over window with her bare fist and helping the princess down to the ground. The princess would be wearing silk and jewels. Parvana would swing her up onto the back of a fast horse, and they'd ride through Kabul in a cloud of dust.

"I'll need a fast horse," she said.

"How about one of those?" Shauzia pointed to a herd of long-haired sheep snuffling through the garbage on the ground of the market.

Parvana laughed, and the girls went back to work.

At her mother's suggestion, Parvana had bought a few pounds of dried fruit and nuts. Nooria and Maryam put them into smaller bags, enough for a snack for one person. Parvana sold these from her blanket and her tray.

In the afternoon, she and Shauzia wandered around the market looking for customers. Sometimes they went to the bus depot, but they had a lot of competition there. Many boys were trying to sell things. They would run right up to someone and stand in the person's way, saying, "Buy my gum! Buy my fruit! Buy my cigarettes!" Parvana and Shauzia were too shy for that. They preferred to wait for customers to notice them.

Parvana was tired. She wanted to sit in a classroom and be bored by a geography lesson. She wanted to be with her friends and talk about homework and games and what to do on school holidays. She didn't want to know any more about death or blood or pain.

The marketplace ceased to be interesting. She no longer laughed when a man got into an argument with a stubborn donkey. She was no longer interested in the snippets of conversation she heard from people strolling by. Everywhere, there were people who were hungry and sick. Women in burqas sat on the pavement and begged, their babies stretched across their laps.

And there was no end to it. This wasn't a summer vacation that would end and then life would get back to normal. This was normal, and Parvana was tired of it.

Summer had come to Kabul. Flowers pushed up out of the ground, not caring about the Taliban or land mines, and actually bloomed, just as they did in peace time.

Parvana's home, with its little window, grew very hot during the long June days, and the little ones were cranky at night with the heat. Even Maryam lost her good humor and whined along with the two youngest children. Parvana was glad to be able to leave in the morning.

Summer brought fruit into Kabul from the fertile valleys – those that had not been bombed into extinction. Parvana brought treats home for her family on the days she made a bit more money. They had peaches one week, plums the next.

The clear mountain passes brought traders from all over Afghanistan into Kabul. From her blanket in the marketplace, and when she walked around selling cigarettes with Shauzia, Parvana saw tribal peoples from Bamiyan, from the Registan Desert region near Kandahar, and from the Wakhan Corridor near China.

Sometimes these men would stop and buy dried fruit or cigarettes from her. Sometimes they had something for her to read or write. She would always ask where they were from and what it was like there, so she could have something new to tell her family when she went home. Sometimes they told her about the weather. Sometimes they told of the beautiful mountains or the fields of opium poppies blooming into flower, or the orchards heavy with fruit. Sometimes they told her of the war, of battles they had seen and people they had lost. Parvana remembered it all to tell her family when she got home.

Through Mother's and Mrs. Weera's women's group, a secret little school was started. Nooria was the teacher. The Taliban would close down any school they discovered, so Nooria and Mrs. Weera were very careful. This school held only five girls, including Maryam. They were all around her age. They were taught in two different groups, never at the same time two days running. Sometimes the students came to Nooria, sometimes Nooria went to the students. Sometimes Parvana was her escort. Sometimes she carried a squirming Ali.

"He's getting too big to be carried around," Nooria said to Parvana on one of their noon-day walks. Mother had allowed Nooria to leave Ali at home, to get a break from him. They only had Maryam with them, and she was no trouble.

"How are your students doing?"

"They can't learn much in a few hours a week," Nooria replied. "And we don't have any books or school supplies. Still, I guess it's better than nothing."

The little gifts from the window kept landing on Parvana's blanket every couple of weeks. Sometimes it was a piece of embroidery. Sometimes it was a piece of candy or a single bead.

It was as if the Window Woman was saying, "I'm still here," in the only way she could. Parvana checked carefully around her blanket every time she went to leave the market, in case one of the gifts had rolled off.

One afternoon, she heard sounds coming from above her. A man was very angry. He was shouting at a women who was crying and screaming. Parvana heard thuds and more screams. Without thinking, she sprang to her feet and looked up at the window, but she couldn't see anything through the painted glass.

"What goes on in a man's house is his own business," a voice behind her said. She spun around to see a man holding out an envelope. "Forget about that and turn your mind to your own business. I have a letter for you to read."

She was planning to tell her family about the whole incident that night, but she didn't get the chance. Instead, her family had something to tell her.

"You'll never guess," her mother said. "Nooria's getting married."

THIRTEEN

"But you've never even met him!" Parvana exclaimed to Nooria the next day at noon. It was the first chance they'd had to talk about it, just the two of them.

"Of course I've met him. His family and ours were neighbors for many years."

"But that was when he was a boy. I thought you wanted to go back to school!"

"I will be going back to school," Nooria said. "Didn't you listen to anything Mother was saying last night? I'll be living in Mazar-e-Sharif, in the north. The Taliban aren't in that part of Afghanistan. Girls can still go to school there. Both of his parents are educated. I can finish school, and they'll even send me to the university in Mazar."

All of this was written in a letter that had arrived while Parvana was out at work. The women in the groom's family belonged to the same women's group as Mother. The letter had passed from one member of the group to another until it finally reached

Mother. Parvana had read the letter, but she still had a lot of questions.

"Do you really want to do this?"

Nooria nodded. "Look at my life here, Parvana. I hate living under the Taliban. I'm tired of looking after the little ones. My school classes happen so seldom, they're of almost no value. There's no future for me here. At least in Mazar I can go to school, walk the streets without having to wear a burqa, and get a job when I've completed school. Maybe in Mazar I can have some kind of life. Yes, I want to do this."

There was a lot of discussion in the following few days about what would happen next. Parvana, out at work, had no voice in these discussions. She was merely informed of the plans when she got home in the evening.

"We'll go to Mazar for the wedding," Mother announced. "We can all stay with your aunt while the wedding is prepared. Then Nooria will go to live with her new family. We will return to Kabul in October."

"We can't leave Kabul!" Parvana exclaimed. "What about Father? What will happen if he gets out of prison and we're not here? He won't know where to look for us!"

"I'll be here," Mrs. Weera said. "I can tell your father where you are and look after him until you get back."

"I'm not sending Nooria off to Mazar all by herself," Mother said. "And since you are a child, you will come with us."

"I'm not going," Parvana insisted. She even stamped her feet.

"You will do as you're told," Mother said. "All this running around wild in the streets has made you think you're above yourself."

"I'm not going to Mazar!" Parvana repeated, stamping her feet again.

"Since your feet want to move around so much, you'd better take them out for a walk," Mrs. Weera said. "You can fetch some water while you're at it."

Parvana grabbed the bucket and got some satisfaction out of slamming the door behind her.

Parvana glowered for three days. Finally, Mother said, "You can take that awful frown off your face. We've decided to leave you here. Not because of your bad behavior. A child of eleven has no business telling her mother what she will and will not do. We're leaving you here because it will be too difficult to explain your appearance. Your aunt will keep your secret, of course, but we can't count on everyone to be so careful. We can't take the chance of word about you getting back here."

Although she was glad to remain in Kabul, Parvana found herself sulking that they weren't taking her with them. "I'm not satisfied with anything any more," she told Shauzia the next day.

"Neither am I," Shauzia said. "I used to think that if only I could sell things from a tray, I'd be happy, but I'm not happy at all. I make more money this way than I did as a tea boy, but it's not enough to make any real difference. We still go hungry. My family still argues all the time. Nothing is better."

"What's the answer?"

"Maybe someone should drop a big bomb on the country and start again."

"They've tried that," Parvana said. "It only made things worse."

One of the women in the local branch of the women's group was going to accompany Parvana's family to the city of Mazar. Her husband would go with them as the official escort. If the Taliban asked, Mother would be the husband's sister, and Nooria, Maryam and Ali would be the nieces and nephews.

Nooria cleaned out the family cupboard one last time. Parvana watched her pack up her things. "If all goes well, we'll be in Mazar in a couple of days," Nooria said.

"Are you scared?" Parvana asked. "It's a long journey."

"I keep thinking of things that can go wrong, but Mother says everything will be fine." They would be traveling together in the back of a truck. "As soon as I get out of Taliban territory, I'm going to throw off my burqa and tear it into a million pieces."

Parvana went to the market the next day to buy

the family some food for the journey. She wanted to buy Nooria a present, too. She wandered through the market looking at things for sale. She finally decided on a pen in a beaded case. Every time Nooria used it at university, and later when she became a real school teacher, she would think of Parvana.

"We'll be gone for most of the summer," Mother reminded Parvana the night before they left. "You'll be fine with Mrs. Weera. Do what she tells you, and don't give her any trouble."

"Parvana and I will be good company for each other," Mrs. Weera said, "and by the time you get back, the magazine should be coming in from Pakistan, all printed and ready to distribute."

They left very early the next day. The mid-July morning was fresh but held the promise of hot weather to follow.

"We'd best be going," Mother said. Since there was no one else on the street, Mother, Nooria and Mrs. Weera had their burqas flipped up so their faces could be seen.

Parvana kissed Ali, who squirmed and fussed, grumpy from being woken up early. Mother got him settled on the floor of the truck. Parvana said good-bye to Maryam after that, then lifted her into the truck.

"We will see you by the middle of September," Mother said as she hugged Parvana. "Make me proud of you."

"I will," Parvana said, trying not to cry.

"I don't know when we'll see each other again," Nooria said just before she climbed into the truck. She had Parvana's gift clutched in her hand.

"It won't be long," Parvana said, grinning even though tears fell from her eyes. "As soon as your new husband realizes how bossy you are, he'll send you back to Kabul as fast as he can."

Nooria laughed and climbed into the truck. She and Mother covered themselves with their burqas. The women's group member and her husband were sitting in the front seat. Parvana and Mrs. Weera watched and waved as the truck drove out of sight.

"I think we could both use a cup of tea," Mrs. Weera said, and they went upstairs.

Parvana found the next few weeks to be a strange time. With only herself, Mrs. Weera and Mrs. Weera's grandchild, the apartment seemed almost empty. Fewer people meant fewer chores, less noise and more free time. Parvana even missed Ali's fussing. As the weeks went by, she looked forward more and more to everyone coming back.

Still, she did enjoy having more free time. For the first time since Father's arrest, she took his books out of their secret place in the cupboard. Evenings were spent reading and listening to Mrs. Weera's stories.

Mrs. Weera believed in trusting her. "In some parts of the country, girls your age are getting married and having babies," she said. "I'm here if you need me, but if you want to be responsible for yourself, that's fine, too."

She insisted that Parvana keep some of her wages as pocket money. Sometimes Parvana would treat Shauzia to lunch at one of the kebab stands in the market. They'd find a sheltered place to go to the bathroom and keep working all day. Parvana preferred to come home at the end of the day, rather than at noon. It meant that one more day was over, and her family would soon be home.

Toward the end of August, there was a bad rainstorm. Shauzia had already gone home. She had seen the darkening sky and didn't feel like getting wet.

Parvana wasn't so clever, and she got caught in the rain. She covered her tray with her arms to keep her cigarettes dry and ducked into a bombed-out building. She would wait out the storm there and go home when it was over.

The darkness outside made the inside even blacker. It took awhile for her eyes to adjust. While she waited for that to happen, she leaned against the doorway, watching the rain turn Kabul's dust into mud.

Gusts of wind mixed with driving rain forced Parvana deeper inside the building. Hoping there were no land mines, she found a dry spot and sat down. The pounding of the rain beat a steady rhythm as it hit the ground. Parvana began to nod. In a little while, she was asleep.

When she woke up, the rain had stopped, although the sky was no lighter.

"It must be late," Parvana said out loud.

It was then that she heard the sound of a woman crying.

FOURTEEN

The sound was too soft and too sad to be startling.

"Hello?" Parvana called out, not too loudly.

It was too dark to see where the woman was sitting. Parvana rummaged around on her tray until she found a box of the matches she sold with the cigarettes. She struck one, and the light flared up. She held the flame out in front of her, looking for the crying woman.

It took three matches before she saw the figure huddled against the nearby wall. She kept striking matches so she could see as she made her way over to the woman.

"What's your name?" Parvana asked. The woman kept crying. "I'll tell you my name, then. It's Parvana. I should tell you that my name is Kaseem, because I'm pretending to be a boy. I'm dressed like a boy so that I can earn some money, but I'm really a girl. So now you know my secret."

The woman said nothing. Parvana glanced out the door. It was getting late. If she was going to be home before curfew, she'd have to leave now.

"Come with me," Parvana said. "My mother is away, but Mrs. Weera is at home. She can fix any problem." She struck another match and held it up to the woman's face. It suddenly dawned on her that she could see the woman's face. It wasn't covered up.

"Where is your burqa?" She looked around but couldn't see one. "Are you outside without a burqa?"

The woman nodded.

"What are you doing outside without a burqa? You could get in a lot of trouble for that."

The woman just shook her head.

Parvana had an idea. "Here's what we'll do. I'll go home and borrow Mrs. Weera's burqa and bring it back to you. Then we'll go back to my place together. All right?"

Parvana started to stand up, but the woman grabbed onto her arm.

Again Parvana looked out the door at the coming night. "I have to let Mrs. Weera know where I am. She's fine with me being out during the day, but if I'm not back at night, she'll be worried." Still the woman did not let go.

Parvana didn't know what to do. She couldn't stay in the building all night, but this frightened woman clearly did not want to be left alone. Groping in the dark for her tray, she found two little bags of dried fruit and nuts.

"Here," she said, handing one to the woman. "We'll think better if we eat."

The woman downed the fruit and nuts in almost one swallow. "You must be starving," Parvana said, passing her another bag.

Parvana chewed and thought and finally decided what to do. "This is the best suggestion I have," she said. "If you have a better idea, let me know. Otherwise, this is what we'll do. We'll wait until it gets very, very dark. Then we'll head back to my place together. Do you have a chador?"

The woman shook her head. Parvana wished she had her pattu, but it was summer, so she had left it at home.

"Do you agree?" Parvana asked.

The woman nodded.

"Good. I think we should move close to the door. That way, when it's time, we can see our way out to the street without lighting a match. I don't want to draw any attention to us."

With a bit of gentle pulling, Parvana got the woman to her feet. Carefully they made their way to a spot just inside the door, but still hidden from the view of anyone passing by. They waited in silence for night to fall.

Kabul was a dark city at night. It had been under curfew for more than twenty years. Many of the street lights had been knocked out by bombs, and many of those still standing did not work.

"Kabul was the hot spot of central Asia," Parvana's mother and father used to say. "We used to walk down the streets at midnight, eating ice cream. Earlier in the evening, we would browse through book shops and record stores. It was a city of lights, progress and excitement."

Parvana could not even imagine what it had looked like then.

Before long it was as dark as it would get. "Stay right with me," Parvana said, although she needn't have bothered. The woman was gripping her hand tightly. "It's not far, but I don't know how long it will take us tonight. Don't worry." She smiled, pretending to be brave. She knew it was too dark in the doorway for the woman to see her smile, but it made Parvana feel better.

"I'm Malali, leading the troops through enemy territory," she murmured to herself. That helped, too, although it was hard to feel like a battle heroine with a cigarette tray hanging around her neck.

The narrow, winding streets of the marketplace were very different in the dark. Parvana could hear their footsteps echo along the narrow corridors. She was about to tell the woman to walk more softly, that the Taliban had made it a crime for women to make noise when they walked, but she changed her mind. If the Taliban caught them out after curfew and with the woman without a burqa or a head covering at all, the noise they were making would be the least of their problems. Parvana remembered the scene in the stadium. She didn't want to know what the Taliban would do to her and her companion.

Parvana saw headlights approaching and pulled the woman into another doorway until the truck filled with soldiers moved on down the street. Several times they almost tripped on the uneven pavement. For one long, heart-stopping minute, Parvana thought she was lost. Finally she got her bearings, and they kept moving.

When they got to Parvana's street, she started to run, and she pulled the woman along with her. She was so scared by this point, she thought if she didn't get home right away, she would collapse.

"You're back!" Mrs. Weera was so relieved, she hugged both Parvana and the woman before she realized what she was doing. "You've brought someone with you! You are very welcome here, my dear." She took a critical look at the woman. "Parvana, you didn't bring her through the streets like that? With no burqa?"

Parvana explained what had happened. "I think she's in trouble," she said.

Mrs. Weera didn't hesitate. She put her arm around the woman. "We'll get the details later. There's warm water for you to wash in, and hot food for supper. You don't look much older than Parvana!"

Parvana took a good look at her companion. She hadn't seen the woman in the light before. She looked a little bit younger than Nooria.

"Fetch me some clean clothes," Mrs. Weera told Parvana. Parvana took a shalwar kameez of Mother's out of the cupboard, and Mrs. Weera took the young woman into the washroom and closed the door.

Parvana restocked her tray for the next day, then spread the meal cloth out on the floor. By the time she had put out the nan and the cups for tea, Mrs. Weera emerged from the washroom with their guest.

Dressed in Mother's clean clothes, her hair washed and pulled back, the woman looked less scared and more tired. She managed to drink half a cup of tea and eat a few mouthfuls of rice before she fell asleep.

She was still sleeping when Parvana left for work the next morning.

"Fetch me some water, please, dear," Mrs. Weera asked before Parvana went off to the market. "That poor girl's clothes need washing."

Finally, that night, after eating supper, the girl was able to talk.

"My name is Homa," she said. "I escaped from Mazar-e-Sharif just after the Taliban captured the city."

"The Taliban has captured Mazar!" Parvana exclaimed. "That can't be! My mother is there. My brother and sisters are there."

"The Taliban is in Mazar," Homa repeated. "They went from house to house, looking for enemies. They came to my house. They came right inside! They grabbed my father and my brother and took them outside. They shot them right in the street. My mother started hitting them, and they shot her, too. I ran back inside and hid in a closet. I was there for a long, long time. I thought they would kill me, too, but they were finished killing people at my house. They were busy killing at other houses.

"Finally I left the closet and went downstairs. There were bodies all over the street. Some soldiers drove by in a truck. They forbade us to move the bodies of our families, or even cover them up. They said we must stay inside.

"I was so scared they would come back for me! When it got dark, I ran outside. I ran from building to building, looking out for the soldiers. There were bodies everywhere. The wild dogs had started eating some of the bodies, so there were pieces of people on the sidewalks and in the streets. I even saw a dog carrying a person's arm in its mouth!

"I couldn't face anything else. There was a truck stopped on the street. Its motor was running. I jumped into the back and hid among the bundles. Wherever the truck was going, it couldn't be worse than where I was.

"We traveled a long, long time. When I finally got out, I was in Kabul. I went from the truck to the building where Parvana found me." Homa started to cry. "I just left them there! I left my mother and my father and my brother lying in the street for the dogs to eat!"

Mrs. Weera put her arms around Homa, but the girl could not be comforted. She cried until she collapsed into an exhausted sleep.

Parvana couldn't move. She couldn't speak. All she could do was picture her mother, sisters and brother, dead in the streets of a strange city.

"There's no evidence your family is hurt, Parvana," Mrs. Weera said. "Your mother is a smart, strong woman, and so is Nooria. We must believe they are alive. We must not give up hope!"

Parvana was fresh out of hope. She did what her mother had done. She crawled onto the toshak, covered herself with a quilt and resolved to stay there forever.

For two days she stayed on the toshak. "This is what the women in our family do when we're sad," she said to Mrs. Weera.

"They don't stay there forever," Mrs. Weera said. "They get up again, and they fight back."

Parvana didn't answer her. She didn't want to get up again. She was tired of fighting back.

Mrs. Weera was gentle with her at first, but she had her hands full with Homa and her grandchild.

Late in the afternoon of the second day, Shauzia showed up at Parvana's door.

"I'm very glad to see you," Mrs. Weera said, nodding toward Parvana. They went out onto the landing to speak for a moment, out of Parvana's earshot. Then they came back in and, after fetching a couple of buckets of water, Shauzia sat down on the toshak beside Parvana.

She talked about ordinary things for awhile, how her sales had been, people she'd seen in the market, conversations she'd had with some of the tea boys and other working boys. Finally she said, "I don't like working alone. The marketplace isn't the same when you're not there. Won't you come back?"

Put to her like that, Parvana knew she could not refuse. She'd known all along that she would have to get up. She wasn't really about to stay on that toshak until she died. Part of her wanted to slip away from everything, but another part wanted to get up and stay alive and continue to be Shauzia's friend. With a little prodding from Shauzia, that was the part that won.

Parvana got out of bed and carried on as before. She did her work in the market, fetched water, listened to Mrs. Weera's stories and got to know Homa. She did all these things because she didn't know what else to do. But she moved through her days as though she were moving through an awful nightmare – a nightmare from which there was no release in the morning.

Then, late one afternoon, Parvana came home from work to find two men gently helping her father up the steps to the apartment. He was alive. At least part of the nightmare was over.

FIFTEEN

The man who came back from prison was barely recognizable, but Parvana knew who he was. Although his white shalwar kameez was now gray and tattered, although his face was drawn and pale, he was still her father. Parvana clung to him so tightly she had to be pulled away by Mrs. Weera so that her father could lie down.

"We found him on the ground outside the prison," one of the men who had brought him home said to Mrs. Weera. "The Taliban released him, but he was unable to go anywhere on his own. He told us where he lived, so my friend and I put him on our karachi and brought him here."

Parvana was down on the toshak with her father, clinging to him and weeping. She knew that the men stayed to tea, but it wasn't until they were getting up to leave, to make it back to their homes before curfew, that she remembered her manners.

She got to her feet. "Thank you for bringing my father back," she said.

The men left. Parvana started to lie back down

beside her father, but Mrs. Weera stopped her. "Let him rest. There will be time to talk tomorrow."

Parvana obeyed, but it took days of Mrs. Weera's careful nursing before Father even started to get well. Most of the time he was too ill and weary to talk. He coughed a lot.

"That prison must have been cold and damp," Mrs. Weera said. Parvana helped her make a broth and fed it to her father hot, off a spoon, until he was able to sit up and eat.

"Now you are both my daughter and my son," Father said when he was well enough to notice her new appearance. He rubbed his hand over her cropped hair and smiled.

Parvana made many trips to the water tap. Father had been beaten badly, and the poultice bandages Mrs. Weera put over his wounds had to be changed and washed frequently. Homa helped, too, mostly by keeping Mrs. Weera's granddaughter quiet so Father could rest.

Parvana didn't mind that he was unable to talk right away. She was overjoyed just to have him home. She spent her days earning money, and her evenings helping Mrs. Weera. When her father felt better, she would read to him from his books.

Homa knew some English from studying it in school, and one day Parvana came home from work to hear Homa and Father talking English to each other. Homa hesitated a lot, but Father's words flowed smoothly into each other.

"Did you bring us home another educated woman today?" Father asked Parvana, smiling.

"No, Father," Parvana replied. "I just brought home onions." For some reason, everyone thought that was funny, and there was laughter in Parvana's home for the first time since her father's arrest.

One thing in her life had been repaired. Her father was home now. Maybe the rest of the family would come back, too.

Parvana was filled with hope. In the market she chased after customers just like the real boys did. Mrs. Weera suggested some medicine for Father, and Parvana worked and worked until she had earned the money to buy it. It seemed to help.

"I feel like I'm working for something now," she told Shauzia one day as they walked around looking for customers. "I'm working to get my family back."

"I'm working for something, too," Shauzia said. "I'm working to get away from Afghanistan."

"Won't you miss your family?" Parvana asked.

"My grandfather has started to look for a husband for me," Shauzia replied. "I overheard him talking to my grandmother. He said I should get married soon, that since I'm so young, I'll fetch a good bride-price, and they will have lots of money to live on."

"Won't your mother stop him?"

"What could she do? She has to live with them. She has nowhere else to go." Shauzia stopped walking and looked at Parvana. "I *can't* be married! I *won't* be married!"

"How will your mother manage without you there? How will she eat?"

"What can I do?" Shauzia asked, the question coming out as a wail. "If I stay here and get married, my life will be over. If I leave, maybe I'll have a chance. There must be some place in this world where I can live. Am I wrong to think like this?" She wiped the tears from her face. "What else can I do?"

Parvana didn't know how to comfort her friend.

One day Mrs. Weera had a visitor, a member of the women's group who had just come out of Mazar. Parvana was at work, but Father told her about the visit that evening.

"A lot of people have fled Mazar," he said. "They are staying in refugee camps outside the city"

"Is that where Mother is?"

"It's possible. We won't know unless we go to the camps and look."

"How can we do that? Are you well enough to travel?"

"I will never be well enough," Father said, "but we should go anyway."

"When do we leave?" Parvana asked.

"As soon as I can arrange transport. Can you

carry a message for me to the men who brought me home from prison? I think, with their help, we can be on our way in a couple of weeks."

Parvana had been wanting to ask her father something for awhile. "Why did the Taliban let you go?"

"I don't know why they arrested me. How would I know why they let me go?"

Parvana would have to be satisfied with that for an answer.

Her life was about to change again. She was surprised at how calm she felt. She decided it was because her father was back.

"We'll find them," Parvana said with complete confidence. "We'll find them and bring them home."

Mrs. Weera was going to Pakistan. "Homa will come with me. We'll put her to work there." They were going to link up with the members of the women's group who were organizing Afghan women in exile.

"Where will you stay?"

"I have a cousin in one of the camps," Mrs. Weera replied. "She has been wanting me to come and live with her."

"Is there a school there?"

"If there isn't, we'll start one. Life is very difficult for Afghans in Pakistan. There is a lot of work to do."

Parvana had an idea. "Take Shauzia with you!"

"Shauzia?"

"She wants to leave. She hates it here. Couldn't she go with you? She could be your escort!"

"Shauzia has family here. Do you mean to say she would just leave her family? Desert the team just because the game is rough?"

Parvana said no more. In a way, Mrs. Weera was right. That was what Shauzia was doing. But Shauzia was also right. Didn't she have a right to seek out a better life? Parvana couldn't decide who was more right.

A few days before they were to leave for Mazar, Parvana was sitting on her blanket in the marketplace when something hit her on the head. It was a tiny camel made out of beads. The Window Woman was still alive! She was all right, or at least well enough to let Parvana know she was still there. Parvana wanted to jump up and down and dance. She wanted to yell and wave at the painted window. Instead she sat quietly and tried to think of a way to say goodbye.

She was almost home that afternoon when she thought of a way.

Heading back to the market after lunch, she carefully dug up some wildflowers that were growing among the bombed-out ruins. She had seen them growing there in other years, and hoped she was right in thinking they were the kind that grew year after year. If she planted the flowers in the spot where she usually put her blanket, the Window

Woman would know she wasn't coming back. The flowers would be something pretty to look at. She hoped they would make a good present.

In her spot in the market, Parvana dug up the hard soil first by pounding into it with her ankle. She used her hands, too, as well as a rock she found nearby.

The men and boys in the market gathered around to watch her. Anything different was entertainment.

"Those flowers won't grow in that soil," someone said. "There are no nutrients in it."

"Even if they grow, they will be trampled."

"The marketplace is no spot for flowers. Why are you planting them there?"

Through the voices of derision came another voice. "Do none of you appreciate nature? This boy has undertaken to bring a bit of beauty into our gray marketplace, and do you thank him? Do you help him?" An old man pushed his way to the front of the little gathering. With difficulty, he knelt down to help Parvana plant the flowers. "Afghans love beautiful things," he said, "but we have seen so much ugliness, we sometimes forget how wonderful a thing like a flower is."

He asked one of the tea boys hovering nearby for some water from the tea shop. It was fetched, and he poured it around the flowers, soaking the earth around them.

The plants had wilted. They didn't stand up properly.

"Are they dead?" Parvana asked.

"No, no, not dead. They may look scraggly and dying now," he said, "but the roots are good. When the time is right, these roots will support plants that are healthy and strong." He gave the earth a final pat, and Parvana and one of the others helped him up. He smiled once more at Parvana, then walked away.

Parvana waited by her flowers until the crowd had gone. When she was sure no one was watching, she looked up at the window and waved a quick goodbye. She wasn't sure, but she thought she saw someone wave back.

Two days later they were ready to leave. They were going to travel by truck, just as the rest of the family had done.

"Am I traveling as your son or your daughter?" Parvana asked Father.

"You decide," he said. "Either way, you will be my little Malali."

"Look at what's here!" Mrs. Weera said. After making sure the coast was clear, she took several copies of Mother's magazine out from under her burqa. "Isn't it beautiful?"

Parvana flipped through the magazine quickly before hiding it again. "It's wonderful," she said.

"Tell your mother that copies are being sent out to women all over the world. She has helped to let the world know what is happening in Afghanistan. Be sure you tell her that. What she did was very important. And tell her we need her back, to work on the next issue."

"I'll tell her." She gave Mrs. Weera a hug. Both Mrs. Weera and Homa were wearing burqas, but she could tell by hugging them who was who.

It was time to leave. Suddenly, just as the truck was ready to pull out onto the road, Shauzia appeared.

"You made it!" Parvana said, hugging her friend.

"Goodbye, Parvana," Shauzia said. She handed Parvana a bag of dried apricots. "I'm leaving soon, too. I met some nomads who will take me to Pakistan as a shepherd. I'm not waiting until next spring. It would be too lonely here without you."

Parvana didn't want to say goodbye. "When will we see each other again?" she asked in a panic. "How will we keep in touch?"

"I've got it all figured out," Shauzia said. "We'll meet again on the first day of spring, twenty years from now."

"All right. Where?"

"The top of the Eiffel Tower in Paris. I told you I was going to France."

Parvana laughed. "I'll be there," she said. "We won't say goodbye, then. We'll just say so long for now."

"Until next time," Shauzia said.

Parvana hugged her friend one last time, then climbed into the truck. They waved to each other as the truck rolled away.

Twenty years from now, Parvana thought. What would happen in those twenty years? Would she still be in Afghanistan? Would Afghanistan finally have peace? Would she go back to school, have a job, be married?

The future stretched unknown down the road in front of her. Her mother was somewhere ahead with her sisters and her brother, but what else they would find, Parvana had no idea. Whatever it was, she felt ready for it. She even found herself looking forward to it.

Parvana settled back in the truck beside her father. She popped a dried apricot into her mouth and rolled its sweetness around on her tongue. Through the dusty front windshield she could see Mount Parvana, the snow on its peak sparkling in the sun.

PARVANA'S JOURNEY

To children we force to be braver
than they should have to be

ONE

A man Parvana didn't know gave one final pat to the dirt mounded up over her father's grave. The village mullah had already recited the jenazah, the prayer for the dead. The funeral service was over.

Small, sharp stones dug into Parvana's knees as she knelt at the edge of the grave and placed the large stones she had gathered around it. She put each one down slowly. There was no reason to hurry. She had nowhere else to go.

There were not enough rocks. The ones she had gathered only went halfway around the rectangle of turned-up earth.

"Spread them out," a man said, and he bent down to help her.

They spread out the stones, but Parvana didn't like the gaps. She thought briefly about taking rocks from other graves, but that didn't seem right. She would find more rocks later. One thing Afghanistan had was plenty of rocks.

"Rise yourself up now, boy," one of the men said to her. Parvana's hair was clipped short, and she wore the plain blanket shawl and shalwar kameez of a boy. "There is no point staying in the dirt."

"Leave him alone," another man said. "He is mourning for his father."

"We all have dead to mourn, but we do not have to do it in the dirt. Come on, boy, get to your feet. Be the strong son your father would be proud of."

Go away, Parvana thought. Go away and leave me alone with my father. But she said nothing. She allowed herself to be pulled to her feet. She brushed the dust from her knees and looked around at the graveyard.

It was a large graveyard for such a small village. The graves spread out in a haphazard pattern, as if the villagers thought that each person they buried would be the last.

Parvana remembered digging up bones in a graveyard in Kabul with her friend, Shauzia, to earn money.

I don't want anyone digging up my father, she thought, and she resolved to pile so many rocks on his grave that no one would bother him.

She wanted to tell people about him. That he was a teacher, that he had lost his leg when his school was bombed. That he had loved her and told her stories, and now she was all alone in this big, sad land.

But she kept silent.

The men around her were mostly old. The younger ones were damaged somehow, with an arm missing, or only one eye, or no feet. All the other young men were at war, or dead.

"A lot of people have died here," the man who had helped her said. "Sometimes we are bombed by the Taliban. Sometimes we are bombed by the other side. We used to be farmers. Now we are targets."

Parvana's father hadn't been killed by a bomb. He had just died.

"Who are you with now, boy?"

Parvana's jaw hurt as she held her face tight to keep from crying.

"I am alone," she managed to say.

"You will come home with me. My wife will take care of you."

There were only men at her father's graveside. The women had to stay in their homes. The Taliban didn't like women walking around on their own, but Parvana had given up trying to understand why the Taliban hated women. There were other things to think about.

"Come, boy," the man urged. His voice was kind. Parvana left her father's grave and went with him. The other men followed. She could hear the scuff of their sandals on the hard, dusty ground.

"What is your name?" the man asked.

"Kaseem," Parvana replied, giving him her boy-name. She didn't think any more about whether to trust someone with the truth about herself. The truth could get her arrested, or killed. It was easier and safer not to trust anyone.

"We will go first to your shelter and retrieve your

belongings. Then we will go to my home." The man knew where Parvana and her father had set up their lean-to. He had been one of the men who had carried her father's body to the graveyard. Parvana thought he might have been one of the men who had checked in on them regularly, helping with her father's care, but she couldn't be sure. Everything about the past few weeks was blurry in her memory.

The lean-to was on the edge of the village, against a mud wall that had crumbled from a bomb blast. There wasn't much to retrieve. Her father had been buried in all the clothes that he owned.

Parvana crawled into the lean-to and gathered her things together. She wished she could have some privacy, so she could cry and think about her father, but the roof and walls were made of a sheet of clear plastic. She knew the man could see her as he waited patiently for her to go home with him. So she concentrated on the task in front of her and did not allow herself to cry.

She rolled the blankets, her extra shalwar kameez and the little cook-pot into a bundle. This was the same bundle she had carried on their long journey from Kabul. Now she would have to carry the other things, too – her father's shoulder bag where he kept his paper, pens and little things like matches, and the precious bundle of books they'd kept hidden from the Taliban.

She backed out of the lean-to, pulling the bundles out with her. She took the plastic down from where it had been spread over a ragged corner of the building, folded it up and added it to her blankets.

"I'm ready," she said.

The man picked up one of the bundles. "Come with me," he said, leading the way through the village.

Parvana paid no attention to the rough mud-walled houses and piles of bomb-damaged rubble that made up the village. She had seen many places like it, traveling with her father. She no longer tried to imagine what the village might have looked like before it was bombed, with homes in good repair, children playing and flowers blooming. Who had time for flowers now? It was hard enough just finding something to eat every day. She kept her head down and kicked at pebbles as she walked.

"Here is my house." The man stood before a small mud hut. "Five times my house has been destroyed by bombs, and five times I have built it back up again," he said proudly.

A flap of tattered green cloth covered the doorway. He held it aside and motioned for Parvana to go in.

"Here is the grieving boy," he said to his wife. The woman, crouching over her needlework, put aside her sewing and stood up. Parvana was young, so the woman did not put on her burqa. Three small girls watched from a corner of the room.

As a guest, Parvana was given the best spot in the

dark one-room house. She sat on the thickest mat on the floor and drank the tea the man's wife brought her. The tea was weak, but its warmth soothed her.

"We lost our son," the woman said. "He died of a sickness, like two of our daughters. Maybe you could stay here and be our son."

"I have to find my family," Parvana said.

"You have family besides your father?"

"My mother, my older sister, Nooria, my younger sister, Maryam, and my baby brother, Ali." Parvana saw them in her mind as she spoke their names. She wanted to cry again. She wanted to hear her mother tell her to do her chores, or Nooria say something bossy, or feel the little ones' arms around her.

"I have family in many places, too," the woman said. She was about to say more when some neighbor men came into the house. She quickly took her burqa down from a nail, put it over her head and fetched the men some tea. Then she sat in a corner, quiet and faceless.

The men sat on the mats along the walls and looked at Parvana. They had been at the graveside.

"Do you have other family somewhere?" one of them asked.

Parvana repeated their names. It was easier the second time.

"Are they in Pakistan?"

I don't know where they are," Parvana said. "My father and I traveled from Kabul to look for them. They went to Mazar-e-Sharif for my sister's wedding, but the Taliban took over the city, and now I don't know where they are. My father and I spent the winter in a camp north of Kabul. He was ill then, but when spring came, he thought he was well enough to continue."

Parvana did not want to talk about her father's growing weakness. For days, it seemed as though he would die while they walked alone through the Afghan wilderness. When they arrived at the village, he just could not go any farther.

For so long now they had been wandering from village to village, from temporary settlement to larger camps for people displaced by the war. There were times on the journey when his cough and his weariness were so bad he could not leave the lean-to. There was never much food, but sometimes he was even too tired to eat what there was. Parvana would scramble through the camp, desperately searching for things that would tempt her father to eat, but often she would come back to the lean-to empty-handed.

She did not speak to these men of those times. She also did not tell them that her father had been in prison, arrested by the Taliban for being educated in England.

"You can stay here with us in this village," one of the men said. "You can make your home here."

"I have to find my family."

"That is important," one of the men said, "but it is not safe for you to wander around Afghanistan on your own. You will stay here. You can continue your search when you are grown."

Weariness hit Parvana like a tank. "I will stay," she said. Suddenly she was too tired to argue. Her head slouched down on her chest, and she felt the woman in the house lay her down and cover her with a blanket. Then she fell asleep.

Parvana stayed in the village for another week. She piled rocks on her father's grave and tried to become brave enough to leave.

The girls in the family helped her feel better. She played string games with the little ones. The older girl, who seemed only a couple of years younger than Parvana, went with her each day to her father's grave and helped carry and pile the rocks to keep him safe.

It was comforting to have a mother taking care of her again, too, cooking for her and watching out for her, even though it wasn't her own mother. It made her feel almost normal to be around the everyday tasks of ordinary living, the cooking and cleaning. As a guest she was not expected to help, so she spent most of her time resting and mourning her father. She was tempted to stay and be a son to the good people who had taken her in. The journey ahead of her would be long and lonely.

But she had to find the people she belonged to. She could not pass as a boy forever. She was already thirteen.

One afternoon toward the end of the week, a group of children poked their heads in the door of the house where Parvana was staying.

"Can we take you today?" they asked. "Can you come now?"

The children had been begging for days for her to go with them to see the village's main attraction. Parvana hadn't felt like seeing anything, but today she said, "All right, let's go."

The children pulled her by the hand up a hill on the far side of the village from the graveyard.

A rusty Soviet tank stood on the top of the hill, hidden by some boulders. The children scrambled on it like it was the swing set Parvana dimly remembered from her old schoolyard in Kabul. They played battle, shooting each other with finger-guns until they were all dead, then jumping up to do it all again.

"Isn't this fine?" they asked Parvana. "We are the only village in this area with its own tank."

Parvana agreed the tank was lovely. She didn't tell them that she'd seen many other tanks, and crashed-down war planes, too. She always avoided them, afraid the ghosts of the people who died in them would jump out and grab her.

Parvana was awakened the next night by a gentle shake. A small hand was pressed over her mouth to prevent her from crying out.

"Come outside," a voice whispered in her ear. The

oldest girl took up Parvana's bundles and went out the door. They had to be very quiet. The rest of the family was asleep in the room.

Parvana held her sandals and her blanket shawl and crept out of the house.

"You must leave now," the girl said once they were outside. "I heard the old men talking. They are going to turn you over to the Taliban. Some soldiers are coming by here any day, and the men think the Taliban will pay them money for you."

Parvana wrapped her blanket around her shoulders and slipped her feet into her sandals. She was shaking. She knew that what the girl was saying was true. She had heard many stories about this in the winter camp where she and her father had stayed.

"Here is some food and drink," the girl said, handing Parvana a cloth parcel. "It's all I dared to take without being caught. Maybe it will last until you get to the next village."

"How do I thank you?"

"Take me with you," the girl pleaded. "My life here is nothing. There has to be some place better than this on the other side of those hills, but I can't go by myself."

Parvana couldn't look at the girl's face. If she took the girl with her, all the men of the village would come after them. The girl would be in terrible trouble for dishonoring her family, and Parvana would be turned over to the Taliban.

She put her arms around the girl, aching for her sisters.

"Go back inside," she said stiffly. "I can't help you." Then she picked up her belongings, turned quickly and walked out of the village without looking back.

She didn't stop walking until the sun hung low in the sky late the next day. She found a spot sheltered from the wind by some boulders and gazed out at the magnificent Afghan landscape. The land was bare and rocky, but the hills picked up the color of the sky and now glowed a brilliant red.

She sat down and ate some nan and drank cold tea. There was not another person in sight, just hills and sky.

"I'm all alone," she said out loud. Her words drifted away into the air.

She wished she had someone to talk to.

"I wish Shauzia were here," she said. Shauzia was her best friend. They had pretended to be boys together in Kabul so they could earn money. But Shauzia was somewhere in Pakistan. There was no way to talk to her.

Or maybe there was. Parvana reached into her father's shoulder bag – her shoulder bag now – and took out a pen and a notebook. Using the surface of the bag as a desk, she began to write.

Dear Shauzia:

A week ago, I buried my father…

TWO

"Fourteen times five is seventy. Fourteen times six is eighty-four. Fourteen times seven is ninety-eight." Parvana recited the multiplication tables to herself as she walked over the barren hills. Her father had got her into the habit.

"The world is our classroom," he always said, before giving Parvana a science or a geography lesson. He had been a history teacher, but he knew a lot about other subjects, too.

Sometimes they were able to ride in the back of a cart or a truck from village to village or from camp to camp as they searched for the rest of the family. Often, though, they had to walk, and the lessons made the journey go by more quickly.

If they were alone, he taught her to speak and read English, scratching letters into the dirt when they stopped for a rest. He told her stories from Shakespeare's plays and talked about England, where he had gone to university.

On clear nights, if he wasn't too tired, he taught her about the stars and the planets. During the long, cold winter months, he told her about the great Afghan and Persian poets. He would recite their poems, and she would repeat them over and over until she knew them by heart.

"Your brain needs exercise, just like your body," he said. "A lazy brain does no one any good."

Sometimes they talked about the family as they walked along. "How big is Ali now?" her father would ask. He had been in jail for many months, and by the time he was released, the little boy had left Kabul with the rest of the family. Parvana would try to remember how big her brother was the last time she'd held him, and then they would imagine how much he might have grown since then.

"Maryam is very smart," Parvana would remember.

"All my girls are smart," her father would say. "You will all grow into strong, brave women and you will rebuild our poor Afghanistan."

Whenever Parvana and her father talked about the family, it was as though Mother and the children were just off on a holiday, safe and happy. They never spoke about their worries.

Sometimes they walked in silence. Those were the times when her father was in too much pain to talk. The injuries he had suffered when his school was bombed had never completely healed. The beatings in prison and the bad food and poor medical care in the camps meant that he was often in pain.

Parvana hated those times, when there was nothing she could do to make anything better.

"We can stop for awhile, Father," she would say.

"If we stop, we die," her father always replied. "We will go on."

Parvana's belly had a familiar ache today. The small bit of cooked rice, nan and dried mulberries given to her by the village girl had lasted three days. She would eat only small portions at each meal, then tie up the food again quickly in its cloth bundle so she wouldn't gulp it all at once. But it had been four days since she left the village, and now everything was gone.

"Fourteen times eight is one hundred and twelve. Fourteen times nine is one hundred and twenty-two...no, that's not right." She tried to figure out her mistake, but she was too hungry to think properly.

A sound reached Parvana's ears across the empty stretch of land – a sound not human, not animal, and not machine. It rose and fell, and for awhile Parvana thought it was the wind whining around the hills. But the day was still. Not even a breeze played around her neck.

Parvana walked through a small valley with not-too-tall hills all around her. The strange sound bounced from hill to hill. She couldn't be sure where it was coming from. She thought about hiding, but there were no trees or boulders to crouch behind.

"I'll just keep going," she said out loud, and the sound of her own voice gave her some small comfort.

She turned down a bend in the valley trail, and the sound came at her in a rush.

It was coming from right above her.

Parvana looked up and saw the crouched figure of a woman sitting on the top of the little hill. Her burqa had been flung back, and her face was showing. The unearthly noise was coming from her.

Parvana trudged up the hill. The climb was hard with the load on her back, and she was sweating and breathing hard by the time she got to the top.

Catching her breath before she spoke, Parvana stood in front of the woman and gave her a little wave.

The wailing did not stop.

"Are you all right?" Parvana asked. There was no response. "Do you have anything to eat or drink?" Still nothing but wailing.

Where could the woman have come from? Parvana could see no village or settlement nearby. The woman had no bags or bundles with her – nothing to show she was on any sort of journey.

"What's your name?" Parvana asked. "Where do you come from? Where are you going?" The woman didn't look at her or show any sign at all that she knew Parvana was standing in front of her.

Parvana dropped her bundles and waved her arms in front of the woman's face. She jumped up and down and clapped her hands right beside the woman's ear. Still nothing but wailing.

"Stop that noise!" Parvana shouted. "Stop it! Pay

attention to me!" She bent down and grabbed the woman by the shoulders and shook her roughly. "You're a grownup! You have to take care of me!"

Still the woman kept wailing.

Parvana wanted to strike her. She wanted to kick her and shove her until the woman shut up and fed her. She was shaking with fury and actually raised a hand to slap her when she took a closer look at the woman's eyes.

The eyes were dead. There was no life left in them. Parvana had seen that look before, in the camp for internal refugees. She had seen people who had lost everything and had given up hope that they would ever have love or tenderness or laughter again.

"Some people are dead before they die," her father once told her. "They need quiet, rest, a special doctor who knows of such things, and a glimpse of something better down the road. But where will they find these things in this camp? It is hard enough to find a blanket. Avoid these people, Parvana. You cannot help them, and they will take away your hope."

Parvana remembered her father's words. She no longer felt like hitting the woman. Since the woman could not help her, and she could not help the woman, Parvana picked up her bundles and went back down the hill. Then she walked quickly away until she had left the sound of the woman's grief far, far behind.

THREE

Later that afternoon, Parvana lay on her belly at the top of a small ridge, peering into the clearing below.

A small group of mud huts – a tiny village – was in ruins. Parvana recognized the sort of damage that came from bombs. There had been a war going on in Afghanistan for more than twenty years. Someone was always bombing someone else. Lots of bombs had fallen on Kabul. Bombs had fallen everywhere.

Nothing was moving below except for a piece of cloth fluttering in a doorway.

Parvana knew that sometimes soldiers would move into a village after bombing it and live in the houses people had abandoned. She had seen them do this in her travels with her father.

She watched the village for a long time but saw no other movement. Slowly she went down the hill. Much of the wall around the village had been destroyed, but there were still many places where soldiers could be hiding.

Parvana walked into the little settlement, stepping

carefully through the rubble. She peered into what was left of the one-room houses. Mattresses, rugs, cook-pots and tea cups were scattered everywhere.

She recognized the look. It was the run-for-your-life look. She had seen her own houses look like this as her family grabbed a few possessions and ran out just ahead of the bombs.

She wondered where the people from these houses had gone. They would probably come back to rebuild when they thought it was safe.

It was eerie standing by herself in the deserted village. She felt as though she were being watched, but there was no one left to see.

A thin wail drifted on the breeze. It sounded like a kitten. Parvana followed the sound.

The cry came from the last house. Parvana stood at the doorway. Part of the ceiling had fallen in, and she looked over the rubble for the source of the sound.

Then she saw it. It wasn't a kitten.

In a corner of the room was a baby, lying on its back. A piece of dirty cloth barely covered it, as if it had been blown there by the wind. The baby cried without energy. It cried as if it had been crying for a long time and no longer expected anyone to come.

Parvana went to it.

"Did they leave you all alone? Come on, you poor thing." She lifted the little creature into her arms. "Did your people get scared and forget about you?"

Then she heard the flies and saw the dead woman crushed under the rubble.

Parvana quickly took the child outside, shading its eyes from the bright sun.

"You weren't forgotten," she said. "Your mother would have taken you if she could."

In the light, Parvana could see that the child was a boy, half naked and filthy.

"We'll have to get you clean," she said. "But first we'll feed you. There must be some food around here somewhere."

Parvana took the baby to the least damaged of the houses. She tried to put him down so she could search for things he needed, but the child clung to her and screeched. He wasn't about to be left alone again!

"It's all right, baby. I won't leave you." She put her father's books and her other things down instead.

The house she was in only had one room. In a corner was a pot with some rice in it. The rice was moldy, but she could scrape off the mold. There was also a small pile of nan, very hard and stale, but what did that matter? It was food.

"We'll have a feast, baby," Parvana said. She had noticed a stream at the edge of the village. She took a pot off the shelf in the house and went to fetch water.

The baby wasn't very good at drinking from a cup. Most of the water went down his front, but Parvana was sure he must have swallowed some. She soaked some stale nan in a bit of water and fed that to the baby, too. He ate everything she gave him, keeping his eyes locked onto hers.

"You're the size my brother Ali was when I last saw him," she said. "No, I'm wrong. You're smaller. Anyway, I know all about the messes babies make. I'll get you clean, and then I'll get myself clean. Then we'll have some more to eat."

She had to go back into the baby's house to see whether there were any clean clothes for him. She found a little knitted suit, some cloths to use for diapers and a little hat for his head. The house was too damaged to hunt for more things, and Parvana didn't like being around the body of the baby's mother.

I should bury her, Parvana thought, but I can't. I just can't.

She tossed a bit of cloth over the woman's face, which might at least keep the flies away. She didn't want to have to come back here again.

Then she took the baby and the clean clothes down to the stream.

"You're such a good boy," she said as she took off his filthy clothes and washed him. She used the silly sing-song voice that people used to talk to babies. "You'll be easy to take care of. No trouble at all. It will be like having a puppy." Parvana had always wanted a puppy.

The water was cold, but the little boy didn't complain. He just kept looking at Parvana. There was a rash on his body from being in dirty diapers for so long, and he was very thin, but otherwise he seemed unhurt.

Parvana dressed him in clean clothes.

"Doesn't that feel better?"

Parvana didn't know whether the boy's family had spoken Dari or not. Maybe they were Pashtun speakers, and he didn't understand a word she was saying. She decided it didn't matter. It was just nice to have someone to talk to.

She propped the baby up between some rocks with a blanket behind him for padding, so he could see that she wasn't going away. Laying her spare shalwar kameez close by, she took off her own filthy clothes and jumped into the water.

"Yes, I know I'm a girl," she said to the baby. "But that will be our secret, all right?" The baby gurgled.

She used sand to scrub the grime off her skin and clothes, which she spread in the sun to dry.

Back in the least damaged house, she shared some more stale bread with the baby. With a full belly, the little boy fell asleep.

Parvana gently put him down on a toshak and covered him up. She sat down beside him and watched him sleep. He was clean and beautiful, and when she touched his little palm, his tiny fingers curled around her bigger one. She could see no war in his sleeping face, or in the way his breathing made his little chest rise and fall.

"I'll call you Hassan," she said, "because everybody has to have a name."

She stretched out beside him. "Pleasant dreams," she whispered. Then she fell asleep herself.

Parvana stretched herself awake the next morning, enjoying the softness of the mattress underneath her. She usually slept on the hard ground. Sleepily, she wondered whether she could roll the mattress into a small enough bundle to carry with her.

Hassan made a noise, and Parvana became fully awake. He was watching her, and when he saw that she saw him, he gave her a goofy little grin and waved his arms around.

"Good morning, Hassan," Parvana said. It was wonderful to have company.

She picked him up and carefully looked outside. Everything was quiet. No army had come into the village while they had been sleeping.

"Are you hungry, Hassan?" she asked. "How about some golden rice pilaf, with extra raisins, and huge chunks of roasted lamb buried in it? Then we'll have some bolani dumplings, and some tomatoes and onions, and lots of sweet noodle pudding. Doesn't that sound good?"

While she described the menu, Parvana settled Hassan onto her hip. He clung there like a monkey she had once seen in her school geography book clutching a tree branch. She scraped the fuzzy green mold off the cold rice in the pot and shared it with him.

After breakfast, they explored the rest of the little settlement for things they could use. Parvana stayed away from the baby's house, and they saw no more bodies.

A tiny building behind the houses turned out to be a small barn with two goats and a few chickens. Parvana had a vague idea how to milk a goat, and she was thrilled when all her squeezing actually resulted in milk spurting into a bowl. She gave a lot of it to Hassan and drank some herself. It was warm and sweet.

The hens didn't want her taking their eggs, and they kept pecking at her hands whenever she got close to them.

"I need those eggs more than you do," she said, finally picking up a bit of old board and swatting at the chickens until they hopped out of their nests, squawking with annoyance. She put the eggs high on a shelf in the house where she slept. She didn't want to step on them by accident.

As long as Hassan could see her, he didn't fuss, so Parvana made sure they were always close together.

She went from house to house, pulling out of the rubble anything that could still be used. She put everything on a long piece of plastic sheeting and dragged it from house to house. When she was finished, everything was spread out before her.

"I don't like taking other people's things," she said to Hassan, "but if I'm going to take care of you, your village will have to help me."

Parvana looked at everything she had scavenged and carefully chose what she could carry with her. She already had a small cook-pot, but she did take a sharp knife, an extra blanket, some candles, a few boxes of matches, a small pair of scissors and a length of rope. She added a long-handled spoon and two drinking cups. The cups were small, and maybe she could teach Hassan to hold one. He looked smart enough.

She made a food bundle, too, with flour, rice, onions, carrots and some dried apricots – all the food she could find. She put a small tin jug of cooking oil into the bundle.

Finally she added a wonderful find – a bar of soap wrapped in paper with roses on it. The wrapping looked old. Parvana wondered where the people had got it and what special occasion they were saving it for.

She placed both bundles by the door of the least-damaged house, next to her other belongings.

"Now we're ready to continue our journey," she said to Hassan. "We're going to find my mother. I'll let her help me take care of you, but I'm going to be your boss, not her, all right? Nooria – that's my older sister – will definitely try to boss you. She can't help it. She's naturally bossy. But I won't let her."

She was ready to leave but didn't want to.

"I'll just tidy up the house first," she said to Hassan, who was watching her sleepily from the toshak.

With a small whisk broom she found hanging on a nail, Parvana gave the floor a good sweeping. There was a lot of dust, and it took her a long time, but the floor looked better when she was finished. The rest of the little house looked dusty now compared to the clean floor, so she left Hassan sleeping on the mattress and ran down to the stream to fill a pot with water. She wiped down all the walls and shelves, going back to the stream twice for clean water. The whole house soon looked much better.

"I could plant some rose bushes outside," she said quietly, so as not to wake the baby. Afghanistan used to have beautiful gardens. She'd heard about them from her parents. The gardens had all been destroyed by bombs before she was born.

She emptied the dusty water outside the door of the house, spread out her cleaning cloth to dry, and realized that she was very tired. She stretched out beside Hassan and soon fell asleep.

She woke up in the middle of the night. Everything was dark, and for a moment she couldn't remember where she was. She began to panic. Then Hassan moved a bit in his sleep. She curled around him, closed her eyes to keep the darkness out, and fell back asleep.

She built a cook fire the next morning down by the stream and decided to fry all five of the eggs she'd found. Too late, she realized she should have put some oil in the cook-pot, because the eggs stuck to the bottom and didn't hold their shape the way fried eggs did when her mother made them. Still, they tasted very good, and she and Hassan ate every scrap. She even scraped the bottom of the pot with a stick to get the last bits.

Eggs made Parvana think of chickens.

"How hard can it be to kill a chicken?" she asked Hassan.

She carried him to the little barn and they drank more fresh goat's milk. Then she propped the baby up against some straw and turned her attention to the chickens.

"One of you is going to be our dinner," she announced. "Any volunteers?"

No chicken stepped forward.

"I'm bigger than you are," she reminded them, turning toward the fattest one. It stared back at her as she crept closer and closer. Then, just as she was about to grab it, it flew out of her way.

Hassan laughed.

"You're not helping," Parvana said, but she was laughing, too.

None of the chickens felt like being caught, and they made Parvana chase them all over the little barn, to Hassan's great delight.

She was just getting ready to make a final great leap on a chicken she had cornered, when something outside the barn window caught her eye.

In the next instant she had grabbed Hassan and

was running madly back to the house where they had slept. She scooped up their bundles of belongings and ran in a panic out of the village.

She had seen, in the distance, the black turbans of Taliban soldiers. They were heading toward her village. If they found her and thought she was a boy, they might force her into their army. If they found her and discovered she was a girl...

That was too horrible to think about.

Parvana didn't think. She just ran, up and over the hill away from the village.

Why Hassan didn't cry out, why the Taliban didn't see her scurrying over the hill, why she didn't stumble under the weight of all she carried, Parvana never knew. She ran and kept running. When she finally stopped, there were three hills between her and the Taliban.

Hassan wasn't at all disturbed at being jostled about. He thought it was great fun and gave her a big grin.

"It must be nice to be young," Parvana said, catching her breath and wiping the drool from Hassan's face.

She knew she could not keep carrying everything. The weight of her bundle would wear her out before she got anywhere. But she dared not get rid of any food.

"We don't know when we'll get more," she said to Hassan.

She opened the other bundles and decided they would probably need everything in them, as well.

That left her father's books.

She opened up that bundle. Four big books with thick hard covers and one small book with a paper cover lay on the cloth. There was also a copy of the secret women's magazine her mother had written articles for back in Kabul. It had been smuggled into Afghanistan by women who had printed it in Pakistan. Parvana was supposed to give it to her mother when they saw each other again.

"I'll bury the biggest three books," she said, "and come back some day and dig them up again."

Using a rock to help her dig through the hard ground, she made a hole big enough for the books. One book was about science, one was about history, and the third was a book of Persian poetry. She couldn't spare a cloth to wrap them in, so the red dirt was plopped right on top of the covers.

She patted down the soil, then kicked some rocks and pebbles on top so no one would be able to tell something was buried there. She thought of her father being underground with his books. Now he would have something to read.

With a heavy heart, Parvana picked up her bundles and the baby, and walked on.

FOUR

Crouching near the mouth of the cave, Parvana listened for the sounds of something that might have gone in there before her.

Hassan fussed and wriggled. Parvana put a finger over his lips, but he either didn't understand or he didn't care. He kept whining and kicking and making screechy little baby noises.

Carrying a baby on a journey was different from carrying a bundle. A bundle could be tossed over one shoulder or the other. A bundle could be dropped when her arms were tired, or even thrown to the ground when she was frustrated and didn't know which way to go next.

But a baby had to be carried carefully and couldn't be dropped, tossed or thrown. Hassan was cute, but he could also be heavy and cranky and smelly to carry.

Parvana's back and shoulders ached. There was no comfortable way to carry everything she needed, and not even multiplication tables took away the pain.

The cave, by a small stream, would be a good place to rest for a few days, as long as there were no wolves inside.

Hassan let out a big squeal, and Parvana gave up any hope of trying to sneak in. She walked up to the entrance and peered in, then stepped inside.

The cave was more of a low-hanging rock than a real cave. As her eyes began to get used to the dimmer light, she could see bits of the back wall. The cave was tall enough for her to stand up in and wide enough for her to stretch out, with plenty of room left over for her bundles. The rocks rose up around it like a cocoon, creating a cozy shelter where she could sleep safely without the risk of anyone creeping up on her. She would stay here for awhile and rest her arms.

"Get out of my cave!"

Parvana spun around and was running away before the voice stopped echoing off the cave walls. Fear kept her legs moving long after she was exhausted.

When she finally slowed down, her brain began to tell her something she had been too scared to hear moments earlier.

The voice that had yelled at her from the back of the cave was a child's voice.

Parvana stopped running and caught her breath. She turned around and looked back at the cave. She wasn't going to let some child keep her from getting a few days of rest!

"Let's go and see who's in there," she said to Hassan.

She went back to the mouth of the cave.

"Hello," she called in.

"I told you to get out of my cave!" the voice shouted. It was definitely a child's voice.

"How do I know it's your cave?" Parvana asked.

"I've got a gun. Go away or I'll shoot you."

Parvana hesitated. Lots of young boys in Afghanistan did have guns. But if he had a gun, why hadn't he shot at her already?

"I don't believe you," Parvana said. "I don't think you're a killer. I think you're a kid just like me."

She took a few more steps forward, trying to see in the dark.

A stone hit her on the shoulder.

"Stop that!" she shouted. "I'm carrying a baby."

"I warned you to stay away."

"All right, you win," Parvana said. "Hassan and I will leave you alone. We just thought you'd like to share our meal, but I guess you'd rather throw stones."

There was a moment's silence.

"Leave the food and go."

"I have to cook it first," Parvana said over her shoulder as she walked away. "If you want it, come out and get it."

Parvana put down the baby where she could watch him and kept talking while she gathered dried grasses and stalks from dead weeds for a cook fire. The water in the stream was clear and moving swiftly, so she thought it would be safe to drink without boiling it first.

She dipped in her pan. "Here's some lovely cool water to drink, Hassan," she said. "Tastes good, doesn't it? Drink it all down, and we'll have a hot tasty supper." She gave him a piece of stale nan to keep him quiet until the meal was ready.

Parvana heard a little shuffling noise. Out of the corner of her eye she saw a small boy peering out from the cave. He was sitting on the ground. She took him some water.

Dirt covered every inch of him, and he stank like the open sewers that ran through the camp where she had spent the winter. One of his pant legs lay flat against the ground, empty where his leg should have been. He was, Parvana thought, nine or ten years old.

She put the water down where he could reach it, then went back to her work. She heard him gulping the water.

"Bring me some food," the boy ordered, tossing the pot at her.

"I don't like having things thrown at me," Parvana said. "If you want food, come and get it yourself."

"I can't walk!" he yelled. "How stupid you are, not to notice that. Now bring me some food!"

Parvana walked over with some stale nan. The

boy glowered at her with hatred and rage. And fear, she thought. His hair was matted with dirt. His face was scratched and his clothes were torn. She kept the bread out of his reach.

"Have you really got a gun?" she asked.

"I'm not telling you." He reached for the bread.

"You give me an answer and I'll give you some food."

The boy flew into a furious burst of temper. He cursed and yelled and threw fistfuls of rocks and dust at Parvana. The fit left him panting and coughing. His cough was deep and used up his whole chest, just like her father's cough had done. Parvana wondered how someone so scrawny found the strength to be so unpleasant.

I could blow on him and he'd fall over, she thought.

"No, I don't have a gun," the boy finally admitted, "but I can get one any time I want, so just watch what you do!"

Parvana gave him the bread. It disappeared in a flash. She fetched more water and put it to boil over the little fire. When the rice was cooked, she put some on a flat rock and took it to the boy.

"What's your name?"

The boy frowned and stared at the rice. "Asif." Parvana gave him the rice. Then she fed Hassan.

"My name is Parvana," she said, putting fingerfuls of rice into Hassan's mouth. "I'm looking for my family. I found this baby in a village that had been bombed. I call him Hassan." She ate some rice herself.

"Why do you have a girl's name?" Asif asked.

Parvana turned suddenly cold. How could she have made such a mistake? Quickly she tried to think of something to say to cover up, but she was suddenly too tired to lie.

"I am a girl," she said. "I pretended to be a boy in Kabul so I could work. When my father and I started out on this journey, it was easier to keep pretending to be a boy."

"Why didn't your father work? Was he lazy?"

"No, my father was not lazy, and don't you dare say another word about him!" Parvana slammed the ground with a rock. The noise startled Hassan and made him cry.

"I'll say what I please. I don't take orders from a girl," Asif taunted.

"You'll take orders from me if you want to eat any more of my food," Parvana yelled. "Oh, be quiet, Hassan!"

Yelling at the baby to stop crying only made him cry louder and longer.

Parvana turned her back on both of them. She tried to ignore them as she watched the flames of her smoky little fire dwindle into embers.

Finally she was calm. Hassan's cry had faded to a thin whimper. Parvana picked him up and held him in her lap until he fell asleep. Then she spread out a blanket and wrapped him up against the night chill.

She had almost forgotten about the cave boy, when he asked her another question.

"So where is your father now?"

Parvana put a few stray strands of camel-grass on the coals and watched as they burst into quick flames.

"He's dead," she answered quietly.

Asif was silent again for awhile. Then he said, "I knew you were a girl. You're far too ugly to be a boy." His voice was weaker than before, as though all the fight had been drained out of him. Parvana saw that he was lying down. She took him a blanket.

"What were you doing in that cave?"

"I'm not answering any more of your stupid questions."

"Tell me, and I'll let you use this blanket."

"I don't want your stinking blanket," he replied, mumbling into the dirt. Parvana wasn't sure whether to kick him or cover him.

Then Asif spoke again, so quietly that she had to lean down to hear him.

"I was chased into the cave by a monster," he said. "I mean, I was chasing a monster. It disappeared into a hole in the cave, and it will probably come out tonight and gobble you up, which will make me very happy."

Parvana walked away without kicking him or covering him. She left the blanket on the ground just out of his reach.

She sat down beside Hassan. There was a tiny bit of light left in the sky. She took out her notebook and pen.

Dear Shauzia:

I met a strange creature today. He's part boy and part wild animal. One of his legs is missing, and he's been hiding in a cave.

You'd think he'd be grateful to me for taking care of him, but he just gets ruder and ruder. How can someone that small be so awful?

Doesn't matter. He's not my problem. In the morning I'll leave him behind. I've got to find my family, and he will just slow me down.

Maybe I should leave the baby behind, too. These boys are not my brothers. They are not my problem.

The evening was too dark to write any more. Parvana put her writing things away. She looked up at the sky for awhile, remembering her father's astronomy lessons.

She got to her feet again and walked back to Asif. He was sleeping flat against the earth, almost hugging the hard ground. She picked up the nearby blanket. She covered him up, then went to sleep beside Hassan.

FIVE

"You need a bath," Parvana said to Asif. "Don't tell me what to do," Asif snapped.

"You stink."

"So do you."

"No, I don't," Parvana said, although she probably did, at least a little. Not as bad as Asif, though.

"If you don't wash, you don't eat," she declared.

"I don't need your lousy food. I've got lots of food in the cave. Good food, too. Not the swill you cook."

"All right, rot away in your stink. I don't care. We're leaving you today anyway, although we'll have to walk miles and miles to get away from your smell. We'll probably have to walk all the way to France."

"France? There's no such place as France."

"You've never heard of France? And you call *me* stupid?"

Asif threw the blanket at her. It didn't go very far, because in mid-throw he started coughing. His shirt was ripped in the middle, and Parvana could see his ribs straining with the effort of trying to breathe between coughs.

She spun on her heels and snapped the blanket in the air to shake the dirt out of it. The dust made her sneeze, which only made her more angry.

"You made my blanket stink," she accused Asif, who was too busy coughing to take any notice of her. She spread the blanket out in the sun to make it smell better. It was something her father had taught her.

"You stink, too," she snarled at Hassan. At least there was someone who had to do what she said. She snatched him away from the stones he was happily bumping together and began undressing him roughly.

Hassan screamed with rage.

"You're doing that all wrong."

Parvana jumped at the suddenness of Asif's voice and turned to see that he had slithered over to the stream on his backside.

"How dare you sneak up on me!"

"You're doing that all wrong," he said again.

"I know exactly what I'm doing. I have a younger brother and sister."

"They must hate you."

"They love me. I'm the best big sister in the whole world."

"They're probably jumping for joy that you're lost out here, because they'll never have to see you again."

Parvana plopped the howling Hassan into Asif's lap. "You think you can do better? Go ahead and try."

Hassan immediately stopped crying. Parvana stared, open-mouthed, as the rage disappeared from Asif's face when Hassan's little fingers reached up and grabbed his nose.

"Go find my crutches," he said to Parvana.

She was about to yell at him for ordering her about, but the crutches seemed like a good idea.

"Where are they?"

"If I knew, I wouldn't tell you to go and look for them," he said with annoying logic.

She found them a little ways from the mouth of the cave. They were not together.

He must have dropped them while he was escaping from whatever was chasing him, she thought. She took the crutches down to the stream.

Asif was sitting in the stream in his clothes, holding onto Hassan. The baby gurgled as Asif rubbed him clean.

She put the crutches down and opened a bundle to take out clean clothes for Hassan. Under the baby's clothes was her spare shalwar kameez. She took that out, too, then got the bar of rose soap from her father's shoulder bag. She unwrapped the soap and put the wrapping back in the bag. It smelled nice.

"You might want this," she said, putting the soap

and clothes on the edge of the stream. She added a clean diaper for Hassan. "Don't eat the soap," she couldn't help adding in a slightly nasty tone.

Asif took the soap from her, but ignored her comment. He was too busy playing with the baby.

Parvana went downstream a little ways and scrubbed Hassan's clothes with sand. She was spreading clean wet diapers in the sun to dry when Asif called out, "He's clean. Take him."

She waited for Asif to hand the baby over to her, then realized he didn't have the strength to do so. She waded into the stream and picked Hassan up.

"Now go away, so I can wash in private."

She took Hassan to the mouth of the cave and dressed him there. He looked rosy and cheerful from his bath. There was still some stale bread left, and she gave him a small piece to chew on.

"Hey, stupid one. Get over here!"

I don't have to answer him, she thought.

"I said, get over here."

Parvana played a little clapping game with Hassan and ignored the boy in the stream.

"I can't remember your name," Asif said in a tone that wasn't quite so nasty.

Parvana picked up Hassan and went down to the stream. Asif had taken off his shirt and tossed it on the shore. He was slumped over, almost as though he couldn't hold himself up any more. His hair was full of soap.

Parvana fetched one of the drinking cups and waded into the stream. He turned his face away from her when she came up behind him.

She gasped when she saw the scars that criss-crossed his back. Some were old and were now a permanent part of his body. Some were fresh, still scabby and infected.

He really was being chased by a monster, Parvana thought.

"Don't just stand there," he growled.

"Put your head back." She dipped the cup into the stream. "Close your eyes," she ordered, "and your mouth." Then, doing for Asif what her mother used to do for her, she rinsed the soap out of his hair.

The effort of washing wore Asif out. He fell asleep in the sun soon after putting on Parvana's spare shalwar kameez.

With the laundry done and spread on the rocks to dry, Parvana put Hassan down on a blanket and took out her notebook and pen.

Dear Shauzia:

It's getting harder and harder to remember what you look like. Sometimes when I think of you, I can only picture you in your blue school uniform with the white chador, back when we were students in Kabul. You had long hair then. So did I.

Sometimes I put my hand behind me on my back

and try to remember how far down my hair grew. I think I know, but I could be wrong.

It's hard to remember that I used to sleep in a bed and had to do my homework before I could watch television and play with my friends. It's hard to remember that we used to have ice cream and cakes to eat. Was that really me? Did I really leave a big piece of cake on my plate one day because I didn't feel like eating it? That must have been a dream. That couldn't have been my life.

My life is dust and rocks and rude boys and skinny babies, and long days of searching for my mother when I don't have the faintest idea where she might be.

SIX

Parvana swept out the little cave using her sandal as a broom. She liked the dirt floor to be smooth, even though it never stayed that way for long.

"We could fix it up," she said to herself. She would have said it to Hassan, but Hassan was with Asif down by the stream. Even though she was alone, she spoke out loud. She liked the way her quiet words bounced around in the little cave.

"We could put some shelves up in this corner," she said, running her fingers on some jagged bits of rock that could hold boards, if she could find any wood. "Maryam and I could sleep at the front, and Mother and Ali could sleep in the back so that Ali couldn't get out without crawling over us."

What about Nooria? Parvana frowned as she measured the little space with her eyes. Then she shrugged. Nooria could sleep outside.

Satisfied for the moment with the cave floor, Parvana put her sandal back on before joining the others at the stream.

"What were you doing?" Asif asked. He was

twisting grass together, trying to make a little boat. Hassan was watching him.

"I was cleaning out the cave."

"Why? It's just a cave. It's stupid to clean it."

"You think you are so right all the time," Parvana said, folding her arms across her chest. "There's a lot you don't know. Maybe it's not just a cave. Maybe it's a treasure cave."

"What are you babbling about? Hassan makes more sense than you do. There's no such thing as a treasure cave."

"There is," Parvana insisted, her voice rising. "In fact, it's exactly the sort of cave Alexander the Great would have used to hide his treasure in." She waited for Asif to ask her who Alexander the Great was so she could show off how much she knew, but he just kept working on his boat.

She tapped her foot several times and then told him.

"Alexander the Great was an army general who lived a long time ago. He took treasures from every place he conquered."

"You mean he was a thief. He should have had his hands cut off."

"He wasn't a thief," Parvana insisted, although even as she was talking, she wondered if that were true. "People loved him. They gave him their treasures."

"You mean he'd ride through a town and people loved him so much they just gave him their things?"

"They did," she insisted.

"Then they were all stupid," Asif declared. "If I had treasure, I wouldn't give any of it away." He finished twisting the grass and put the little boat in the stream. The children watched it float away with the current.

"Why would he bury his treasure anyway?" Asif asked. "Why wouldn't he keep it with him?"

"Probably there was too much to carry," Parvana said. "He had so much treasure his horses were weighed down with it, and he had to bury some or their backs would break."

"So why didn't he come back for it?"

"Maybe he forgot which cave it was in. Maybe he had so much treasure that he didn't even need to think about it once he buried it. How should I know?" Parvana's mind flashed briefly on the memory of her father's books, stuck in a hole in the ground, covered up with dirt. How would she ever find them again? She chased the question from her head. It was making her sad, and she didn't want to be sad when she was busy being annoyed at Asif.

"You think there's treasure in that dirty old cave?"

"I'm sure of it," Parvana said. Why wouldn't there be? The more she thought about it, the more she was certain that a box of gold coins and big jewels lay under the ground in the cave, just waiting for her to dig up.

"If there's any treasure there, it belongs to me," Asif insisted. "I found the cave first."

Parvana sputtered with anger. "You're wearing my clothes, eating my food, and that's how you say thank you? You really are a terrible boy."

"All right, all right. I'll share it with you."

"You certainly will."

Asif pulled himself up with his crutches. He only got halfway up, when he started to fall back. Parvana put her hands under his arms and gave him a boost.

"Let's go," he said.

"Where?"

"To the cave. To start digging." He shook his head with disgust. "What did you think I was talking about? Better find something to dig with." He hobbled off.

The treasure was by now so real in Parvana's imagination that she barely minded being ordered around. She found a couple of good-sized rocks with points at the ends, picked up Hassan and joined Asif in the cave.

The floor soon lost its smoothness as Parvana and Asif scraped away at it with their rocks. Sometimes one of their rocks hit a clunk, and they got very excited until they realized they had only hit another rock.

"What will you do with your share of the treasure?" she asked Asif.

"Horses," he answered. "I'll buy lots of horses, fast ones. I'll ride and ride, and when the horse I'm riding gets tired, I'll buy another one, then another, then another. I'll never have to stop moving."

"What about food?"

"What will I need food for? I'll be riding, not walking."

"I'll buy a big house," Parvana said. "A magic house where bombs just slip off the roof without exploding. It will be a white stone house just like the one I used to live in, only bigger, with a separate house in the yard for my sister Nooria, so I wouldn't have to see her all the time. And I'll wear beautiful clothes and lots of jewels, and I'll have lots of servants so I'll never have to do housework again." She could see herself in her mind, dressed up in a glowing red shalwar kameez like the one her aunt made her that she had to sell, long ago in Kabul, so that her family could buy food to eat.

"All the jewels in the world wouldn't make you look pretty," Asif said. "What good are jewels, anyway? You can't eat them or burn them to keep you warm at night, or – "

Parvana's rock suddenly clunked against a hard surface.

"I think I've found something."

"It's just another rock."

She scraped away some more dirt. "No, I don't think so." She dug in harder. "I think it's a box!"

Asif dug his rock in close to hers. "It is! It is a box!"

They dug faster and faster, dirt flying up and around the cave.

"Watch out for Hassan. He's right behind you," Parvana managed to say while she was huffing and puffing with exertion. Asif adjusted his digging so the dirt wouldn't fly near the baby.

Bit by bit, the box emerged. Parvana got up onto her knees to pull it out, and Asif leaned in to help. With a giant grunt, they pulled the box out of the ground. It was made of green metal, twice as long as Parvana's sandal and one sandal width wide.

"It's smaller than I thought a treasure box would be," Asif said.

"Diamonds don't have to be big," Parvana replied. "Let's take it out in the sun so that the jewels will really sparkle when we open it." She dragged the box out of the cave into the sunshine. While Asif scooted out on his bottom, she went back for Hassan, so he could be there for the treasure-box opening, too.

Asif pounded on the dirt-encrusted lock with a rock until it broke apart.

"It's rusty," he said.

"It's been under the ground for thousands of years," Parvana said. "You'd be rusty, too."

Asif pulled the broken pieces of padlock away from the clasp.

"Ready?"

"Ready." She put her hands near his, and they opened the box together.

It was full of bullets.

The children looked down and stared, too shocked to speak. Hassan gurgled and reached out to touch the shiny little objects.

Asif slammed the box shut.

"Some treasure," he yelled. "Why do I listen to you?" He pulled himself up on his crutches, yanking away from Parvana's offer of help. He knocked her with his shoulder as he hobbled away from the cave.

Parvana opened the box again. Maybe her eyes had played tricks on her.

But they hadn't. All she saw were rows of tightly packed bullets, and when she ran her hands through them, no jewels winked out at her. Only bullets.

They weren't buried by Alexander the Great. Bullets hadn't been invented back then. They were probably buried by the men who had fought in the war that had started long before she was born. Maybe the man who buried them had died. Maybe he forgot which cave they were in. Maybe he had so many bullets he didn't need these.

It didn't matter. There was no treasure.

With great effort, Parvana lifted the box over her head and threw it as far away as she could. It landed with a thud, the bullets spilling out over the ground. They looked like seeds on the earth, but Parvana knew they would not turn into food.

She picked up Hassan and sat with him, looking away from the cave. She turned Hassan so that he couldn't see her face. She was ashamed of herself for getting caught up in a stupid dream, as though she were still a child.

SEVEN

"I'm leaving tomorrow," Parvana told Asif the next morning. They had all slept outside. Parvana didn't feel like smoothing down the floor of the cave again. She didn't feel like being reminded of her foolishness.

"Where are you going?" Asif asked.

"To look for my mother."

"But where are you going to look?"

Parvana gazed around and picked a direction. "Over that way."

"Why that way?"

"Because it's part of my plan."

"You have a plan?"

"Of course I have a plan." Parvana's only plan was to keep walking in the hopes of bumping into her mother somewhere. "But I see no reason to tell you what it is."

"I don't want to know anyway," Asif said. "It's probably a stupid plan."

It will be wonderful to leave you behind, Parvana thought. How lovely and quiet my days and nights will be.

"I suppose you think I'm going to come with you," Asif said.

Parvana pretended she didn't hear him.

"I suppose you think I'd be grateful to go with you," Asif continued. "I suppose you think I can't look after myself out here."

Parvana kept quiet, feeling very superior for having the patience to not answer back.

She decided to wash all the clothes so everything would be clean when she started walking again.

Asif kicked at the ground with his one leg. "I suppose you'll take the baby."

"You want me to leave him with you?"

"I don't care."

Parvana picked up Hassan and the soiled diapers and carried them down to the stream. She was still scrubbing the first diaper when she heard Asif's crutches coming up behind her.

"You'll probably walk right by your mother," he said. "You'll be walking in one direction, and she'll be walking in another, and you'll pass right by each other and keep on walking forever and ever until you both run out of ground to walk on," Asif said. "It makes more sense for you to stay here. Your mother will probably walk by here any day looking for you. In fact, I think she'll come soon, and she'll be very angry when I tell her you couldn't wait around for her."

"What makes you think my mother will be here soon?" Parvana asked. Could he be right? She felt a flicker of hope.

"Just a feeling," Asif replied. "Do you want to take that chance?"

He doesn't know anything, she realized. He's just talking. She felt disappointed but not surprised.

She washed the rest of the diapers and spread them out to dry. "I wish you could wash out your own diapers," she said to Hassan.

Hassan reached for a shiny stone, ignoring Parvana's complaints.

"It would probably really annoy you if I came with you, wouldn't it?" Asif said. "You'd probably hate it. You're probably wishing and wishing that I'll stay behind."

Parvana smoothed the wrinkles out of one of the washed diapers. She didn't say anything.

"In that case," Asif said, "I'll come. Just to annoy you."

Parvana felt a strange, surprising relief. She had known, deep inside, that she wouldn't have been able to leave him behind.

"Please don't," she said.

"Forget it," he said. "My mind is made up. And don't try to sneak away without me, because I'll catch you, and you'll be sorry."

The idea of Asif catching up with anything faster than a worm almost made her smile, but she caught herself in time. She got her shoulder bag and sat down to write to her friend.

Dear Shauzia:

We're moving away from here tomorrow. I like staying in one place, but each time I do, it gets harder to leave. After all the moving around that I've done, I should be used to it. But I'm not.

We have to leave, though. We're running out of food. We're down to four scoops of rice and a bit of oil.

I don't know if there will be food where we're going, but I do know there won't be any more here.

Maybe we'll find a really wonderful place with lots of food, and grownups who can look after Hassan, and a room I can sleep in that's far away from everyone who bothers me.

Was I always this grumpy?

I hope there's lots of food where you are. I wish you could send us some.

Until next time,

Your friend,

Parvana

The next morning, Parvana washed out the diapers Hassan had dirtied again and wrapped them in a cloth. She would spread them out to dry when they stopped for a rest.

She started to bundle up the food.

"What if there's no water where we're going?" Asif asked. "How will you cook the rice? You didn't think of that, did you?"

She hadn't, although she hated to admit it. She took the cook-pot out of the bundle.

"I guess I should cook it all up now," she said. "I don't like to do that. I don't know how long it will last without growing moldy if it's cooked."

"We'll eat it before it gets moldy," Asif said. "There's not that much left."

Parvana knew he was right. Four little cups of rice would not last long with two children and one baby eating it. She gathered some grasses and dried weeds. Asif broke them into the right size, struck a match, and soon had a fire going. Parvana fetched water, and they cooked the rice.

"We could eat some while it's hot, couldn't we?" Asif asked.

Parvana thought that would be a good idea. "We'll only eat a little bit," she said. "It's got to last until we find more food."

They ate the hot rice right out of the pot. Hassan sat on Asif's lap, and Asif fed him, too.

It seemed like they had just started eating when Parvana noticed the pot was only half filled with rice.

"Stop eating!" she cried, snatching the pot away from Asif's hands. "This has got to last!"

"Why did you eat so much, then?"

"Don't blame me! You're the one who kept shoveling it in, as if we were rich people with bags of rice all over the place." Parvana flung her arm so violently in anger that the pot of rice slipped out of her fingers and flew off into the dirt.

It landed bottom up.

Neither child spoke. They stared at the up-turned pot.

After a long, terrible moment, Parvana walked over to the pot and carefully lifted it up. Most of the rice was still stuck to the bottom. She must have cooked it too long.

There was still some rice on the ground. Asif shuffled over on his behind, and together they picked up the rice, grain by grain, and put it back in the pot.

When everything was packed up, Parvana took out her notebook.

Dear Shauzia:

I hate it when I make things worse. Why do I behave so badly? Why can't I be nice?

She helped Asif stand up, picked up the bundles and the baby, and the children walked away from the cave. They didn't look back.

EIGHT

They walked for two days before the food ran out, and then they walked for two days more.

Parvana's belly had that ache it got when she didn't feed it. It was a mixture of pain and emptiness. Her head felt empty, too, and she felt dull and stupid.

Hassan wailed the first day after the rice was gone, but by the second day the wail had dwindled to a thin whine, like the sound he had been making when Parvana first found him.

"Hassan needs to rest," Asif said. Parvana suspected it was Asif who needed to rest, but he would never admit that. He moved more and more slowly, and his face had the same expression her father's face had when he was in pain.

Parvana put Hassan on the ground, then her bundles. She held onto Asif's arm as he sat down. When he was tired, he often slipped and rolled onto his side when he was trying to sit. This embarrassed him and made him grumpy.

"Is there any water left?" Asif asked.

Parvana untied the bundle with the plastic water

bottle in it and shook the bottle so Asif could hear that there was still a bit sloshing around. He reached out his hand, and she passed it over.

She was going to remind him to take it easy, to not drink too much, but what was the point? It didn't make any difference whether Asif took two swallows or one. They still needed to find more water soon.

Asif poured a little bit of water into the cap of the bottle. Parvana watched him pour it, bit by bit, into Hassan's mouth, not spilling any.

"Isn't that good?" he asked. "Would you like some more?" He gave Hassan three capfuls of water before taking a swallow himself. Then he passed the water bottle back to Parvana.

"Do you have any brothers or sisters?" Parvana asked Asif. She realized that she didn't know anything about this boy who was traveling with her. She knew he came out of a cave, but she didn't know where he came from before that. She knew he was annoying, but she didn't know why. She didn't know who had hated him enough to tear up his back.

"I'm alone," Asif replied shortly.

"So am I," Parvana said, "but I've got family somewhere. What about you? Do you have a family somewhere else?"

Asif tried to get Hassan to play with his finger, but Hassan didn't seem interested in playing. He didn't seem interested in anything.

"No," Asif said finally.

"Did they go away? What happened to them?"

"I had a family. Now I don't. That's all there is." He wouldn't say any more, and Parvana wondered why she'd bothered to ask.

She took out her notebook.

Dear Shauzia:

Another day of being hungry, with nothing around that looks like food. I don't even know if I am hungry any more. I'm just tired, and I feel like crying all the time. We're almost out of water, and I don't know what to do.

Remember those fairy stories we read in school, where someone taps a magic wand on a rock and water pours out of it, or where someone rubs a lamp and a genie comes out to grant three wishes? I believed in that when I was little, but now I know that a rock is just a rock, and that rubbing a lamp only makes it shiny.

Maybe when I'm old and spend all my time dreaming in the sun, I'll be able to believe in those things again. But what do I believe in until then?

"You're not very smart," Asif said, "to be carrying all those things in your bag. It's tiring you out and making you mean. You're stupid."

Parvana slammed down her notebook. "How dare you call me stupid? I *have* to carry all these things. Who else is going to carry them?"

"I could carry something. I could carry Hassan."

"Don't be silly. You can barely walk."

"I could carry him on my back. It's not so sore now." Asif took off his blanket shawl and tied it into a sort of a sling. "Hassan can sit in here, and I'll tie this end around my neck."

Parvana thought of her aching arms. "Do you think it will work?"

"Of course it will work. I've been thinking about it for awhile."

They tried it out. Parvana had to help Asif stand, and she had to tie the baby sling on him, but it did appear to work all right. Hassan didn't seem to care. He whimpered, but he whimpered when Parvana carried him, too, so she didn't think it was because he was on Asif's back instead of in her arms.

Asif could still manage his crutches with the baby on his back, so the three children moved on. They followed a dirt road because it was flat and easier to walk on. Sometimes a truck went by, or a donkey cart, but although Parvana waved for them to stop, they just kept going.

Toward the end of the day they came to a tiny village, almost as small as the one Hassan had come from. This one hadn't been bombed or, if it had, the people had long since rebuilt it.

Old men sat on the ground outside their homes, shading their eyes from the sun as they watched Parvana, Asif and Hassan move slowly down the middle of the road that ran through the village. Parvana felt uncomfortable with their eyes on her, but there was nothing she could do about it.

"Do you think we should ask them for water?" she whispered to Asif.

"They don't look very friendly. They might ask a lot of questions and make trouble for us," Asif said. "Let's see if we can find someone else to ask. Maybe we can find a child."

They saw a few small boys playing with an oddly shaped soccer ball. There wasn't enough air in it, and it didn't go very far when they kicked it.

"Where can we get some water?" Asif asked them.

"There's a tea house down there," one of the soccer players said. "Do you want to play with us?"

"I'm thirsty," Asif said. "Maybe later."

The boys went back to their game. Parvana and Asif walked a little farther down the road and came to the tea shop.

"We don't have any money," Parvana said. "We'll have to beg."

"I don't beg," Asif said. "I can work."

Parvana sighed. She was too tired to work. Begging would have been much easier.

The tea shop was a little mud hut with a few tables in it. There were three men inside sitting in silence. A large tea urn was at one end of the room.

Shauzia had been a tea-boy back in Kabul, running around the marketplace delivering trays full of cups of tea to merchants in their stalls. But there didn't seem a need for that sort of person in this village.

"We're looking for work," Asif said.

One of the men shifted in his chair. "There's no work here, boy. Do you think we'd be sitting still if there was work available?"

"We'll do anything," Parvana said, "and you don't have to pay us. Just give us something to eat and drink."

The man took a swallow of tea and took his time answering, as though Parvana and Asif were well-fed children asking for work for the fun of it.

"You can't work," he finally said, looking at Asif.

"My brother will look after the baby," Parvana said quickly. "I can do the work of two."

"What is your name?" the man asked.

"Kaseem," Parvana replied, giving her boy-name.

"My chicken house needs cleaning," he said. "If you do a good job of that, I'll give you some food, but then you'll have to be on your way. I only have one chicken house, and I'm not about to give away food for free."

The chicken house stood at the back of the small yard. It was filthy.

"There's water there if you want a drink," the

man said, pointing at a rain barrel. "If the water's good enough for the chickens, it's good enough for you. I'll bring you food when you finish the work." And he went back to his friends.

The yard was surrounded by a fence that was falling apart more than it was standing up, although the fence around the chicken house was in good repair. Parvana lifted Hassan off Asif's back and helped the two of them settle in a bit of shade under two scraggly trees. She brought them a ladle of water, but Asif motioned for her to drink first. She emptied the ladle in a second, then filled it again. Asif gave some to Hassan before drinking himself.

Parvana thought of the chickens that had bullied her in the bombed-out village. She wasn't in the mood to be bullied today, and the chickens seemed to sense that. They scurried out of her way.

She worked steadily, scraping away chicken muck with an old board and pushing filthy straw out into the yard, trying not to get too much muck on herself. As soon as she got the job done, they could eat.

Nestled in some straw, she found some eggs the owner had forgotten to collect. How could she take them? They would show, and probably break, if she put them in her pocket. She looked over at Asif, asleep with Hassan, using their blanket bundle as a pillow.

Parvana looked around. It was wrong to steal. She had seen what happened to thieves under Taliban law. They had their hands cut off. She didn't want that to happen to her. But she did want those eggs!

She cupped the eggs in her hands and checked to make sure the coast was clear. She would dash across the yard, tuck the eggs into the blanket bundle and dash back into the hen house.

But she couldn't do it. Her father would not be proud of her if she stole. They were often hungry when they were traveling together, and although the opportunity to steal came up, her father wouldn't hear of it. "Our bellies would be full tonight," he would say, "but could we live with ourselves in the morning?"

Parvana put the eggs back and went back to cleaning the hen house. It was filthy, but at least it was small, and soon she was finished.

"Here is your food," the man said, bringing a small bowl of rice into the yard.

"There are three of us," Parvana said.

"But only one of you worked. Do I look like a rich man?"

"You are richer than we are," Parvana said. "We are children."

"If I help all the hungry children in Afghanistan, I would soon be as poor as you. If you don't want the rice, I'll take it away."

"We want it," Asif said. But the man stood there and held the bowl just out of Asif's reach.

"Please," Asif said. "Can we please have the rice." Parvana could see his hand trembling.

The man finally handed the bowl to Asif, then went back inside.

The children shared the small amount of rice, eating in grim silence. It didn't take long to empty the bowl. Then Parvana filled their water bottles, and Asif rinsed out a few diapers for Hassan.

"Grownups shouldn't turn their backs on children," he said angrily as he squeezed water out of the diapers.

"I wish I had taken those eggs of his," Parvana muttered, casting a dark look at the tea house.

"Go and get them now," Asif said.

"It's too risky."

"Then we'll come back."

They found a spot at the edge of town where they couldn't be seen. They spread the diapers out to dry and waited until night came.

Leaving Hassan asleep in the hiding spot with their belongings, Parvana and Asif snuck back into the village and into the back yard of the tea house.

Parvana found the eggs she had left behind and put them into her shoulder bag next to her letters to Shauzia.

Asif, moving slowly, picked up a chicken so smoothly and calmly that the chicken didn't even squawk. He put his shawl around it and handed it to Parvana. Then they crept out of the yard.

On the edge of the village, they picked up Hassan and their belongings and kept walking until the village was far behind them.

"People who cheat children deserve to have bad things happen to them," Parvana said. "I don't feel the least bit sorry."

"Eggs for breakfast," said Asif.

Then they laughed.

NINE

Parvana couldn't sleep. Her belly was empty, and it hurt.

When they had the chicken and the eggs, it felt like they had all the food in the world. Hassan couldn't eat chicken very well because he only had a few teeth to chew with, so Parvana and Asif decided to let him have the eggs. Parvana cooked them up nice and soft. There was no oil left to cook with, but she watched them carefully, and they did not stick to the pan too badly.

Asif killed the chicken simply and quickly, and Parvana began to think there were things he could do besides complain and annoy her.

They ate the chicken for as long as they could, feeding Hassan the softer parts. They all felt better when they were eating. Hassan took an interest in things again, and Parvana wasn't nearly so grumpy.

But eventually there was nothing left to eat, and they all became hungry again.

Had it been a week since the chicken ran out? Parvana could no longer keep track of time. She lay on the hard ground, wondering what the point was of eating one day, when they just got hungry again the next day.

She closed her eyes and tried again to sleep.

She had chosen her sleeping spot carelessly. There was a rock in the ground that jutted into her back. No matter how she changed her position, she was still uncomfortable. But the night was cold, and at least she was warm. If she got up to find a more comfortable place, she'd get cold. If she stayed warm, she'd be uncomfortable.

At least she didn't have to worry about waking Hassan if she got up. He slept with Asif all the time now.

The rock dug into her again, and she decided to move. She could always get warm again.

"One, two, three," she whispered, then flung back her blanket.

The cold air grabbed at her. She tried to move quickly before it really chilled her, but she couldn't find a smooth place to put her blanket. So she wrapped her blanket around her shoulders and sat on the ground.

"Maybe I'm the only person awake in the whole world," she whispered. "Everyone else is sleeping and dreaming, and I'm awake, watching over all of them. Parvana the Protector." She smiled.

She started humming a song about the moon that she had learned at school. The music went out into the cold night air and seemed to make the stars twinkle more brightly.

There was a shuffling behind her. She knew without turning that Asif was awake, and she waited for him to say something rude about her singing.

Instead, he shuffled over to her on his bottom. He gently tugged at the corner of her blanket, and she wrapped it around both their shoulders. She added words to the song she'd been humming. Then Asif sang something he knew, then they sang something together that they both knew.

They sat and sang and watched for shooting stars, until they were both so tired they were able to fall asleep again, even with the ache in their empty bellies and the sharp rocks under their backs.

TEN

Dear Shauzia:

We're going to have to walk again today, although I would rather just sit. I'm so tired. But I keep thinking of what my father always said. "If we stop, we die."

Hassan flops around. He's like a sack of rice. His eyes are dull, and he doesn't respond when we talk to him. It's like he's already gone away.

The grass we ate yesterday upset our stomachs. We all have nasty stuff pouring out the bottom of us. It's bad enough for Asif and me, but it's worse for Hassan, who has no clean clothes left. It's a good thing the sun is warm today, because he's naked until his laundry dries. One of us has to keep fanning him to keep the flies away.

Wait a minute, Parvana thought. Hassan hadn't eaten any grass. They had tried to feed him some, but he wouldn't take it. So why was he sick?

Then she knew. She had forgotten to boil the water before they drank it.

She knew well enough to do that. Even back in Kabul, where the water came from a tap in the street, it had to be boiled before you could drink it. Unboiled water could make people sick. Everybody knew that.

She looked out at the little pond they'd been living beside and drinking from for three days. Fast-moving streams were sometimes safe, but water in ponds always had to be boiled. How many times had her father told her that? No wonder they were all sick.

She took up her pen again.

I'm tired of having to remember things. I want someone else to do the remembering.

Parvana put her writing things back in her shoulder bag and gathered some dried grasses to build a fire so she could boil some water. Until someone else came along, she would have to take care of things.

"At least with our stomachs upset, we don't feel like eating," she said, when the baby's clothes had dried and they were walking again.

Asif didn't answer. It seemed to take all of his energy to simply keep moving. Parvana knew she should carry Hassan for him, but she didn't offer.

Two more days passed. The children stopped for yet another rest.

Parvana sat with her writing things in her lap.

She was going to write another letter to Shauzia, but couldn't bear to write again about how hungry they were, or how thirsty, or how much Hassan stank. She was tired of writing those things. She wanted to be able to write something new.

If only the world were different, she thought. She closed her eyes and imagined a cool, green valley, like the one her mother's family came from, only better and brighter than the way her mother had described it. She thought of the sort of place where she would like to live. Then she opened her eyes and began to write.

Dear Shauzia:

This morning we came to a hidden valley in the Afghan mountains, so secret that only children can find it. It's all green, except where it's blue or yellow or red, or other colors I don't even know the names of. The colors are so bright you think at first they will hurt your eyes, but they don't. It's all so restful.

Parvana kept writing, and as her words filled the page, she could see Green Valley more clearly in her mind. It almost became real.

"Writing to your friend again?" Asif asked from where he was sitting.

"Do you want to hear it?"

"Why would I want to hear what a couple of girls have to say to each other?"

"You'll like this," Parvana said. "Let me read it to you."

Asif didn't say yes, but he didn't say no, so Parvana read out what she had written.

Green Valley is full of food. Every day we eat like we are celebrating the end of Ramadan. I just finished eating a big platter of Kabuli rice with lots of raisins and big hunks of roasted lamb buried inside it. After that I ate an orange as big as my head and three bowls of strawberry ice cream. No one in Afghanistan has ice cream any more, except for the children of Green Valley, and we can have as much as we want.

You would love it here. Maybe when you get tired of France you could come here, and this is where we could meet instead of the Eiffel Tower. Now that I've found this place, I never want to leave.

We can drink the water here without boiling it, and we don't get sick. The other children tell me it's magic water. All the children here have both arms and legs. No one is blind, and no one is unhappy. Maybe Asif's leg will even grow back.

Parvana finished reading. She sighed deeply and put the letter down. It sounded foolish. While she was writing it, she could see everything so clearly! But now she could only think about her empty belly,

Asif's terrible cough and blown-off leg, and the horrible smell coming from Hassan.

"Green Valley." Asif kicked at the dirt with his foot. "There's no such place."

"No," Parvana said flatly. "There's no such place. I made it up."

"Why?"

Parvana shrugged. "I just thought... I guess I just thought that if I could imagine it, I could make it real."

"Just like Alexander the Great's treasure in the cave," Asif taunted.

Parvana was furious with herself for sharing her dream with Asif, but mostly for having a dream in the first place. His leg would not grow back, there would never be enough food, and unboiled water would always make people sick.

She ripped the paper out of the notebook, balled it up and threw it into the field.

A breeze picked up the little ball of paper and sent it back to her. It landed just out of her reach.

She picked up a stone and threw it at the paper. She missed, then threw another stone angrily.

"Those are lousy throws," Asif said.

"Oh, you think you could do better with those skinny arms of yours?"

"I could throw better than you if I had no arms!"

The challenge was on. Parvana helped Asif stand up, and she handed him some stones. He leaned on one crutch as he threw. His first throw went a lot farther than hers.

"I told you!"

"My first throws didn't count," Parvana insisted. "I wasn't trying." She threw another rock. This was much better.

They kept throwing. Sometimes Asif's throw went farther, sometimes hers did. She kept handing Asif rocks, and he kept throwing them.

"Anyone can throw these small stones," Asif said. "Get me some big rocks, and I'll show you how to really throw."

Parvana made a little pile of rocks big enough to need two hands to throw. She had to hold him up while he threw these, because he couldn't throw and hold onto his crutches at the same time. The effort made him cough, but he kept trying.

Parvana picked up the largest rock in the pile. It was quite heavy. She put all her strength behind it and heaved it into the field.

The ground roared and rose up in front of them, as if a monster was punching its way through from below.

The children screamed. They screamed and screamed, and kept screaming as the dust settled.

Asif threw a stone at Parvana's shoulder. "You led us into a mine field!" he hollered, his rage making his voice even louder than Hassan's screams. "You are the stupidest girl. With all your writing and all your France, you don't know what you're doing! We will all be blown up! You are stupid, stupid, stupid!" As he yelled at her, his hand kept grabbing at the place where his leg used to be.

Something made Parvana put her arms around Asif's frail body. They dropped to the ground, gathered up the stinking, weeping Hassan, clung to each other, and cried and cried.

ELEVEN

Parvana didn't know how long they sat like that. It seemed like hours and it seemed like minutes.

She shielded her eyes and looked out at the rocky, dusty field. She couldn't tell by looking at it how deadly it was.

Sometimes land mines were spread on top of the ground, brightly painted to look like pretty things. People would try to pick them up and get their arms blown off. Most of the land mines were buried just a few inches under the ground. People didn't know they were stepping on them until the bombs exploded.

Parvana didn't know what to do now. If they were in a mine field, all they had to do was take one wrong step, and the earth would rise up beneath them.

Should they head out across the field and maybe get blown up? Should they stay where they were and wait to die from hunger and thirst? How could she know what was the right decision? She was too tired and sad to even guess. Either way, it looked as though they were all going to die. She would never meet up with Shauzia after all. She thought of her friend, sitting at the top of the Eiffel Tower, waiting and waiting and waiting.

Parvana rested her chin on Asif's shoulder as their crying subsided into quiet sobbing. She looked out at the field. All she saw was rocks and dust and hills with more rocks and dust.

Something caught her eye. It was moving toward them. She blinked a few times to be sure she was seeing correctly, then sat up straight.

"Someone's coming," she said, "across the mine field."

Asif turned and looked where she was pointing.

"I think it's a girl," he said.

"I think you're right," Parvana said, seeing the chador flow out from the girl's head as she ran toward them.

"Do you think she's real?" Asif asked.

Parvana wasn't prepared to guess. Things that seemed real to her turned out to be things she had just dreamed up.

"We can't both be imagining her, can we?"

Before they had time to wonder, the girl herself was there.

"Children!" she exclaimed. "It's been ages since I've seen children!" She bent down to hug them.

Parvana and Asif were too stunned to hug her back.

The girl was smaller than Asif. She wore a filthy green chador over her hair. "And you have a baby. Oh, this is wonderful! Did anybody die?"

Parvana's brain, sluggish from hunger, was slow to respond.

"What?"

"The explosion," the girl said, waving her hands in the air. "Is anybody dead?"

"No, no, there's no one dead."

"What's the baby's name?" the girl asked.

Asif answered. "His name is Hassan."

"It's too bad you're all boys," she said. "I've been wanting and wanting a sister."

"She's a girl," Asif said, jerking his thumb at Parvana.

"Are you? You're a very strange-looking girl."

Asif giggled. Parvana frowned at him. She could say the same about this girl. She wore a dress that looked like a long piece of flowered cloth with a hole cut out for her head. Her belt was a rope. Her face was covered with sores like the ones Parvana had seen on other children. Her father had told her they came from disease and infection. The girl wore an assortment of bangles and necklaces made from objects Parvana couldn't completely identify – a nail in the necklace, and something that looked like the twisty end of a broken lightbulb. The jewelry clanked and jingled as the girl pranced around them.

Parvana felt too overwhelmed by the girl's energy to ask her any questions.

"Well, let's go," the girl said.

"Go where?"

"To my house, of course. I always take what I find in the mine field back to my house. You are even better than a wagon or a donkey. Have you ever eaten donkey? Of course, I couldn't get the whole donkey home. I had to cut off a bit of it, just big enough to carry. I came back for more, but by then the flies and the buzzards had found it. I don't like to eat things if the flies have been on it, and those buzzards scare me."

The girl kept talking as she picked up the two bundles and walked away, leaving Parvana to pick up Hassan and Asif to pick up himself.

"Wait!" Parvana called after her. "What about the land mines?"

"Land mines won't hurt me," the girl called back. "Just follow me and they won't hurt you, either."

The girl headed out across the mine field. She moved so quickly, skipping along, that Parvana had to call her a few times to wait for them. The mine field was dotted with animal skeletons, broken wagon wheels and bits of soft-drink bottles.

The girl led them down a short canyon and into a small clearing sheltered on all sides by rocky hills.

"Welcome to my house," she said, spreading her arms as if she were welcoming them to a palace.

It was the stench that hit Parvana first. The smell of rotting meat seemed trapped in the clearing. She saw half-butchered sheep and goats on the ground, covered with flies.

The house was a mud shack like many others Parvana had seen in her travels. It was coming apart in many places. The mud was patched in spots, but only a short ways up. Parvana realized that the girl, who looked to be no more than eight years old, could not reach any higher. A cloth that was more holes than material hung over the doorway.

Apart from the animal carcasses, there was litter all over the yard–broken boards, empty bottles, bits of leather harness, frayed ropes, filthy bits of cardboard and tangles of weeds. There was another smell, too. Parvana guessed the girl had been using the yard as a latrine.

There was no one else in the yard, and no one came out of the house to greet them.

"Do you live here all alone?" Parvana asked.

"Oh, no. I live here with my grandmother. Come and meet her. She'll like you a lot."

She led them into the house. It was dark inside, and it also stank.

"I've found some children, Grandmother. Isn't that wonderful? Say hello to my grandmother," she urged Parvana and Asif.

At first Parvana thought the girl had gone completely mad, that there was no one else in the room. Slowly, her eyes adjusted to the darkness of the little house.

She saw a tall cupboard, some shabby mats against the walls and a pile of clothes in the corner.

The little girl went over to the pile of clothes, knelt down and appeared to be listening to it. "Grandmother says she's very glad to see you, and to please stay as long as you like."

"We'd better take the kid with us," Asif whispered to Parvana. "She's as crazy as you are."

Parvana was about to agree with Asif when she took a closer look at the mound of clothes.

She knelt down and put her hand on it. She felt the boniness of a human spine and the slight rise and fall of breath.

The girl's grandmother was curled into a ball on a thin mattress, with her back to the door. She had a dark cloth draped over her whole body. Even her face was covered. She did not move or make a sound. Only the tiny movement of her breathing and the absence of the death smell proved to Parvana that the woman was alive.

The little girl didn't seem to notice anything was wrong. She took them back outside.

"Grandmother needs a lot of rest," she said, before twirling around in a dance of activity.

Parvana remembered that her own mother had been like that, lying on the toshak at home when her father was in jail. She remembered the woman on the hill.

This was what happened to grownups when they

became too sad to keep going. She wondered whether it would ever happen to her, too.

She had a hundred questions for the girl, but for the moment she just asked one.

"What is your name?"

"Leila," the girl said, and she fetched them some water and cold rice.

The food and drink revived Parvana and Asif, but neither of them could coax Hassan to eat. He just didn't seem interested.

"He's almost dead," Leila said very matter-of-factly.

"No, he's not," Asif insisted. "He's going to be fine." He soaked the edge of his shirt with water and put it in Hassan's mouth. For a long minute it seemed as if Hassan would just let it sit there. Then he started sucking the water out. "See? He's going to be fine." He made a paste out of a bit of rice, and Hassan ate that, too.

There was a well in the clearing with a hand pump, and they were able to wash. Leila brought out clean clothes for them.

"These were my mother's," she said.

Parvana felt very proud of herself for not laughing at Asif as he came out of the house dressed in a lady's shalwar kameez until his own clothes were washed and dried. His stick-thin body was lost in the grownup clothes, and a glower covered his whole face.

Parvana liked being back in girl clothes. The shalwar kameez Leila gave her was light blue with white embroidery down the front. It made her feel almost pretty again.

In the yard there was a cook-fire with rocks around it that made a place to set pots on. Leila cooked some rice and meat stew for supper. Before serving it, she took a pinch of food from the pot and put it in a little hole she made in the ground with her fingers. Parvana was too tired to ask what she was doing.

"It's pigeon stew," the little girl said. "I hope you like it."

Parvana wouldn't have cared if she were eating vulture. Any food was good food. Asif spooned broth from the stew into Hassan's mouth. Hassan swallowed everything, keeping his eyes on Asif's face.

They ate their evening meal in the one-room house with Leila's grandmother. Leila talked nonstop as she put some food on a plate, lifted her grandmother's head cover a little and placed the plate underneath it.

Parvana watched closely. Eventually she saw slow movements under the cover as the old woman lifted morsels of food from her plate to her mouth.

Through it all, Leila talked and talked. Words spilled out of her like she was a pot boiling over.

"I know I'm talking a lot," she said, "but it's

been such a long time since I had anyone to talk to, especially children. Of course, I have Grandmother, but she doesn't talk much."

As far as Parvana could see, Grandmother didn't talk at all.

"Was she always so quiet?" she asked Leila.

"Oh, no. She used to talk all the time. All the women in my family are big talkers. She didn't go quiet until my mother wandered off."

"Mothers don't just wander off," Asif said.

"Well, really she went looking for my brother and father. Someone came by and told us they were killed in the fighting, but she didn't believe them and went off to look for herself. She hasn't come back yet. I sit up on the hill every day and watch for her, but she hasn't come back yet." She looked confused, Parvana thought, as if she couldn't understand why her mother was taking so long.

Asif asked the question Parvana was almost too afraid to ask.

"How long ago did she leave?"

Leila seemed puzzled.

"Did she leave before last winter?" Parvana asked.

"Yes," Leila said. "Before the winter. The nights were still warm when she left."

That was months and months ago.

"You've been alone all that time?"

"Not alone," Leila insisted. "With Grandmother."

Asif and Parvana exchanged looks. Being alone with a grandmother like that was as bad as being all alone.

"Go ahead and talk all you want," Parvana said. "We'll listen."

TWELVE

They spent the night in the little house. Leila shared her mattress with Parvana, and Asif slept next to Hassan. Parvana slept deeply and did not dream.

The flies woke her up.

We'll have to do something about that, she thought as she scratched at the flea bites on her ankles. They would have to do something about the bugs in the beds, too.

She realized she had decided to stay for awhile.

The others were still sleeping. Parvana gently lifted Leila's arm from where it had fallen across her chest and went outside.

The clearing was a little world by itself. The way the hills surrounded it, it was hard to tell there was a world outside at all.

Parvana walked around the little house. In the back was a patch of dirt that looked as if it might have been a vegetable garden at one point. There were sticks in the ground that could have staked tomatoes, like the ones she had seen in gardens in the villages she had passed through with her father.

Near the garden was a rusty wire cage full of pigeons. The cage was taller than Parvana, but the perch had broken and was lying on the ground covered with droppings. Most of the pigeons hopped around in the muck on the bottom. One was trying to work its way through a hole in the wires. Parvana put her hand against the hole and felt the bird's soft head butt against her palm.

"We ate one of those last night," Leila said, coming up behind her. "We eat some, and they keep having babies, so we have more to eat."

Leila took Parvana on a tour of the clearing. "These are apple trees," she said, pointing to two scraggly trees with shiny green leaves and little green apples on the branches. "The apples will be ready in the fall. They're good, but you have to eat around the worms."

In another part of the yard were sacks of flour and rice. Parvana could see mouse holes in some of the bags.

"Come and see my treasure house," Leila said.

The treasure house turned out to be some boards leaning up against a rock. Leila pulled one of the boards away. Parvana peered in and saw cans of cooking oil, several bolts of cloth, a box of light bulbs, cooking pots, sandals of many sizes, men's caps, lengths of rope, several thermos flasks, and a box of bars of soap, some chewed by mice.

"Where did all this come from?" Parvana asked.

"A peddler got blown up in the mine field. That was a really good day. We got all these things. I made myself this dress from some of the cloth."

Parvana struggled to understand. "You mean you go out into the mine field when you hear an explosion?"

"Of course. That's how I found you."

"What happened to the peddler?"

"Oh, he was blown up. His cart and clothes were all blown up, too. Nothing there we could use. I had to make a lot of trips to carry all these things back."

Parvana had an image of Leila as a spider, waiting for a fly to become trapped in her web.

Asif had joined them in time to hear the last part. "You actually go into the mine field? That's stupid."

Parvana frowned at him.

"He means it's dangerous."

"Not for me," Leila said. "The ground likes me. Every time I eat, I put a few crumbs in the ground to feed it. That's what keeps me safe. Oh, no, it's not dangerous for me. Do what I do, and it won't be dangerous for you, either."

"You're a little bit crazy, aren't you?" Asif said.

"Pay no attention to him," Parvana said, putting her arm around the girl's shoulder. "He's always in a bad mood."

"You two belong together," Asif said over his shoulder as he hobbled away to answer Hassan's call from inside the house. "You're both dreamers."

Leila smiled at Parvana.

"Let's be sisters," she said.

Being sisters sounded fine to Parvana.

"All right. We'll be sisters."

"Can your brothers be my brothers?"

"You mean Asif and Hassan? They're not my brothers. We just sort of found each other."

"That makes them your brothers," Leila said.

"Yes, I guess it does," Parvana agreed, and she wondered how Asif would feel about having her for a sister.

"And that makes them *my* brothers, and my grandmother is *your* grandmother."

Parvana didn't say how she felt about having a lump on a mattress for a grandmother. It didn't matter. A grandmother was a grandmother, and it was nice to have one.

"Who taught you to cook and take care of things?" Parvana asked.

"I used to watch my brother and father do things before they went off to the war. My grandmother and my mother taught me other things, and some things I just made up." Leila skipped off to build the fire up to make the morning tea.

Parvana found Asif shuffling through a pile of broken bits of board by the pigeon house.

"I think I'd like to stay here for awhile," she told him.

"If you think I'm going to stay here with that

crazy girl and her crazy grandmother, you're as crazy as they are."

"I didn't ask you to stay," Parvana said. "I just said I'm staying. Hassan, too," she added.

"You're probably hoping I'll go," Asif said. "It will probably make you miserable if I stay."

Parvana knew what was coming. She kept quiet.

"So I will stay," Asif decided, "but only because it will annoy you." He poked a crutch at the rubble one more time before walking away.

Parvana sighed. He really was a tiresome boy.

Dear Shauzia:

We've found a real Green Valley. It's a little rough still, and it will take a lot of work to make it beautiful, but we can do it.

This is a place where children are safe. No one is hurt or beaten or taken away in the night. Everyone is kind to everyone else, and no one is afraid.

We won't let the war in here. We'll build a place that is happy and free, and if any war people come they will feel too good to keep on killing.

Parvana looked around the clearing. There was so much work to do. She smiled.

They would begin by cleaning up the yard.

THIRTEEN

Parvana kept her plan to herself for the first few days. She and Asif needed to rest and take care of Hassan, and she wanted Leila to get used to them before she started changing things.

She did use an old board to scoop dirt over the animal carcasses. They'd have to be properly buried, but she didn't have the strength to do that just yet.

"The dirt might help keep the flies away," she explained to Leila, who had taken to following her everywhere.

"I never thought of that," Leila said. "Nobody told me." She looked down at her feet. "I try to do things right."

Parvana bent down so she could look Leila in the eye. "You do all kinds of things right," she said. "If you don't know, you don't know. No shame in that."

Parvana brushed some hair out of the little girl's face so Leila could see her smile. She suddenly drew back and then forced herself to look again.

Underneath the hair that fell over Leila's forehead was a large sore, like the smaller ones on the lower part of her face. But this one had small white worms wiggling in it.

"Come with me," she said, and she led Leila to a sunny place in the yard.

"What are you up to?" Asif asked.

Parvana showed him the sore.

"Let me take care of it," he said. "I've got more patience than you do."

Parvana was about to argue, but she realized that he was right. He was more patient. She went to heat up some water to wash the wound. That was what her mother always did.

"Do you realize you've got worms crawling in your face?" she heard Asif ask Leila.

"Sometimes I feel them and I try to brush them away, but I can't always feel them."

Parvana fetched a bit of soap from the treasure house and built up the fire under a pot of water. She cut some strips of cloth and carried everything over to Leila and Asif. On her way, she checked on Hassan. He was napping in the little house, not far from Grandmother.

"You'll need these," Parvana said to Asif and Leila. But they didn't even hear her. Leila was talking a mile a minute while Asif patiently pulled the tiny worms from her wound.

"It's the flies," he said. "They lay eggs in the sore, and the eggs grow into worms."

"How did you get to be so smart?" Leila asked.

Anyone knows that, Parvana was about to say, then bit her words back. Asif was actually smiling.

"I can take over," Parvana said.

"Why? We don't need you." Asif finished with the worms and gently dabbed at the wound with a cloth soaked in hot water. "You need to keep your face clean," he said to Leila. "In fact, you need to keep your whole self clean."

"I know I should," she said. "Now that you're all here, I will. When it was just Grandmother and me, I forgot."

Parvana left them to it. She wasn't sure what she was feeling. Was she jealous? Of what? Mentally, she gave herself a kick. Here they were, finally safe, with food to eat and water to drink, and she was getting all moody. What was wrong with her?

Whatever it was, she couldn't understand it yet. What she could understand was work. She changed into her old boy-clothes so she wouldn't get the girl-clothes dirty, and got busy.

Bit by bit, Green Valley took shape. The worst job was hauling the animal carcasses out of the clearing and burying them outside the canyon. Asif attached ropes to them, Parvana and Leila pulled them out, and all three children dug the holes. Then they dug a proper latrine and cleaned up the yard of everything that attracted flies. There was a lot less buzzing after that.

"How do you know how to do all this?" Leila asked after every new thing they did.

Parvana wasn't sure. "My mother liked everything to be clean, and she always made me help her. I also saw how people did things in the camps and villages I traveled through with my father. And some things are just common sense."

"You? Common sense?" Asif laughed.

Parvana ignored him. She had come to the conclusion that Asif could be pleasant to everyone but her.

"We need to keep the mice out of the rice and flour," he said. He rummaged through the junk in the yard until he came up with enough boards and plastic sheeting to build some mouse-proof containers. He used rope to bind them together when he couldn't find enough nails.

"You girls clean out the rest of the rice and flour," he ordered, "and I'll make plastic pouches for the food that's still good."

Parvana noticed that Asif was always cheerful when he was giving orders.

Parvana and Leila hauled the mouse-tunneled sacks up to the top of the look-out hill.

"We can watch for my mother while we clean the rice," Leila said. "We can watch for your mother at the same time."

"Why not?" Parvana replied, flicking a mouse turd down the hill.

"Maybe your mother and my mother will meet each other, and they'll come walking across the field together. Wouldn't that be great?"

"It would be great, but it's not likely to happen."

"But it *could* happen," Leila insisted. "Don't you think so? Don't you think it *could* happen?"

"All right," Parvana relented. "It could happen."

This set Leila off on a long, detailed fantasy about how their mothers would meet and mysteriously know their children were together and decide it was time to come back to them. By the time she stopped to catch a breath, Parvana almost believed her.

"Asif's mother is dead," Leila said. "So is his father. So is everyone else."

"How do you know that?"

"He told me. He was living with an uncle who beat him, so he ran away."

"Why did he tell you? He never told me," Parvana said, but Leila was already talking about something else. Parvana stopped listening. She was too busy being annoyed at Asif.

As the days went by, Green Valley began to look better, and so did the children. Leila's sores started to heal, and one day Parvana washed and combed out the little girl's long hair. She didn't have a real comb and had to use her fingers, but Leila's hair looked much better when she was finished. Parvana tied it in two long braids and laughed as Leila swung her head from side to side, feeling the braids move.

Hassan lost the floppy-baby look.

"He's like a plant," Parvana said. "If you don't water a plant, it wilts, but then when you start watering it again, it bounces back." He started crawling. "You were much easier to look after when you stayed where we put you," Parvana told him. They had to watch him carefully, as he put everything he found into his mouth, whether it was good for him or not.

Hassan would allow himself to be fed by anybody, but he clearly prefered Asif. When he got bored with Asif, he crawled around looking for other fun things. He loved to watch the pigeons, and when the children couldn't find him, that's usually where he was.

"Hassan is standing up!" Asif yelled one day. The others came running. Hassan had hauled himself up by holding onto the wires of the pigeon cage. He grinned and laughed as he reached for the pigeons, but when he let go of the cage, he fell back on his rump. He looked surprised, then reached out and hauled himself back up again.

Then one morning, the children couldn't find Hassan. He wasn't at the pigeon cage or inside the house. Parvana got a cold feeling in her stomach.

"He can't be in the mine field!"

"Well, don't just stand there. Run after him!" Asif yelled.

Leila was faster. Hassan had crawled through the

little canyon and was right on the edge of the mine field. Leila snatched him up.

"You can't go there," she said, as Hassan screeched. "You're not protected yet." She handed him over to Parvana as he squirmed and fussed.

The children discussed the problem. "We can't let him crawl into the mine field," Parvana said, "but we don't want to chase after him all day, either."

Asif came up with a solution.

"Tie a long rope around his waist. Then he can crawl around without going anywhere he shouldn't." They tried this, and it worked fine.

As long as he had something to lean against, Asif found that he was very good at patching mud walls. He fashioned a device with long boards that let him reach the high spots. Soon the house looked stronger.

Leila and Parvana dug up some wildflowers from the edge of the mine field and replanted them in the yard. Leila edged the little flowerbed with rocks. Parvana remembered the flowers she had once planted in the marketplace in Kabul. She wondered whether they were blooming.

None of the children knew anything about growing vegetables, but when Parvana pulled the weeds and dead plants out of the garden, she found some things growing there already.

"Maybe seeds fell from last year's vegetables," she said to Leila, who was helping her.

"Maybe it's magic," Leila said. "I told you, the ground likes me."

Leila started burying bits of Hassan's food along with hers at the start of each meal. After some prodding, Parvana began to do the same thing. She felt foolish at first, but then it became a habit.

Asif refused. "There's no protection against land mines," he insisted. "You two are idiots."

"Is that how you lost your leg?" Parvana asked. She had never dared ask him before, but if he was willing to tell Leila about his family, maybe he was prepared to talk about his leg, too.

She was wrong.

"No, it wasn't a land mine," he said, glaring at her. "It was...a wolf who ate my leg, but I ate the wolf, so I won that battle."

"You're very brave," Leila said. Asif smiled at her and stuck his thin chest out a little.

Parvana just rolled her eyes.

Every afternoon, Parvana went to a shady spot in the yard and wrote to her friend.

Dear Shauzia:

We patched up the pigeon cage this morning and cleaned it out. I wish we had some vegetable seeds. With all the fertilizer from the pigeons, we could have a wonderful vegetable patch.

Some chickens would be nice, too. Pigeons are good to eat, but I prefer chicken.

Maybe another peddler will get caught in the mine field, a peddler with chickens and seeds and lanterns and lantern oil, and toys for Hassan, books for me, a false leg for Asif, real jewelry for Leila and some new toshaks. Fluffy ones without bugs in them.

Until then, we'll have to make do with what we have.

Parvana read back over what she had written, thinking how lovely it would be to have all those things. Then she realized that for her wishes to come true, some peddler would have to die.

For a moment she wondered what she was becoming. Then she dismissed the question. "I didn't create this world," she said to herself. "I only have to live in it."

FOURTEEN

Leila and Parvana took turns taking care of Grandmother. She didn't need much attention. She just stayed in her corner, eating and sleeping. A few times a day Parvana or Leila would take her a pan, give her some privacy while she used it, and then they would take the pan away again to empty it in the latrine.

At first the children were careful to be quiet around Grandmother, but they soon forgot to worry about her and chattered as much inside the house as they did outside. Sometimes Hassan would use her as a prop when he worked on his standing skills. If Grandmother minded any of this, she gave no sign.

Parvana found some needles and thread in the treasure house.

"Let me fix your dress," she said to Leila. "What you've done is pretty, but I think I can make it even prettier."

Although the dress Parvana made for Leila had sleeves that weren't even – she wasn't very good at sewing – it did look a little more normal than what

Leila had been wearing, and the material she used brought out the blue in the little girl's eyes.

One day, weeks after they had arrived, Parvana decided to wash the dust off the shelves in the little house. She remembered how her mother and Nooria had endlessly washed out the cupboard in the tiny room the family shared in Kabul, using up the water she'd had to walk so far to fetch.

Maybe they could add a room to their Green Valley house, or even two rooms. Her mother, Grandmother and Nooria could sleep in one room. Hassan would make a great little brother for her brother, Ali, and Asif could share a room with them and watch out for them. She could sleep in the third room with her little sister Maryam and Leila. It would be so wonderful to have everyone together.

A pang of missing her family shot through her.

She dropped the cloth back in the bucket and dashed up the hill to the look-out point. Leila was already up there.

"See anything today?"

"I saw some tanks drive by," Leila said, "but I don't think they saw me, because they didn't shoot me."

"The war won't find us here," Parvana said, stroking Leila's hair. "The road is far away. See any mothers yet?"

Leila peered out at the landscape again.

"No, no mothers today."

"Maybe tomorrow," Parvana said.

"Maybe tomorrow."

Parvana squatted down beside her new sister. "If they don't show up soon, I'll have to go looking for them again."

"We could take turns sitting up here," Leila said. "If one of us was always here, they wouldn't be able to slip by without us spotting them."

I have to continue my journey, Parvana thought. She remembered the long months of being hungry and tired, walking through the countryside. She would be alone this time, too. She couldn't ask Asif to go with her. He was making this place his home. And it would be wrong to take Hassan away from where he was fed and happy.

"You're going to stay here forever, aren't you?" Leila asked, entwining her fingers with Parvana's. "We're sisters. You have to stay."

"I'll stay," Parvana said, but she did not say forever. She gave Leila's hand a squeeze, then went back to her house cleaning.

"I will continue my search," she vowed out loud as she finished scrubbing the shelves. "I will. Just...not quite yet."

That decided, she felt much better, and she took a deep, satisfied breath. Then she looked around the tiny one-room house for something else to do.

She had already swept the floor mat with a leafy branch, but she wasn't pleased with the result. It really ought to be taken outside to have the dust beaten out of it. The toshaks should all be aired out, too. Maybe the warm sun would drive the bed bugs and lice out of them.

"Mother wouldn't recognize me," Parvana laughed, "doing housework without being told." She was even wearing girl-clothes all the time again, except when she did nasty cleaning jobs. Her hair was growing back, too. Soon she would be able to tuck bits of it behind her ears.

She pulled two of the three toshaks out of the house and into the yard. Then she bent down, grabbed a corner of the mat and tugged. But the mat wouldn't move.

Grandmother – that was the reason! The mat ran under the toshak where Grandmother crouched.

"You need to be aired out just like the furniture," Parvana said. She laughed at herself. She sounded just like her mother's bossy friend, Mrs. Weera.

Parvana went out into the yard. Leila had come down from the look-out and was hitting one of the toshaks with a stick to beat out the dust and bugs. Asif was keeping Hassan entertained with a piece of wood he moved in the dirt like a toy car. He made car noises that Hassan tried to mimic.

"Can your grandmother walk?" Parvana asked Leila.

"She could before Mother left."

"Let's bring her outside," Parvana said. "It will

be good for her, and it will give us a chance to give the inside of the house a good cleaning."

Asif couldn't help much, but he went into the house with them with Hassan crawling along behind. He liked to try to grab at Asif's crutches as he walked.

Parvana and Leila crouched down in front of the old woman.

"We're going to take you outside now, Grandmother," Leila said.

The woman didn't respond.

"How will we do this?" Leila asked. "We can't carry her."

"Pull her out on the toshak," Asif suggested. As if he could understand, Hassan crawled up onto the mattress beside Grandmother. He giggled.

The girls grabbed the end of the mattress and slowly pulled it across the room and out the door. Parvana saw Grandmother's old thin hands grip the sides of the mattress so she wouldn't fall off, but she made no other movement. Hassan laughed at getting a free ride.

"Let's put her in the sun for awhile," Leila suggested. "If it gets too hot, we can move her into the shade."

Hassan thought the old woman was something to climb on, so Asif led him back to the game they had been playing.

Parvana and Leila brought the floor mat outside, beat the dirt out of it and left it basking in the sun.

Then they gave the inside of the house a good hard scrubbing until it smelled much better and looked much brighter.

They brought Grandmother outside every day after that. One afternoon, when they weren't watching Hassan closely enough, he snatched the chador off the old woman's head, tossed it on his own and laughed out loud.

Grandmother crouched down to cover her face. Leila took the chador away from Hassan and was going to give it back to Grandmother when Parvana stopped her. "Let's wash it first."

While it was drying, Leila combed the old woman's long, graying hair with her fingers. Slowly, her body began to unfold, and her face lifted to the sun. Parvana wasn't absolutely certain, but she thought she saw the old woman smile.

Days and weeks went by – golden days full of sun and enough food and lots of happy work. The sores on Leila's face completely healed, Hassan grew strong, and Asif stopped coughing. Often at night they would sit around the cook-fire and tell stories or sing songs. Hassan usually fell asleep in Asif's lap, but sometimes, if Grandmother sat out with them, he would fall asleep against her, and Parvana would see her gently stroke the little boy's hair as he slept.

Dear Shauzia:

On good days, Grandmother sits facing the door

when she's inside. Sometimes she has harder days and goes back to facing the wall. I tell her it's okay. I know all about bad days.

No sign of our mothers yet. Leila says it's just a matter of time. I hope Nooria doesn't go all bossy as soon as she gets here. I hope she respects that I found this place before she did, and what I say goes, but that might be too much to hope for.

On very, very good days, Grandmother practices standing up. Her legs are not strong enough yet to hold her up for very long.

Sometimes Hassan tries to stand at the same time. They practice together, and they look so much alike that it really is very funny to watch. Even Asif laughs, although that isn't very fair of me, because he laughs all the time now. We tell Grandmother we're laughing at the baby, but really we're laughing at them both.

"I don't know how to write," Leila said, crouching beside Parvana. "I've never been to school. My mother didn't go. Neither did my grandmother. They wanted to send me, but now there's no school."

"I can teach you how to read and write," Parvana said. Asif was sitting nearby holding Hassan's hands and trying to get him to stand on his own. Parvana saw him raise his head, although he didn't say anything.

"Can you teach Grandmother, too?"

Parvana nodded. "Sure."

"She always wanted to own a book," Leila continued. "She used to tell me that if she had a book, she'd learn to read it, and she would sit and read her book when the work was done for the day. She said it would give her new things to think about, and she'd like that."

Parvana knew at once what to do.

There were two of her father's books left. One was a small book with a paper cover. The other was large with a hard cover. She took the large book inside to Grandmother.

Grandmother was having a bad day. She was back in her usual spot, facing the wall, her head covered over again.

"I have a present for you, Grandmother," Parvana said, sliding the book onto the mattress. She placed the old woman's hand on the book's cover. "It's a book, for your very own. And I will teach you how to read it."

The thin, wrinkled hand slowly stroked the book's cover and thumbed the pages. Parvana was about to go back to Leila when the old woman grabbed her hand and squeezed it.

"You're welcome," Parvana said. She slipped her father's last book into her shoulder bag where she kept her letters to Shauzia.

Her father would be pleased, she thought. And she smiled.

FIFTEEN

The weeks sped by. Parvana knew that time was passing, but she didn't think to keep track of the days. Some days it rained, but most days were sunny. She knew by the coolness of the evenings that the summer was turning into autumn.

"We're down to the last sack of flour," Asif said one morning. He had appointed himself in charge of food supplies. "There's only one full can of cooking oil left, and one and a half sacks of rice."

"Are you sure?" Parvana asked.

Asif just looked at her with disdain before turning his back and walking away.

Parvana climbed up to the look-out point to watch for her mother and think. The breeze at the top of the little hill was chilly.

She tried to figure out how long the food would last. They had apples now, too, but not very many.

"Even if we're very careful, the food won't last the winter," she said to the air. She had been too busy enjoying herself when she should have been worrying about the coming winter.

Leila climbed up the hill and sat down beside her. One of her braids had come loose. Parvana rebraided it as they talked.

"Any mothers yet?" Leila asked.

"Not today."

"Maybe tomorrow."

"We're running out of food," Parvana said, then wished she could snatch the words back. It wasn't right to worry the little girl. But she would have to know soon, wouldn't she?

"Don't worry," Leila said. "The mine field will take care of us."

"I hope it happens soon."

They watched as a group of planes streamed across a corner of the sky. A moment later there was a sound like thunder rumbling in the distance. Then they saw dust rise up from the far hills.

The girls had seen these planes before. They were nothing special.

"Grownups killing each other," Parvana said, and she turned away to look for her mother in the other direction.

"I kill," Leila said.

Parvana looked at her.

"I kill pigeons," Leila said. "I don't like to do it, but it's not hard. It must be much harder to kill a goat or a donkey. Is it hard to kill a child?" she asked suddenly.

"It should be," Parvana said, "but some people seem to find it awfully easy."

"As easy as killing a pigeon?"

"Easier, I think."

"We eat dead pigeons," Leila said. "What do they do with all the dead children?"

Parvana didn't even try to answer that question. She put her arm around her new little sister, and together they watched the bombs go off, way in the distance.

As the days went by the children saw many more planes in the sky. The sound of explosions went on around them all night, night after night.

"I can't sleep with all that noise," Leila complained. "Don't those grownups know there are children trying to sleep down here?"

"Maybe we should go somewhere else," Asif said.

"Nothing will happen to us here," Parvana said. "Besides, Grandmother can't walk very far yet." The old woman had worked up to taking a few steps in the yard, but she was still very slow.

All night long the sky would rumble like a thunderstorm. The noise stopped in the morning, and the children sometimes stayed in bed until midday, catching up on the sleep they had lost.

In the afternoons, Parvana taught school. Leila was eager to learn, but she found it hard to keep still and silent during lessons. Grandmother sat beside Leila, holding her book and listening. Parvana wasn't sure how much she was learning, but she liked having her there.

"I don't need your stupid school," Asif announced. He took care of Hassan during the lessons, but Parvana noticed they were always close enough to be able to hear what she was saying. Sometimes she saw him trying to draw the letters in the dust with the tip of his crutch, but he always made sure to rub out his efforts afterward.

One afternoon Parvana was teaching Leila how to count using piles of stones. Hassan was standing on Asif's foot, his arms clinging to Asif's leg. Every time Asif took a step, Hassan swung and giggled. Parvana kept frowning at them – the giggling was distracting – but they kept doing it anyway.

Then they heard the sound of an explosion in the field beyond the canyon.

"Did you hear that?" Leila yelled as she jumped to her feet. "I told you the mine field would take care of us!" She sprinted off down the canyon toward the mine field. Parvana followed her.

"Are you two crazy?" Asif hollered. "Get back here!"

Parvana paid no attention to him. Although Leila had a head start, Parvana's legs were longer, and soon she was right behind the little girl. They dashed through the field to the place where the dust was still billowing from the explosion.

"It's a goat!" Leila exclaimed. "The mine only got a part of it. Most of it is still here!"

They each took hold of one of the dead goat's

legs and dragged it back across the mine field. Parvana thought again about a spider snatching a fly that flew into its web.

Asif waited for them at the mouth of the canyon. He was waving a crutch and yelling at them.

"You are both idiots! You could have been killed!"

"If you call us idiots, we won't give you any meat for supper," Parvana said. She and Leila laughed as they ducked away from the waving crutch.

They put on their most tattered clothes and got the goat ready for cooking. Asif peeled away the skin and chopped the carcass into pieces. They decided to roast most of the meat and put the smaller bones in a pot to boil for soup.

"Let's all get cleaned and dressed up," Parvana suggested, after the nasty part of the job was done and they had buried the remains outside the canyon. "Let's have a party."

Leila loved the idea and, as suppertime grew near and the smell of the roasting goat filled Green Valley, even Asif got into the spirit of it. He washed and put on clean clothes and got Hassan clean and dressed up as well.

After helping Grandmother clean and change, Parvana scrubbed herself and put on Leila's mother's blue shalwar kameez. Her hair felt soft from the washing. She shook her head to feel it fluff out around her neck. It really was growing back!

On impulse, she took a flower from the bottle full of wildflowers Leila kept on the windowsill and tucked it behind her ear.

"Oh, Parvana, you look really pretty!" Leila said. "Doesn't she look pretty, Asif?"

Asif looked at Parvana and made throw-up noises. Parvana turned her back on him. She would not let him ruin the party for her.

The roasted goat was delicious. Parvana wasn't sure how long the cooked meat would last without going bad, so everyone ate as much as they could.

There was still a bit of light in the sky. Parvana fetched her shoulder bag from the house. She meant to write to Shauzia about the meal from the mine field, but when she got back to the fire, Leila and Asif were singing. She slung the bag over her shoulder and joined them until the fire burned down into deep red embers.

They were still singing when night came and the bombs started falling again.

The thunder noise was much louder tonight. Parvana could feel the earth vibrate beneath her. She put her arm around Leila. Asif held Hassan in his lap.

Parvana's heart beat hard in her chest as the children kept singing. The louder the bombs, the louder they sang. Parvana was too scared to be able to think of what else to do.

Then a bomb fell right outside Green Valley. The earth shook violently. The noise sounded right through the hands they clamped over their ears. Hassan screamed.

Parvana and Asif moved the younger ones over beside the boulders on the edge of the clearing.

"Grandmother! Come over here!" Leila yelled.

But Grandmother had rolled back up into a ball and covered her head.

Leila tried to go to her but Parvana wouldn't let her. With one hand she held onto Leila. With the other hand she held onto Asif, who shielded Hassan with his body.

Parvana held on tightly as the earth shook more and more. She held on even though Leila writhed and screamed to get to her grandmother.

She was holding on when a bomb fell directly on Green Valley.

Dust, rocks and debris fell on the children's backs. Parvana couldn't tell who was screaming. Maybe it was her.

They clung to each other through the darkness of the night, as the bombs continued to fall all around them.

Silence came with the morning light.

There was a large crater in the yard.

Grandmother was gone. The house was gone.

Green Valley was gone.

SIXTEEN

Dear Shauzia:

We're back on the road. It almost feels like we never left. Maybe Green Valley was just a dream. I should stop dreaming. All my dreams turn into garbage.

As hard as it was before, it seems harder this time. It's harder to sleep on the bare ground after months of sleeping on a mattress. It's harder to be hungry after months of eating every day. And it's harder to spend the days wandering after having a home again.

I hope you are living somewhere wonderful. You will have to have a truly spectacular life to make up for the waste mine has become.

Leila didn't want to leave the clearing. She kept saying her mother would come back and not find her. She made me leave a note for her mother. I'm glad Leila can't read much, because I had to put in the note that I have no idea where we are going.

Hassan cries and cries and cries. I felt sad for him at first. Now I just hate the noise.

As if he knew what she was writing, Hassan let out an extra-loud wail.

Parvana threw down her notebook.

"Shut up!" she yelled. "We've tried to help you and we can't, so stop crying!"

"He doesn't understand you," Asif said, taking the baby onto his lap. "He got used to eating, and he's angry at us for not feeding him."

Parvana hated it that Asif was behaving better than she was. She picked up her notebook and put it back in her shoulder bag. Then she noticed that Leila was crying again, too.

"Do you want a reading lesson?" Parvana asked her gently. "My father used to give me lessons when we took breaks."

Leila shook her head and wiped away some of the tears that were rolling down her cheeks.

"I should have gone to Grandmother," she said. "You should have let me go."

Parvana tried to hug the little girl, but Leila pulled out of her grasp. Leila cried quietly – not loud like Hassan – but Parvana was just as tired of hearing it. She walked away and sat down with her back to them. She had no idea what to do.

A row of tanks rolled by in the distance, and two planes flew in the sky above her, although she didn't see any bombs falling from them. Parvana didn't pay them any attention. Tanks were normal. Bombs were normal. Why couldn't eating be normal?

They had salvaged what they could after the house was bombed. There was a bit of rice spilled on the ground. They picked it out of the dirt grain by grain. There wasn't enough water to cook the rice, and no cook-pot, so the children had to chew the rice kernels raw.

The food and water lasted them for a few days. Then it ran out. That was two days ago. It was longer for Hassan, because he couldn't chew raw rice.

Their only blanket was the blanket shawl Asif had been wearing around his shoulders when the bomb hit. That, plus Parvana's shoulder bag, was all they had. Hassan had no change of clothing, and already he stank again.

Parvana carried him most of the time. He wanted to be crawling, so he kicked and fussed whenever he was carried. He stank, so Parvana stank. Her once beautiful light blue clothes were now a stinking mess.

"We're worse off than we were before," Parvana said to the air. To top it off, she was dressed in girl clothes. Whatever she did now, she'd have to do it as a girl – a girl who was getting to be too old to be uncovered in public, according to the Taliban. She didn't even have a head covering. She had been enjoying her hair too much on the night of the party to cover it up.

"Are you just going to sit there like an idiot?" Asif yelled. He had to yell loudly to make his voice heard over Hassan's screeching.

She sat with her back to them for awhile longer, then got to her feet. She went back to the others, lifted Hassan, helped Asif stand up, and gently nudged Leila.

"Let's go," she said.

The children started walking again, because there was nothing else to do.

Toward the middle of the afternoon, Asif let out a shout. "There's a stream!"

Parvana looked where he was pointing. He was right. It wasn't much of a stream, but at least it was wet.

"We should boil it first," Parvana said, but Asif and Leila were already scooping water into their mouths. Parvana realized she was being a fool. There was no way they could boil water. If they got sick, they got sick. It was better than dying of thirst.

She made a cup with her hands and drank deeply. The water was muddy, but that didn't matter. She scooped up water for Hassan to drink, too.

She started to undress the baby.

"What are you doing?" Asif asked.

"I'm going to wash him and wash his clothes. In case you haven't noticed, he stinks."

"I thought that was you."

Parvana snatched the blanket shawl from Asif's shoulders. "To keep the baby warm," she said. For a moment she hoped Hassan would wet the blanket – it would serve Asif right – but quickly changed her mind when she remembered that they all had to sleep under that blanket.

They stayed by the stream for the rest of the day, drinking water whenever their bellies felt empty again.

"Hassan's clothes aren't dry," Leila said as night fell. "We can't dress him in wet clothes. He'll catch cold. You should have waited until tomorrow to wash his clothes."

Asif took off his shirt and wrapped it around the baby. Parvana could feel Asif shivering all night long.

The next morning was chilly. Hassan had messed Asif's shirt, so Parvana had to wash it out. Asif kept the blanket around his shoulders, while he waited for his shirt to dry, but it took too long in the cold air. He eventually put it back on while it was still wet.

"You don't know where we are, do you?" Asif accused Parvana, as his thin body cringed at the touch of the cold, wet cloth on his skin.

"No, I don't," Parvana said, too tired to try to think up something reassuring.

"Do you know where we're going?"

"We're going to find food," Parvana replied. "Now you know as much as I do, and if you don't like it, you're free to go off on your own."

"Don't think I won't do that," Asif grumbled.

"Is there any food in your bag?" Leila asked.

"No, of course not."

"Why don't you check?" Leila suggested. "Maybe there's something in there you forgot."

"I wouldn't forget about food. There's no food in my bag."

"Then why don't you check?" Asif said. "If you don't check, it's because you're hiding something. You probably have all kinds of food in there that you eat when we're asleep."

Parvana let out a deep, annoyed breath and dumped the contents of her shoulder bag onto the ground so everyone could see.

"Matches, notebook full of letters to my friend, pens, my mother's magazine, book." She touched each item as she identified it. "No food."

"What is that book?" Leila asked.

Parvana picked up the small book with the paper cover. "It's in English," she said, pointing at the letters.

"You know some English," Leila urged. "Tell us what it says."

Parvana's English was not very good, and she had to concentrate, which was hard. Her brain had that sluggish feeling it always got when she was hungry. She sounded out the words the way her father had taught her, then translated them.

"To Kill a Mockingbird," she said slowly.

"What's a mockingbird?" Asif asked.

Parvana didn't know. "It's like a…a chicken," she said. "This book is about killing chickens."

"That's dumb," Asif said. "Why would anyone write a whole book about killing chickens?"

"There are lots of ways to kill a pigeon," Leila

said. "Maybe there are lots of ways to kill a chicken. Maybe it's a book that tells us the *best* way to kill a chicken. Or maybe it's about what to do with a chicken once it's been killed. You know, different ways to cook it."

"I like it cooked over the fire the best," Asif said. "Remember the chicken we stole?" he asked Parvana. "That was delicious."

Parvana agreed. That had been a particularly good meal.

"My mother used to make a stew with chicken," she said. "She made it for my birthday once, back when we lived in a whole house with lots of rooms. We had a party. Even Nooria was nice that day." More out of habit than hope, Parvana quickly looked around in case her mother was coming.

"Do you suppose the book tastes like chicken?" Leila asked.

"No, I wouldn't think so," Parvana said.

"It probably does," Asif said. "She's probably keeping it all for herself. She's mean like that."

"Parvana's not mean," Leila insisted, which was the first nice thing she had said about Parvana since the bombing. "If that book was good to eat, she'd share it with us."

"She's meaner than an old goat," Asif insisted.

"Oh, here, see for yourselves!" Parvana tore some pages out of the mockingbird book and handed them out.

"What about you?" Leila asked. "You must be hungry, too."

Parvana tore a page out for herself and one for Hassan, but Hassan was getting that floppy-baby look again and wasn't interested.

"What are we waiting for?" Parvana asked. She bit into the page, tearing a chunk off with her teeth. The others did the same.

The book didn't taste like chicken. It didn't taste like anything, but it was something to chew on, and each child ate another page after they finished the first.

"Where do we go from here?" Asif asked.

"Someone else decide," Parvana said, stretching out on the ground. "I'm tired of being the leader."

"If it doesn't matter where we go, why don't we follow the stream?" Leila suggested. "At least we'll have something to drink that way."

Parvana sat up and looked at the girl with admiration. "At least one of us is thinking," she said.

"I was just going to suggest that," Asif insisted.

The children looked up and down the stream. "There are some trees up this way," Asif said. "Maybe we'll find something to eat."

It was good to have a plan, even a small one, so the children headed off again.

SEVENTEEN

The bombing continued night after night. Sometimes it was far away, sometimes a little closer, but always, when darkness fell, thunder sounds rolled across the sky.

"Who is under the bombs?" Leila asked one night. All four children were huddled together under the one blanket. The two youngest ones were in the middle where it was warmer. Parvana had the old rocks-in-the-back problem, but moving herself would have meant moving all four of them. Asif and Hassan were sleeping.

"Parvana, who's under the bombs?" Leila asked again.

"I don't know," Parvana whispered back. "People like us, I guess."

"Why do the bombs want to kill them?"

"Bombs are just machines," Parvana said. "They don't know who they kill."

"Who does?"

Parvana wasn't sure. "Since the bombs come from airplanes, someone must have put them there, but I don't know who, or why they want to kill the people they're killing tonight."

"Why did they want to kill Grandmother? She never knew anyone who put things on planes, so how would they even know her to kill her?"

"I don't know," Parvana said. She took hold of Leila's hand under the blanket. "We're sisters, right?"

"Yes, we're sisters."

"As your big sister, it's my job to protect you," she said. "That's why I had to keep you from going to your grandmother that night. Do you understand?"

"I understand," Leila said. "You were doing your job. I was angry at you, but I'm not any more."

"When my father died, it made me feel better to remember things about him. Why don't you tell me something you remember about your grandmother?"

"She used to sing," Leila said, after thinking for a moment. "She taught me a song about a bird. Would you like to hear it?"

Parvana said she would. Leila sang the song.

"It's like she's still here when I remember her like that," she said. "Do you think she's happy now? What do you think she's doing?"

"I think people get to do what they want after they die," Parvana said. "Your grandmother wanted to read, so she's probably sitting in the warm sun surrounded by books, reading and smiling."

"I'd like to be surrounded by pretty things," Leila said.

"You *are* a pretty thing," Parvana told her.

"So are you. We're both pretty things," Leila giggled.

"Can't you girls ever stop talking?" Asif complained. He turned his back to them, yanking the blanket with him.

Parvana didn't yank it back. Asif's cough had returned. She moved in closer to Leila for warmth against the cold, dark night.

For the next few days the children stuck close to the stream as it got thinner and thinner. The water made them all sick, but they kept drinking it anyway. They ate leaves and grass and some more pages from the mockingbird book.

Hassan stopped crying. He barely whimpered now, and he wouldn't eat any of the leaves they tried to put in his mouth. He didn't turn his head away or spit them out. They would just fall from his lips because he couldn't hold them there.

The ground by the stream was rocky and hard to walk on. They had to move slowly so Asif wouldn't fall. Sometimes they saw people in the distance, but they had no energy to rush over to them for help, and their voices would not carry that far.

They had been walking for four days when Leila suddenly spotted something up ahead.

"Look," she said.

Parvana had been keeping her eyes on the ground, looking for the smoothest way for Asif's crutches. She looked up. Not too far in front of them were some people on a cart. They didn't appear to be soldiers.

"Maybe they'll give us a ride," Parvana said.

"I'll run ahead and see," Leila said.

As they got closer, Parvana could see a woman in a burqa and children in the cart, and a man standing beside it.

They caught up with Leila. She looked up at them and shook her head, then nodded at the broken cart wheel.

"We cannot help you," the man said. "We cannot even help ourselves."

"Can you at least give us food for the baby?" Parvana asked, holding Hassan out to show them what bad shape he was in.

The woman in the cart uncovered the baby she was carrying. It looked like Hassan. Parvana noticed the other children also had dull eyes and sores on their faces like Leila used to have.

"Our baby will soon die," the man said. "Yours will, too."

"He won't," Asif said.

The man went on as if Asif hadn't spoken.

"I am a farmer, but the bombs made holes in my land. There has been so little rain – nothing to help the land recover from the bombs. This stream used to be a river. I caught fish here as a boy. The water was good to drink. Now there are only rocks. Can we drink rocks? Can we eat rocks?" He touched the broken cart wheel gently, too worn out for anger.

"Where do we go now?" Parvana asked him.

"We have heard there is a camp in that direction." He pointed across the river. "I don't know exactly where. Go that way. You will meet others. There are many people trying to get away from the bombing."

Parvana reached out and took hold of the hand of the woman under the burqa. The woman squeezed her hand back. Then the children went on their way.

"This must be the river bank," Parvana said when they got to the edge of the rocky surface. "See where the water cut through the soil?"

The river bank was steep. Asif had to go up backwards on his bottom while Leila carried his crutches. It was slow going, and the effort made him cough a lot. They had to rest before they could go on.

"I smell smoke," Leila said later that afternoon. "Maybe there are people ahead cooking supper. Maybe they have lots of food and will share some with us."

"I don't think anyone around here has lots of food," Parvana said. She could smell the smoke, too. "But we might as well go and see."

They headed toward the smell. They found it at the bottom of a small hill.

The children stood on the hill and looked down

at a forest of blackened trees. Some of them were still smoking.

"What is it?" Leila asked.

"It's an orchard," Asif said. "See how the trees are in rows? It's a place to grow fruit."

The trees would grow nothing now.

"My uncle had an orchard," Asif said. "He grew peaches, mostly, and rows of berry bushes. He accused me of stealing berries from him. Is it stealing to take food when you're hungry? I worked and worked for him, and he didn't give me enough food."

"Is that why he whipped you?" Parvana asked. If Asif wanted to talk, she wanted to listen.

"He never told me why he whipped me. I don't think he needed a reason. When he caught me eating the berries, he locked me in the shed. He said he was going to get the Taliban to cut off my hands."

"How did you get out?"

"Crutches are good for breaking locks," Asif said. Then he headed down the hill into the burnt-out orchard. The others followed him. They soon came across bomb craters in the ground.

Parvana didn't like it in the orchard. She kept thinking she saw things moving among the silent black tree trunks. She wondered what sort of trees they had been. Peach? Apricot? Cherry?

There were no birds singing. That's why it was so quiet.

"Leila, teach us the bird song your grandmother sang to you."

"I don't feel like singing."

"But I do. It will help me to not be afraid."

Leila taught them the song. They sang it until they were out of the orchard. It was a place of death, and Parvana was glad to leave it behind.

EIGHTEEN

Dear Shauzia:

The man with the broken cart was right. We see a lot of people now, traveling like we are. We beg from everyone we see. We even beg from people who are trying to beg from us. Most people don't have anything. If they do, they share it with us – sometimes just a mouthful, but it helps us stay alive another day.

People keep telling us to take Hassan to a doctor, but we don't know any doctors, and we have no money to pay for one.

I wonder if that man ever got his cart out of the river bed. I wonder if their baby will live.

I wonder if we will live.

The children followed a road now, going in the same direction as the other travelers. Sometimes a truck full of soldiers passed them. Once a short line of tanks rumbled by, and everyone had to get off the road to let them pass. Parvana remembered the tank the children had played on in the village where her father died. She wondered if children would play on these tanks one day.

Later they heard the tanks shooting at something.

The planes were bombing in the daytime now, as well as at night. Some of the bombs were so loud that the noise knocked the children to the ground. Asif cut his face when he fell against some rocks. A lot of blood ran from his forehead. He had to keep wiping the cut with his blanket, because they had no bandages.

More bombs fell. One exploded just ahead of them. People scattered, huddling in clumps on each side of the road.

"Get down!" people shouted. "Take cover!"

Parvana ran with the baby to the side of the road. Asif was close behind her. She was face down in the dirt, dust and rocks billowing around her, when she realized Leila wasn't with her.

She peered out through the falling rubble and saw Leila still standing in the road. The little girl had her hands cupped over her mouth, and she was shouting something into the sky.

Parvana slid Hassan over to Asif and ran into the road. As she got closer, she could hear what Leila was saying.

"Stop!" Leila shouted at the airplanes. "Don't do this any more!"

The airplanes ignored her. The bombs kept falling.

Parvana would never know how she found the strength. She picked Leila up and ran with her to the side of the road, then lay on top of her to keep her from rushing out again. Her free hand found Asif's. They stayed like that until the planes finished their bombing.

When everything was quiet except for the crying of people who had lost loved ones, and the screaming of those who had been injured, the children got up and started walking again. They couldn't help anyone, and no one could help them.

Parvana saw a man cradling a dead boy, an injured woman with her burqa flipped back from her face, gasping for air, a child shaking a woman on the ground who was not responding.

The children had to walk around dead pack animals and broken wagons and bits of people's belongings scattered in the road – shoes, pots, a green water jug, a broken shovel. There was smoke and the smell of gasoline, and the sounds of agony and madness. It all made Parvana feel as if she were walking through a wide-awake nightmare.

"Do you suppose we're all dead?" Asif asked.

Parvana didn't even try to answer. She just kept walking.

The children walked for the rest of the day. They were just four more bodies in a long line of people moving forward only because there was nothing to go back to.

"I don't even feel like me any more," Parvana said, talking more to herself than to anyone else. "The part of me that's me is gone. I'm just part of this line of people. There's no me left. I'm nothing."

"You're not nothing," Asif said.

Parvana stopped walking and looked at him.

"You're not nothing," he said again. Then he grinned a little. "You're an idiot. That's not nothing."

Before he could stop her, Parvana wrapped his frail body in a gigantic hug. To her great surprise, he hugged her back before pushing her away with mock disgust.

They kept walking.

As the sky grew darker, mountains and hills became balls of fire and pillars of smoke from the bombs dropped on them. Parvana's eyes stung from the thick smoke in the air. Her throat, already parched from thirst, burned when she tried to swallow.

Night was almost upon them when they reached the top of a small ridge and looked down.

Spread out below them, as far as they could see, was a mass of tents and people.

Parvana knew what they were looking at. She had stayed in a place much like it, with her father, last winter.

It was a camp for Internally Displaced Persons. It was a camp for internal refugees.

It was a home for four tired and hungry children.

NINETEEN

"We have hundreds of people a day flooding in here," the nurse in the Red Crescent Clinic said to Parvana and the others as she took charge of Hassan. "Things were bad enough already. Then someone dropped a bomb on our supply depot. Tents, blankets, food and medicine all went up in smoke before – "

"Will Hassan be all right?" Asif asked.

The nurse had Hassan stripped, washed and diapered with a few quick, practiced movements.

"He's suffering from severe malnutrition and dehydration," she said, putting a needle into Hassan's arm and taping it down.

"What does that mean?" Asif asked.

"It means he's hungry and thirsty," the nurse said.

"I *know* that," Asif almost yelled. "I asked you if he's going to be all right."

"We'll do the best we can," she said, and she began to head off to another patient.

"That's no answer." Asif stuck out his crutch to block her way, and for once Parvana was glad for his rudeness.

The nurse stopped and turned around.

"He's in very bad shape," she said. "I don't know if he'll be all right or not. I've seen sick babies like him recover, though, so don't lose hope. Now, I'm sorry, but you'll have to leave."

Asif lowered himself to the floor beside Hassan's crib. Parvana and Leila sat down beside Asif.

"Where's the rest of your family?" the nurse asked.

"We're it," Parvana said.

The nurse nodded. "Don't get in the way," she said, but gently.

The clinic was just a big tent. They had stood in line for hours to get in. From her spot on the floor, Parvana couldn't see much of what was going on, but she could hear the moans and the weeping, and the sounds from the camp that filtered in under the tent canvas.

Asif and Leila stretched out on the floor under Hassan's crib and were soon asleep, but Parvana was quite content to sit. She felt as though she could sit for the rest of her life.

The nurse came back after awhile. "Here's another blanket for you. Don't tell anyone you got it here. There aren't enough to go around, and we don't want a riot on our hands." She also gave Parvana some bread and mugs of tea. "You won't be able to stay here all the time," she said, "but you can for now."

For now sounded fine to Parvana. "You're not Afghan," she said to the nurse, who spoke Dari with a foreign accent.

"I am from France," the nurse said. "I am here in Afghanistan with a French relief agency."

"Do you know the fields of purple flowers?" Parvana asked, so excited that she gripped the nurse's arm. "My friend Shauzia is going there. Do they really exist?"

"Yes, I have seen the fields," the nurse said. "The flowers are called lavender. They are made into perfume. Your friend picked a beautiful spot to go to. Now, drink your tea while it's hot. Wake up your brother and sister. They should have a hot drink. They can sleep later."

Parvana woke them up. They drank the tea and went back to sleep.

Parvana spent the night hovering between sleeping and waking. She would start to drift off, then bombs would explode in the distance. Or she would start to dream that they were still walking, walking, walking, and she would wake up again. Every time she did, she checked on Hassan. He looked so small in the crib with a tube sticking out of him. Sometimes when she got up, Asif was already standing there watching the baby.

After a couple of days, the hospital was so crowded that the nurse had to ask the children to leave.

"I'm sure we can find some families who will take you in with them."

"We'll stay just outside the clinic," Parvana said. "We want to stay near our brother."

The nurse gave them a letter. "The World Food Programme has set up a bakery on the other side of the camp," she said. "Give them this letter, and you'll be able to get some bread every day... well, almost every day. I'll get food to you when I can, but it won't be very much or very often."

As a final parting gift, she also gave them a piece of plastic sheeting. Parvana was grateful. She knew how to build a shelter with that.

Outside the clinic, Parvana draped the plastic against the barrier separating the clinic from the rest of the camp. She made a little tent, with enough plastic left over to line the floor.

"We've only been here a few days, and already we have food, shelter and an extra blanket, and Hassan has seen a nurse," Parvana said, forcing her voice to sound cheerful.

"I don't like it here," Leila said. "It's noisy and crowded and it smells bad. Can't we go back to Green Valley? Maybe Grandmother is all right now. Maybe she's sitting on top of the hill waiting for us to come home."

"We're here for the winter," Parvana said firmly. She didn't remind Leila that Grandmother was dead. "We're a family. We stick together. I'm the oldest, so you have to do what I say."

She didn't add that her legs had no more steps in them. As bad as this place was, at least it was somewhere. There were grownups around, and the possibility of regular food. Besides, she wouldn't know where to go from here.

"I'll go and get our bread," Asif offered. He was already lying down in the lean-to, coughing. Both he and Leila were coughing all the time now.

"No, it's all right, I'll go," Parvana said.

She didn't want to go. She didn't want to wade into the sea of desperate people. She knew from her experience at the other camps that going for bread or anything else meant standing in line for hours. She couldn't let Asif do it.

"We need you here to guard our belongings," she told him. To Leila, she said, "You should stay here, too, so that one of you can sleep while the other stands guard."

She told them not to expect her back until the end of the day. Then she put her bag over her shoulder and headed off in the direction the nurse had shown them.

Parvana's days fell into a pattern. She began to move through them as though she were dreaming.

Dear Shauzia:

I can't sleep at night. I doze off for a bit, then Asif coughs, or Leila coughs, or they cry out in nightmares, or the neighbors yell, and I wake up again. I can't sleep during the day because I have to spend my time standing in lines.

Often my time in lines is wasted. Three times I've lined up for bread only to have the bakery run out before I got there.

Two days ago there was a rumor that someone was in the camp to choose people to go to Canada. I stood in that line all day, but nothing happened. The line fell apart, and I never found out if the Canada people were really here or not. Either way, I missed lining up for bread that day.

When we first set up our lean-to we were alone on that patch of ground. By the end of the day, when I got back with our bread, there was barely an inch of bare ground around our shelter. I couldn't find our place at first, and ran around in a panic before finally getting home.

Asif's cough is worse. Leila's cough is worse, and we are very cold at night. Hassan is getting better, though. Asif goes to see him every day, leaving Leila to guard our few things. He said yesterday that Hassan was able to grip his fingers, and that he laughed when Asif made funny faces. He said there is another baby sleeping on a mat under Hassan's crib, so the nurse wasn't lying when she said there was no room for us.

Everywhere I go, I look for my mother. I should do a proper search, tent to tent, but I spend all my time standing in lines. I'm not even going to hope that I'll find her. Hope is a waste of time.

The nurse told me the purple fields of France really do exist. I hope you're there. I wish I was.

Parvana put her notebook away and shuffled forward a few inches with the rest of the line. She really should be more grateful, she thought. After all, they weren't alone any more, and a proper adult was caring for Hassan. She tried to make herself feel grateful as she stared out over the tents made of rags, stretching all the way to the horizon.

"Excuse me, what is this line for?" a boy asked her.

For a long moment Parvana couldn't remember. She had been standing in the line for such a long time. "Water," she recalled, and held up the empty cooking oil can she had begged from someone else.

Eventually it was her turn at the water truck, and she lugged the full can back to the lean-to.

The bombing was still going on, and refugees kept pushing their way into the camp, squeezing into every square inch of land.

"Why do they have to squash in here?" Parvana complained, as new arrivals threatened to take over the children's lean-to. "There's a whole field on the other side of the clinic. Why don't they go there?"

"It's a mine field," Asif said.

"How do you know?"

He looked at her with his usual scorn. "I know lots of things you don't."

Parvana felt as if she were back in the tiny one-room apartment she had shared with her family in Kabul. Whenever she got angry with Nooria, there was nowhere to go to get away from her. Now with all the bare ground being taken up with tents and shelters, there was nowhere to go to get away from Asif.

She looked out the flap of the lean-to. Inches away was the neighbor's tent. The man and his wife were arguing loudly in a language Parvana didn't understand.

Is this it? she wondered. Have I come so far, just to be here? Is this really my life?

TWENTY

Weeks went by. The weather grew colder. There were days without any bread because a convoy of food trucks had been bombed.

"Maybe the mine field will give us something to eat," Leila said.

"Oh, sure, and what will we cook it with," Parvana said roughly. "Stop dreaming and grow up."

Leila started to cry. Parvana left her alone in the tent. Asif was visiting Hassan, who was much better but was being kept in the clinic because it was warmer there. Parvana was glad she didn't have to worry about him.

She stomped between the tents, pretending to look for her mother, but really just trying to get rid of her anger.

The camp stank of unwashed bodies. There was no place to wash, and it was too cold to get wet, anyway. Parvana didn't have a sweater or a shawl, and the cold made her mood worse.

"Cover up!" a man spat at her. "You are a woman. You should cover up!"

Mind your own business, Parvana thought. He wasn't the first man in the camp to say that to her. She would cover up if she had something to cover up with, preferably something warm. She changed direction and walked away from him.

Most of the women stayed inside the tents. The men and boys stood outside wherever there was room to stand, watching and waiting because there was nothing else to do. Everywhere Parvana went she heard coughing and crying, saw children with ugly sores and runny noses, saw people without limbs and people who seemed to have lost their minds. Some of these people talked to themselves. Some of them did a strange dance, rocking and weeping.

Even after being there for weeks, Parvana hadn't seen the whole camp. Maybe it didn't end. Maybe it just went on and on – an endless sea of crying, stinking, hungry people.

A man walked by carrying a baby. "Someone please buy my baby so I can feed my family," he pleaded. "My other children are starving. Someone please buy my baby!"

A loud, desperate cry reached Parvana's ears, and she realized it was coming from her own mouth.

A woman in a burqa, her face hidden, came up to Parvana and put her arms around her. She spoke softly in Pashtu. Parvana couldn't understand the words, but she leaned against the woman's comforting shoulders, returning the hug. Then the woman hurried off to catch up with her husband.

Nothing had changed, but Parvana suddenly felt calmer and stronger. She went back to the lean-to to apologize to Leila and pass the hug along.

Later that day, they heard a plane overhead.

"It's going to bomb us!" Leila cried, hiding herself under a blanket.

"It doesn't sound like a bombing plane," Asif said. "Let's go and see."

He and Parvana left the lean-to. A lot of little yellow things were falling from the sky.

"Leila, come out and see," Parvana called, as one fell not far from where they were standing. "It's all right. There's no bomb."

The people in the camp stared at the bright yellow package for a long minute, wondering if it would explode. A teenaged boy finally walked right up to it, kicked it a bit and then picked it up. He turned it around in his hands and tore open the yellow plastic covering.

"It's food!" he exclaimed. Then he slammed the parcel close to his chest and ran off.

Food! Parvana could see a few other parcels on the ground, and she ran toward them, but so did a lot of other people. Fights broke out as a hundred people dived for one package. Parvana was jostled by the crowd. She kept a firm grip on Leila and Asif.

"We might as well go back to our lean-to," she told them. "There's nothing for us here."

"There's lots more parcels over there," Leila said, pointing toward the mine field. "They look like flowers."

Parvana looked. The field was dotted with bright yellow.

The children were jostled again as the frustrated crowd surged on the edge of the mine field. Parvana and the others were pushed near the front of the flimsy barrier that separated the safe place from the dangerous place.

"Get back!" Some men with sticks tried to bring order. "Stay out of the field! It's dangerous!"

But people kept pushing.

"We need that food!"

"My family is starving!"

Parvana heard bits of cries from others, all saying the same thing.

Parvana felt a tug on her arm. She bent down.

"I can get the food parcels," Leila said into Parvana's ear. "The land mines won't hurt me."

"You stay with me." People kept shoving and shouting around them. "Do you hear me?" Parvana yelled at Leila. "You stay with me."

"I'll be right back," Leila said, and she darted away.

Parvana reached through the crowd and grabbed Leila's arm. She held on, even though the little girl kept pulling to get away.

"We should get Leila out of here before she does something stupid," Parvana shouted to Asif, but her words were lost in the noise of the mob.

Asif shook his head. He couldn't hear her.

Parvana took a deep breath and was just about to shout her message out again when there was an explosion in the mine field.

Horrified, Parvana gave a great yank on the arm she was clutching, and a child came crashing against her. Parvana stared at the girl in shock.

It was not Leila.

"Leila!" she screamed, pushing her way to the barrier. She saw her sister lying in a heap on the mine field.

The crowd was now silent. Parvana could hear Leila moaning.

"She's still alive!" Parvana cried. "We have to go and get her!"

"We must wait until the mine-clearing team gets here," one of the men guarding the field told her.

"When will that be?"

"We expected them two days ago."

"I have to go and get her!" Parvana started to duck under the string barrier. The guard grabbed her around the waist and held her back.

"You cannot help her! You, too, will be killed."

"She's our sister!" Asif started hitting the man with his crutch. "Let her go!"

When the guard raised his arms to protect himself from Asif's crutch, Parvana broke away and slipped under the barrier.

She didn't think about the mines planted in the ground. She didn't think about the crowd yelling at her from behind the barrier. All she could think of was Leila.

She finally reached the little girl. Leila was covered with blood. The mine had damaged her belly as well as her legs. She looked up at Parvana and whimpered.

Parvana knelt down beside her and stroked her hair. "Don't be afraid, little sister," Parvana said. Then she gathered Leila up in her arms and walked back across the mine field to the camp.

Their nurse friend was waiting for them at the barrier. People helped Parvana put Leila gently on the ground. Parvana sat down and held Leila's head in her lap. She was dimly aware of Asif kneeling beside her, and of the nurse trying to help.

Leila was trying to say something. Parvana leaned down so she could hear.

The little girl's voice was thin with pain. "They were so pretty," she said. And then she died.

A great deal of activity began to swirl around Parvana, but none of it touched her. She knew Asif was crying beside her. She knew the crowd was talking and that people were pushing in to see what had happened, but the grief inside Parvana was a solid blackness that kept everything away. She kept her head down, looking into Leila's face. She closed Leila's eyes and smoothed down her hair.

"Another dead child!" a woman cried out. "How many dead Afghan children does the world need? Why is the world so hungry for the lives of our children?"

The woman knelt beside Leila's body.

"Whose child is this?" she asked.

"She is the sister of these two children," someone said.

"Where are her parents? Does she have parents? What have we come to, that a girl can die without her mother?"

Something in the woman's voice reached through Parvana's blackness.

Parvana raised her head. The woman was wearing a burqa. Parvana reached out her hand and raised the front of the burqa.

Her mother's face looked back at her.

Parvana started to cry. She cried and cried and did not think she ever would be able to stop.

TWENTY-ONE

Dear Shauzia:

I'm writing this letter while I sit at the edge of another cemetery. It's the only quiet place in the camp. I'm wearing a warm sweater Mother found for me.

We buried Leila yesterday. I put rocks around her grave, just like I put them around my father's grave so long ago.

It's not the same, though. I'm not alone this time. I have my old family – Mother, Nooria and my little sister Maryam. And I have my new family – my two brothers, Hassan and Asif.

My baby brother Ali died last winter. Mother thinks he died of pneumonia, but she's not sure. There was no doctor around at the time.

I told them how Father died. My mother says it wasn't my fault.

There's a lot I haven't told her yet, but there's time. Our stories can wait.

It was pure chance that we found each other again. Mother's tent is on the far side of the camp. She was at the clinic with a neighbor woman who was too shy to go by herself to see the nurse. When she heard the explosion, she came running out.

I would have found her eventually, though. It just would have taken me awhile.

She and Nooria are part of a women's organization in the camp. The Taliban are busy fighting the war so they don't bother women in the camp very much.

The women's organization runs a small school and tries to match up people who need things with the things that they need. Mother said Nooria is especially good at this. I can see how she would be. She'd be good at anything that allows her to boss people around.

She hasn't been bossy to me yet, but just wait. A mean old nanny goat doesn't change into a dove just because a little time has passed.

It's wonderful to be complaining about Nooria again! It makes me feel all warm inside, like there is at least something normal in the world.

I gave mother the women's magazine I'd carried all the way from Kabul. She was very happy to see it. She's going to pass it around to other women in the camp to cheer them up.

We hear a lot of rumors. Some people say the Americans are doing the bombing. Some people say the Taliban have left Kabul. People say a lot of things. They even say that someone sitting comfortably in one city can press a button and destroy another city, but I know that can't be true.

"Writing another letter to your friend?" Asif hobbled over and eased himself down to the ground beside her.

Parvana didn't answer him, hoping he'd take the hint and leave her in peace.

"I'm surprised you even have a friend," Asif said. "You probably made her up. You're probably writing all those letters to yourself."

"Oh, go away," Parvana said.

Asif, of course, stayed where he was. He gave her a few moments of silence and then said, "I've just been talking with your mother. I talked with your sisters, too. They're both much prettier than you are. I don't think you're even from the same family."

"You and Nooria should get along well," said Parvana. "You're both unbearable."

"You're probably going to stay here with your family now, aren't you?"

"Of course I am. Why wouldn't I?"

"Well, if you think I'm going to stay with you and them, you can forget it."

Here we go again, thought Parvana. "I don't recall asking you to stay."

"I mean, your sisters are pretty, and your mother is nice, but deep down, they're probably all as crazy as you are."

"Probably."

Asif was quiet again for a moment. Parvana knew what was coming. She waited.

"You probably want me to go," he said. "Why don't you just admit it?"

"I want you to go."

"You'd probably hate it if I stayed."

"Yes, I would."

"All right then," said Asif. "I'll stay. Just to annoy you."

Parvana smiled and turned back to her letter.

It's been a long journey, and it's not over yet. I know I won't be living in this camp for the rest of my life, but where will I go? I don't know.

What will happen to us now? Will we be hit by a bomb? Will the Taliban come here and kill us because they are angry at being made to leave Kabul? Will we be buried under the snow when it comes and disappear forever?

These are all worries for tomorrow. For today, my mother is here, and my sisters, and my new brothers.

I hope you are in France. I hope you are warm and your stomach is full and you are surrounded by purple flowers. I hope you are happy and not too lonely.

One way or another, I'll get to France, and I'll be waiting for you at the top of the Eiffel Tower, less than twenty years from now.

Until then, I remain,

Your very best friend,

Parvana.

MUD CITY

To children lost and wandering,
far from their homes

ONE

"When did Mrs. Weera say she would be back?"

Shauzia had asked that question so many times that the woman in Mrs. Weera's hut didn't even look up. She simply raised an arm and pointed at the door.

"All right, I'm going," Shauzia said. "But I'm not going far. I'll sit in the doorway until she comes back."

But the woman at the makeshift table was absorbed in her work. Not only was this the office for the Widows' Compound, the section of the refugee camp where widows and their children lived. It was also the office for a secret women's organization that operated on the other side of the Pakistan border in Afghanistan. The Taliban were still in power there. Mrs. Weera's organization ran secret schools, clinics and a magazine.

Shauzia was tempted to jump onto the table and kick the papers onto the dirt floor, just to get a reaction. Instead, she went outside and plunked herself down beside the doorway, her back slumped against the wall.

Jasper, her dog, was taking up most of the sliver of shade by the hut. He lifted his head a few inches off the ground in greeting, but only for a moment. It was too hot to do anything more.

The streets and walls of the camp were all made of mud, which soaked up the heat like a bread oven, baking everything inside, including Shauzia. Flies landed on her face, hands and ankles. Nearby, the resident crazy woman rocked and moaned.

"Remember when we were in the high pasture?" Shauzia asked Jasper. "Remember how cool and clean the air felt? How we could hear birds singing, not women moaning?" She reached under her chador to lift up her hair, which was sticking to the back of her neck. "Maybe we should have stayed with the shepherds," she said, brushing off a fly and redraping her head and shoulders with the chador. "Maybe I should have kept my hair short like a boy's instead of letting it grow back. That was Mrs. Weera's idea. Mrs. Weera orders me around, has dumb ideas, and won't even get me a decent pair of sandals. Look at these!" She took off a sandal and showed it to Jasper, who kept his eyes closed. The sandal was barely held together by bits of string.

Shauzia put it back on her foot.

"It's not fair for you to be in this heat, either,"

she told Jasper. "You're a shepherding dog. You should be back in the mountains with the sheep or, even better, on the deck of a big ship, next to me, with the ocean wind all around us."

Shauzia wasn't completely sure whether there was wind on the ocean, but she figured there must be. After all, there were waves.

"I'm sorry I brought you here, Jasper. I thought this place would be a stepping stone to some place better instead of a dead end. Do you forgive me?"

Jasper opened his eyes, perked up his ears for a moment, then went back to his nap. Shauzia took that as a yes.

Jasper used to belong to the shepherds, but as soon as he and Shauzia met, they realized they really belonged together.

Shauzia leaned back and closed her eyes. Maybe she could remember what a cool breeze felt like. Maybe that would cool her down.

"Shauzia, tell us a story!"

She kept her eyes closed.

"Go away." She wasn't in the mood to entertain the compound's children.

"Tell us about the wolves."

She opened one eye and used it to glare at the group of youngsters in front of her.

"I said go away." She never should have been nice to them. Now they wouldn't leave her alone.

"What are you doing?"

"I'm sitting."

"We'll sit with you." The children dropped to the dirt, closer to her than was comfortable in this heat. A lot of them had shaved heads because of a recent outbreak of lice in the compound. Most had runny noses. They all had big eyes and hollow cheeks. There was never enough food.

"Quit butting into me," she said, pushing away a little girl who was leaning on her. The orphans Mrs. Weera was always finding and bringing into the compound were especially clingy. "You're worse than sheep."

"Tell us about the wolves."

"One story, then you'll leave me alone?"

"One story."

It would be worth the effort, if they really did go. She needed some quiet time to plan out what she was going to say to Mrs. Weera. This time, she wouldn't be put off by a request to do one of those "little jobs."

"All right, I'll tell you about the wolves." Shauzia took a deep breath and began her story.

"It happened while I was working as a shepherd. We had the sheep up in the high pastureland in Afghanistan, where the air is clean and cool."

"I can make Afghanistan with my fist."

"So can I."

A dozen grubby fists were thrust into Shauzia's face. The thumbs were stuck out to represent the skinny part of the province of Badakhshan.

"Don't interrupt. Do you want to hear the story or not?" Shauzia said, waving the hands away.

"We were up in the pastureland, where everything is green – grass, bushes, pistachio trees, great oak trees – a beautiful green."

Shauzia looked around for something to compare it to. The compound was all yellowish-gray mud. Most of the children had spent their whole lives there.

"Look at Safa's shalwar kameez. Up in the high pastureland, the whole world is green like that." There was green under the dirt of Safa's clothes. The water supply was low, and no one had been able to do laundry.

The children oohed and aahed and started babbling about colors. Shauzia had to shut them up so she could finish the story. Then maybe they'd leave her alone.

She pictured the pastureland in her mind and, for a moment, she was taken away from the noise, dirt and smell of the refugee camp. "I was sitting up with the sheep one dark night, guarding them, because sheep are so stupid they can't look after themselves. The other shepherds – big grown men – were asleep. I was the only one awake. I sat by a small fire, watching the sparks fly up into the sky like stars.

"There was an eerie silence in the hills. All I could hear was the sound of the shepherds snoring. Then, suddenly, a wolf howled!"

Shauzia howled like a wolf. Some of the children gasped and some of them laughed, and the women in the embroidery group nearby stopped chatting for a moment.

"That was followed by another howl, and then another howl! There was a whole pack of wolves in the forest, wanting to gobble up my sheep.

"I stood up and saw the wolves begin to creep out from the shelter of the trees. They wanted to eat the sheep, but first they had to deal with me. I counted four, then five, then six – seven giant wolves coming toward me, tense on their haunches, ready to spring.

"I bent down and grabbed two burning sticks from the fire. I held them up just as the wolves jumped at me. They were hungry and strong, but I was angry that they had disturbed my quiet night, so I was more than a match for them. I kicked at them and waved the burning sticks until they were so tired out that they collapsed at my feet and fell asleep. In the morning, they were so embarrassed, they simply slunk away back into the forest, grateful that I didn't laugh at them."

"Hello, children!" Mrs. Weera swept into the compound like a strong wind. "Every time you tell that story, you add another wolf," she said, whooshing past her into the hut.

Shauzia jumped to her feet and followed her inside.

"Mrs. Weera, I need to talk to you."

"Another one of our secret girls' schools has been discovered by the Taliban," Mrs. Weera was saying to her assistant. "We must see what we can – "

"Mrs. Weera!"

But Mrs. Weera ignored Shauzia.

Shauzia felt Jasper's solid dog-body beside her, and it gave her strength.

"Mrs. Weera, I want to be paid!" she shouted.

That got Mrs. Weera's attention. "You want to be paid? For telling stories? Whoever heard of such a thing?"

"Not for telling stories."

Mrs. Weera was already striding away on those strong, phys-ed teacher legs of hers.

"Mrs. Weera!" Shauzia shouted. "I need to be paid!"

Mrs. Weera came back. "Which is it? Want or need? I'm sure we all want to be paid, but do we need to be? And are you not already being paid? Did you not eat today? Will you not sleep under a roof tonight?"

I will not back down this time, Shauzia vowed to herself. "I told you my plans when I first came here. I told you I'd need to earn some money, but you've kept me so busy with your little jobs, I haven't had time to look for real work."

"I would have thought bringing comfort to your fellow Afghans in a refugee camp could be considered enough real work for a lifetime."

"A lifetime!" Shauzia exclaimed in horror. "You expect me to do this for a lifetime? I didn't leave Afghanistan just to live in mud!" She flung her arms at the mud walls surrounding the Widows' Compound, knowing that on the other side of them in the regular part of the refugee camp were more mud walls. Maybe the whole world was mud walls now, and she'd never get away from them.

Mrs. Weera gave Shauzia a hard look. "This isn't that France nonsense again, is it?"

"It's not nonsense."

"She thinks she'll just go to the sea, hop on a ship, sail to France and be welcomed there with open arms," Mrs. Weera announced to the growing crowd that had gathered to see what the excitement was. As others laughed, Shauzia realized that was what she hated the most about living in a refugee camp. She couldn't even have an argument in private.

"She wants to spend her life sitting in a cornfield!" Mrs. Weera continued.

It's a lavender field, Shauzia thought, but she didn't bother saying anything. And I don't want to spend my life there. I just want to stay there long enough to get the sound of your voice out of my head.

"Why won't you go into the nurses' training program like I arranged for you? In a few years, you might be able to work as a nursing assistant and earn money that way. The sea isn't going anywhere. Neither, as far as I know, is France."

"A few years? I can't spend a few years here! I'll go crazy! I'll be like her!" Shauzia pointed at the crazy woman. A woman with no name, she had been found rocking and moaning on the streets of Peshawar. Aid workers had brought her to the Widows' Compound. She still rocked and moaned but, as Mrs. Weera said, "At least she's safe here from the beatings the street boys gave her."

"Shut up!" Shauzia yelled at the woman, unable to stand the noise any longer. The woman ignored her.

"Use some respect in your voice when you speak," Mrs. Weera said sternly. "Why can't you be more like your friend Parvana? She always spoke most respectfully."

Parvana didn't like you any more than I do, Shauzia thought, but again, she kept her mouth shut. Mrs. Weera, she'd discovered, had the talent of hearing only what she wanted to hear.

"If you can't pay me for the work I do here, I'll have to leave and find work that will pay me money."

Mrs. Weera's voice softened. "You don't know what it's like out there. You've always been taken care of. You won't be able to manage on your own."

"What do you mean, I've always been taken care of? I've always taken care of myself! My family certainly didn't take care of me." An unwanted image came into Shauzia's mind, of coming home after a day of working in the streets of Kabul to a dark, crowded little room, to people saying, "How much money did you make?" instead of "How are you?"

"Your family, flawed though they were, also waited for you to come home every evening. You earned money to buy them food, but they cooked the food for you and provided you with a place to be each night. When you lived in the mountains, the shepherds watched out for you, and now all of us in the Widows' Compound watch out for you."

"Watch out for me? You don't even get me proper sandals like you promised. All you do is boss me around. Why don't you go back to Afghanistan and boss the Taliban around instead of me?"

"Shauzia, stop this. You are far too old to be acting like a child."

"Then stop treating me like a child! Stop treating me as though I were one of them!" Shauzia gestured toward the group of small children who were following the argument with open-mouthed delight. She suspected they found it even more entertaining than her wolf story.

Mrs. Weera took a deep, slow breath. "You want me to treat you like an adult?" she said calmly. "All right, I will. As an adult, make your choice. If you decide to stay here, you stay without complaint. You will contribute your time and talents to the best of your ability, without expecting money, because you'll understand that there isn't any. If you decide that life here is not for you, you know where the main gate of the camp is. We have enough problems helping those who want our help. Take a few days to think about it, then give me your decision."

Shauzia was stunned into silence. She stared hard at Mrs. Weera, and Mrs. Weera stared hard right back at her.

"I don't need a few days to think about it," Shauzia said coldly, hoping she sounded braver than she felt. "I'm leaving tomorrow, and I'm going to find a great job and become rich, and go to France, and never come back here again!"

"Very well," Mrs. Weera said quietly. "We'll have a farewell party for you tonight."

With that, she walked away.

TWO

There was no escaping the sound of Mrs. Weera's snoring, and by now Shauzia knew better than to try. She used to put a pillow over her ears, or toss and turn and make loud sighing noises, hoping to wake Mrs. Weera, but nothing worked. Mrs. Weera slept the way she did everything – full out – and she didn't waste time worrying about whether she was bothering anyone else.

Shauzia sometimes went to another hut to sleep, but Mrs. Weera's hut gave her something no other place did – a little bit of privacy. Shauzia slept on a toshak spread out under the table. A blanket hung over the side of the table created a tiny, private space.

"It doesn't keep the snoring out," she said to Jasper, who usually slept with her. "But it does make me feel like there is some place in the world that is mine."

Shauzia lay awake in her little room late on the night after Mrs. Weera left her in the courtyard. The rest of the day had gone from bad to worse.

At Shauzia's goodbye party that evening, everyone in the compound ate together around the cook fire in the courtyard. Mrs. Weera made a speech about how much she had appreciated all of Shauzia's hard work.

"I know Shauzia will be successful in reaching her goal of getting to the sea, and of building a fine new life for herself in France." She went on to talk about how beautiful she had heard France was, and how she was sure Shauzia would have a marvelous time wandering through the cornfields.

All the time she spoke, Shauzia's fists were tightly clenched in anger.

After Mrs. Weera had finished talking, the other women also said nice things about Shauzia. How helpful she was, how clever, how they knew she had a brilliant future ahead of her.

And then the children piped up.

"Don't go, Shauzia!" they cried, the little ones sobbing and crowding in on her. "Stay and tell us stories!"

Shauzia was furious. She knew Mrs. Weera had staged this party to make her want to stay in the refugee camp.

Then Mrs. Weera said, "I have good news, Shauzia. I've arranged a job for you in Peshawar. You will be a housemaid in a women's needlework project and daycare center. You can live at the center, and the job will pay enough that you'll have a bit of money to save even after you pay for your rent and food. Isn't that wonderful? Plus, I'll be able to come and visit you every week when I meet with the project. I'll take you there tomorrow and help you get settled."

The other women applauded and talked about how lucky Shauzia was, but Shauzia was seething.

She was still seething as she lay on her mat, with Mrs. Weera's snores all around her.

"She thinks she can control everything," she whispered to Jasper. "She thinks she can control me."

She remembered her first day at the Widows' Compound. She had been wandering around the camp after being dropped off there by the shepherds, and was directed to the compound by an aid worker.

As soon as she walked through the door in the compound wall and saw Mrs. Weera, she wanted to back out, but it was too late.

"I know you!" Mrs. Weera exclaimed in her loud, booming voice. Everyone in the compound stopped what they were doing and stared at Shauzia. "You're Parvana's little friend."

Mrs. Weera had been a physical education teacher and field hockey coach before the Taliban closed all the schools for girls and made the female teachers leave their jobs. She had lived with Parvana's family in Kabul for awhile. Shauzia remembered how bossy she had been then, and wasn't surprised that she was still bossy.

In a few strides, Mrs. Weera's long legs crossed

the courtyard. She stood in front of Shauzia. Shauzia could imagine what the older woman saw – a skinny girl whose face carried on it months of living out in the sun and the wind, clothes filthy and tattered, but with her back straight and her head up high.

"You stink of sheep," Mrs. Weera said, "but we can fix that. And I see you still look like a boy. We can fix that, too." She hollered out an order for hot water and girls' clothes.

"I'd rather keep looking like a boy," Shauzia said. "If I look like a girl, I can't do anything."

"Nonsense," Mrs. Weera said. It was a word Shauzia was to hear her use many times. "The Taliban are not in charge here. I am. Oh, you have a dog, too." She bent down and peered intently at Jasper, who wisely took two steps back. "A most adequate dog," was her verdict.

She turned away, and Shauzia allowed herself a small smile of relief. Mrs. Weera obviously didn't remember how angry she had been with her the last time they had met in Kabul.

The smile came too soon.

"You left Kabul without a thought to how your family would survive without you."

"They didn't like me!" Shauzia yelled. "They were always shouting, and they were going to marry me off to some old man I didn't even know, just to get some money. I meant nothing to them!"

"You don't abandon your team just because the

game isn't going your way," Mrs. Weera replied. "Now then, before you get settled, I have a little job for you."

Shauzia had been doing Mrs. Weera's little jobs ever since.

"No more," she told Jasper. "And I won't be a housemaid for her, either. I don't need a house to sleep in. I slept outside with the shepherds. I can sleep outside in the city. Then all the money I make can go toward getting to the sea."

She reached under her pillow, where she kept her most valuable possession – a magazine photo of a lavender field in France. She couldn't see the picture in the darkness, but she felt better with it in her hand.

That was where she needed to be, in a field of purple flowers, where no one could bother her. She would sit there until the confusion left her head and the stink of the camp left her nostrils. When she had had enough of that, she would go to Paris and sit at the top of the Eiffel Tower until her friend Parvana joined her there, the way they had promised each other. They would spend the rest of their days drinking tea and eating oranges and making fun of Mrs. Weera.

She pushed herself up on her elbows. "Let's leave tonight," she said to Jasper. He thumped his tail, and that was all the encouragement she needed.

She got up and groped around in the corner until she found the bundle of her old boy clothes. She changed into them. Then she grabbed a fistful of hair and, using the scissors from the table top, cut and cut until the hair on her head felt short again. She put on her cap, tossed the blanket shawl around her neck and picked up her shoulder bag. She didn't have any other belongings.

Resisting the urge to yell "Goodbye!" in Mrs. Weera's ear, Shauzia quietly left the hut with Jasper right behind her.

They passed the hut used for embroidery training, and the one used to teach older women how to read. They doubled as sleeping huts for some of the families.

Shauzia went into the food storage hut. There wasn't much there, but she took the few pieces of nan left over from the day's meals and wrapped some cold cooked rice in a bit of cloth. She put the food and a small plastic bottle for water in her shoulder bag.

Back out in the courtyard, she looked around the compound one last time. Everything was quiet except for the sound of Mrs. Weera's snoring and, farther away, the sound of someone crying outside the Widows' Compound.

There was no reason to stay. The camp was dark. Shauzia began to regret her decision to go off in the middle of the night. But before she could talk herself out of it, she turned and walked through the compound door and continued on her journey to the sea.

THREE

There was a loud honk from behind. Shauzia jumped out of the way, and a huge truck roared past her. The exhaust fumes made her cough.

Jasper stuck close to her legs – so close that she was finding it difficult to walk. She could feel him trembling.

"It's all right, Jasper," she said, patting him, but she was feeling pretty shaky herself.

It had been dark when they walked away from the refugee camp, and they had kept walking right through dawn. Now the day was in full swing, and the closer they came to the nearest city, Peshawar, the crazier the traffic became.

The highway was clogged with every type of vehicle. There were buses so full that men clung to the outsides, and little three-wheeled cars that looked like toys zooming in and out of traffic. They were all brightly painted, with many colors and designs. There were white vans and taxicabs and regular cars. It seemed to Shauzia that they were all honking their horns at the same time.

They shared the road with motorcycles that had whole families piled on them, and bicycles loaded down with parcels. There were carts pulled by horses, donkeys, buffalo and even a camel. Shauzia watched an old man use all his strength to pedal a bicycle loaded down with lumber. The bike teetered and weaved and was almost run into by a passing bus.

It was too much. Shauzia took Jasper to a shady spot under a tree. They sat and watched the traffic speed by while they caught their breath.

"I wonder if we made a mistake coming here." Shauzia said. "I didn't think it would be so noisy. I didn't think it would be so...confusing." She scratched Jasper behind one of his ears, more for her comfort than for his.

"Maybe we should even have stayed with the sheep," she said. "At least the air was easier to breathe, and not so hot. Besides, the sea is such a long way away. What if we never make it? We'll be stuck here."

Jasper nudged her hand so she would keep scratching.

"Do you think we'll make it?" she asked him. He wagged his tail and licked her face.

Shauzia took the photo of the lavender field out of her pocket and looked at it for what was probably the millionth time.

"This is where I'm going," she said, more to herself than to Jasper. "And to get there, first I have to be here."

She put the picture back in her pocket, stood up and took a deep breath full of gasoline fumes.

"Let's go," she said to Jasper. Then she grinned. "I'll pretend to be a mighty warrior, like that Ghengis Khan who conquered Afghanistan. I'll invade this puny city. Nothing stands in my way!" She swaggered back to the highway in what she imagined was a Ghengis Khan strut, got honked at again and resumed her journey along the side of the road. She went back to being just Shauzia, but at least she was moving forward.

"I remember trucks and cars from Kabul," she told Jasper, keeping her hand on his head to reassure him. He was still trembling. "All you've known is sheep. Don't worry. You'll get used to this."

Jasper wasn't so sure. He darted away at the sound of every horn or loud rumble. Shauzia was afraid he would get confused and run into the traffic instead of away from it. When she spied a length of blue binding twine on the ground, she picked it up, tied part of it around Jasper's neck and used the rest as a leash.

"It's for your own good," she said. "Just until you're not scared anymore."

Jasper scratched twice at the rope. Then he licked Shauzia's cheek, and they started to walk again.

"There are so many Afghans here, it looks like Kabul," she said. Even the market looked like Kabul's market, with fruit piled high on outdoor platforms and skinned goats hanging on hooks. Butchers fanned newspapers over them to keep the flies away.

Two things were different, though. One was that although some women wore the burqa, others had their faces showing, and no one beat them for it.

The other thing that was different was that all the buildings were intact. No bombs had fallen here. Shauzia had lived among bomb rubble all her life. It felt strange not to see any.

"There must be lots of ways to make money here." Shauzia doubted Jasper could hear her in the noise of the crowd, but she spoke to him anyway, just to have someone to talk to.

All around her, boys her age and younger were working. She saw them in auto repair shops, pounding metal at a blacksmith's, selling oranges off a cart and carrying trays of tea. She saw boys hanging off the sides of buses. They hopped off and urged in customers, taking their money, then climbed back onto the railing as the bus pulled away from the curb. She passed a construction site and saw small boys covered in dirt, leading donkeys loaded down with bricks.

Languages swirled around her. She recognized the Afghan languages – Pashtu, Dari and Uzbek – and she heard others, too, that she thought must be the Pakistani languages.

The crowd got thicker, and Shauzia kept a good grip on Jasper's leash.

A foul-smelling, slow-moving river divided the

two sides of the market. Shauzia saw shops that sold jewelry and canned goods. She saw a shop that sold nothing but burqas, lined up on the walls, hanging like blue ghosts. Everywhere there were people selling goods off trays and karachis.

Shauzia walked around the market looking at all the shops and trying to imagine herself working in them. When she was too tired to walk anymore, she found a place on the ground in a bit of shade from a building and leaned back against the wall. Jasper sat beside her. She took out her plastic bottle, drank some water and poured some in her hand for Jasper. They shared a piece of the bread she'd brought with them from the camp. Then they each drank more water, to wash down the bread.

It was good to eat and drink. Shauzia felt completely worn out. She closed her eyes to rest.

"This is my spot."

Shauzia opened her eyes. Standing in front of her was a woman covered by a burqa.

"This is my spot," the woman said again. "I come here every day."

"I'm just sitting," Shauzia said.

"Sit somewhere else."

Too tired to argue, Shauzia and Jasper got to their feet.

The woman took their place. "Help me," she begged to a passerby, who ignored her. "Just one or two roupees?" she called to another.

"Do you make much money that way?" Shauzia asked.

"Maybe ten roupees a day."

"Is that a lot?"

"It's enough to keep my children hungry."

"Maybe if you lifted your burqa so people could see who you are… " Shauzia suggested.

"What do you know?" the woman replied angrily. "I keep my face covered when I beg so that no one can see my shame. I was an office manager in Afghanistan. I've graduated from university. And now look at me! No, don't look at me! Go away!"

Shauzia stood there for a moment feeling awkward that she'd hurt the woman's feelings, and angry that the woman had made her get up just when she had gotten comfortable. Finally, since she didn't know what to do with either her awkwardness or her anger, she just walked away, and Jasper went with her.

The woman had scared her. If someone who had been to university was reduced to begging, what hope did Shauzia have?

She knelt down beside Jasper and pretended to fuss with his leash. She kept her head low so no one could see her crying.

"I don't like it here," she whispered. Jasper licked at her tears. Shauzia hugged him close. Then she stood up and kept walking.

There were a lot of beggars in the market. Some

were women, covered and uncovered. Some were sick people with twisted limbs. Others were children her age. People walked past the beggars' outstretched hands as if they were invisible.

"The people they're begging from look as poor as they are," Shauzia said. She turned away. It was all too awful to watch.

They walked through the market again.

I've got to ask someone for a job, she thought, but each time she got close to approaching a shopkeeper, she felt too shy to do it.

"You can't possibly manage on your own," Mrs. Weera had said. Shauzia remembered how everyone had laughed.

She took a deep breath and headed to the nearest shop, a bookstall.

"Give me a job!" she demanded of the man behind the stack of books.

She was quickly ordered out of that shop, and away from the four other shops she went to.

The day slipped away. The market stayed open after dark, but the bare lightbulbs hanging here and there from poles and wires created weird, frightening shadows in the streets. Shauzia and Jasper squeezed themselves into an alcove between shops. She could tell from the smell that they were sharing the space with decomposing fruit and other garbage, but at least they were out of the way of people, cars and shadows.

She leaned against the wall, missed Mrs. Weera's snoring, and fell asleep sitting up.

Shauzia woke to a gray predawn morning, her head pillowed on a pile of rotting cabbage. Jasper was already awake, chewing on something he had found in the garbage.

She got up and they went to a water tap she'd seen in the market. She threw water on her face, and she and Jasper had long drinks. The water filled up her belly – for awhile.

She spent the day looking for work. Many of the shopkeepers told her she was too dirty to work in their shops. Others already had all the help they needed.

The sun was starting to go down when she passed a butcher shop, almost empty of meat, full of dirt and dried blood.

"Your shop needs cleaning," she said to the butcher, who was sitting on a stool just inside the doorway and drinking a cup of tea. "I could clean it."

The butcher swallowed a mouthful of tea, looked her up and down and said, "This is a man's job. You're a small boy. Go away."

Shauzia didn't budge. "I can clean your shop," she said again. She put her hands on her hips and stared right at him. She was hungry and tired and not in the mood for nonsense.

The man drank some more tea and swirled it around in his mouth before swallowing it.

"That's a fine dog," he said finally, nodding at Jasper. "He looks hungry."

Of course he's hungry, Shauzia thought. So am I.

"Wait." The butcher disappeared into the shop and came out again with chunks of meat on a piece of newspaper.

"That's good meat," the butcher said, rubbing Jasper's ears while he gulped down the meat. "Good meat for a good dog." He stood up. "Be here early in the morning. I'll give you half a day's work cleaning the shop. You do a good job, and I'll pay you. You do a bad job, and I'll toss you out." He disappeared into the shop, but appeared again a moment later. "You can bring your dog," he said, before disappearing for good.

"Thank you," Shauzia called after him. She knelt down and threw her arms around Jasper.

"I have a job!" She felt like singing.

She had to have something to eat. As soon as Jasper was finished with the meat, they went to the bread bakery, which was starting to close up.

"If you let me have a piece of bread tonight, I'll pay you for it tomorrow," she said. "I'll have a job in the morning."

The baker picked up a loaf of nan from a small stack and tossed it at Shauzia. She wasn't expecting it, and it landed in the dirt. She quickly picked it up.

"How much do I pay you tomorrow?"

"Go away, beggar. I've given you food, so go away."

Shauzia's face burned with shame. She wasn't a beggar.

She opened her mouth to say something, but changed her mind. She might need free bread again.

She shared the bread with Jasper. Then they both had a drink of water at the tap. The food felt good in her stomach.

The marketplace was quiet. All the stalls were shut down. Shauzia saw people sleeping in the shadows and doorways.

She and Jasper went back to the butcher shop. It, too, was closed. They settled down in the doorway.

"This way, I'll be sure to be on time for work in the morning," she said. The doorway smelled funny, but she was so tired that she fell right asleep.

FOUR

Shauzia woke to the sound of the butcher unlocking the iron grill over his shop.

"Your dog will get too hot out here," he said. "Bring him through to the back. There's a pan on the shelf. Give him some water."

Shauzia and Jasper followed the butcher through the shop to a small cement yard in the back. There was just enough room under an awning for Jasper to stretch out in the shade.

Shauzia found the pan, filled it with water and took it out to Jasper.

"Wait here for me," she said. "If I do a good job, maybe he'll give me more meat for you, or at least some bones for you to chew."

"Clean the shop," the butcher said. He showed her where the bucket, brushes and cleaning solution were kept. "I'm going to go out to have my breakfast now. I'll be back soon to check on you."

Shauzia got to work. She worked quickly, washing down the empty shelves and trays where the meat would go when it was delivered. She wasn't bothered by the dried blood. One of her jobs as a shepherd was to pick up sheep dung and flatten it into cakes. They used the cakes for fuel when they couldn't find wood.

That had been a nasty job. Dried blood was nothing.

If the man liked her work, he might have other jobs for her.

The disinfectant he told her to use smelled strong but clean.

Shauzia had an idea.

She took the bucket into the little walled yard, stripped off her clothes, washed herself all over with the clean-smelling water, then quickly washed her clothes as well.

"I know I look funny," she told Jasper as she put on her shirt that was wrung out but still wet. "It will dry, and at least I'm clean enough now for people to hire me."

She got back to work.

"Spilled a bit of water on yourself, I see," the butcher said when he returned from his breakfast. He nodded at the work she had done and poured her a cup of tea from the thermos he had filled at the tea shop. "Take some bread," he said, pointing to a small stack of nan wrapped in newspaper.

Shauzia tore a loaf in half and took half out to Jasper, who gulped it down, then sniffed the ground for more.

"Maybe later," she said, and he thumped his tail.

By the time she had finished the job, the heat of the morning had almost dried her clothes.

"Do you have any more work for me today?" she asked.

"Not today. I am closed today, so there will be no deliveries or customers. You are a hard worker. Maybe I will have jobs for you from time to time. I just said maybe," he added, when Shauzia's face lit up. "Fetch your dog, and I will pay you."

Shauzia got Jasper.

The butcher peeled a ten-roupee note from a bundle he pulled out of his pocket. He hesitated for a moment, then added another ten-roupees.

"Take the rest of the bread," he said. She did.

"Look," she showed Jasper. "Three loaves. We'll eat like kings today and still have some for tomorrow. Food, money and clean clothes, and we only just got to the city! This will be easy."

But she had no more luck that day, or the next. The day after that, her sandals fell apart. She tied them together with a bit of twine that she found on the ground, but that only held for a half a day. It wasn't just the straps that were broken. She'd worn one sole clean through to the pavement.

"I can't go on like this," she said, looking at the bloody mess the bottom of her foot had become.

They sat at the side of the road for a good long while, wondering what to do.

In the middle of the afternoon, a peddler with a karachi full of rubber sandals pushed his cart slowly past her.

"That's what I need!" Shauzia called for him to stop and walked gingerly over to him, her bare feet tender against the hot pavement.

"How much for a pair of sandals?" she asked.

The peddler named a price. It was more than Shauzia had in her pocket.

"I don't have enough." She felt like crying. Her bare feet burned. She had to hop from one foot to the other.

The peddler watched her for a moment, then rummaged in the bottom of his cart. Finally he handed her several sandals that did not match.

"Try these," he said. Shauzia tried them on until she found a sandal to fit each foot. One was brown, and one was green.

"Why do you have all these sandals that don't match?" she asked.

"People with one leg need sandals, too," he replied.

"How much for these?"

"How much do you have?"

Shauzia showed him the money in her pocket.

"That will do," he told her. He took it all.

Now she had sandals, but she had no money.

"It's all Mrs. Weera's fault," she said to Jasper, as they watched the sandal man wheel his cart away.

"If she had got me new sandals like she was supposed to... " Shauzia didn't complete the thought. Blaming Mrs. Weera suddenly seemed like a waste of time. There was never any money in the compound for things like sandals.

"What do I do with these?" she asked Jasper, holding up her old torn sandals. She decided to leave them on the sidewalk. She put them down, but before she had taken a few steps, a young man swooped down and picked them up.

Maybe she should have kept them after all.

Shauzia slept in a different spot each night for the first few nights she was in Peshawar. The city was never quiet at night. There were always the sounds of gunshots, arguments and trucks. There were sounds that could have been crying and could have been laughing. Sometimes it was hard to tell the difference.

When people passed by they ignored her, or stared down at her. Sometimes they dropped trash on her. She told herself it was because they didn't see her. The more it happened, though, the harder that was to believe.

One day, after she and Jasper had been in Peshawar for more than a week, Shauzia found a good sleeping spot between two buildings, off a quiet street. It was a sort of a shelf, big enough for her and Jasper to sleep on.

"This will make a good home for us," she told Jasper.

In a nearby garbage dump she found an old cardboard box. She tore it up and used the pieces to line the cement shelf.

She sat on the cardboard to test how it felt.

"We'll be the most comfortable sleepers in the city," she said to Jasper, who joined her on the bed and wagged his tail.

Shauzia stepped up her job search. She did many different jobs, some lasting a few days, some just a few hours. In the cloth market, with rainbows of fabrics hanging over the walkway like a multicolored forest, she helped unload bolts of cloth and sorted buttons into jars.

She did a bit more work for the butcher, cleaning the shop again, and one day she set up sheep's heads on the table outside the store. He gave her a good-sized bone for Jasper at the end of that day. He also recommended her to his friend with a grocery store, and she got a day's work there, cleaning the place.

Everywhere she went, she saw groups of small children dragging blue plastic sacks, poking through garbage.

"I'll do that if I have to," she told Jasper, "but I don't see how I could make much money that way."

She got a few days' work as a tea boy while the tea shop's regular delivery boy was sick. This was work she had done in Kabul, delivering trays of tea in metal mugs to merchants who couldn't leave their shops for a break. She was good at it, too, and could rush through the narrow streets of the market without spilling a drop. Everywhere she took tea, she asked if there was work for her. She was rewarded with a job sweeping out a furniture warehouse.

One day, instead of looking for work, she went down to the train station.

"Do any of these trains go to the sea?" she asked the man behind the ticket counter.

"You want to go to Karachi," the man said.

"Karachi," Shauzia repeated. "Like the cart. Is it expensive?"

"Return?"

"One way."

The ticket seller told her the price. It was much, much more than she had saved in her money pouch. She thanked him and headed out. She was almost back on the street when some people going on a journey gave her a few roupees to help them carry their bundles.

After that, on the days when she didn't have other jobs, she went to the train station and carried people's bags for tips. She couldn't go there often. There were men whose regular job was to be porters, and they chased her away if they saw her.

It was just as well. She found it hard being at the station, watching other people get on the trains, heading off on a trip.

When would it be her turn?

"I work cheaper than the other porters," she told Jasper one evening. "Some day, someone is going to work cheaper than me, and I won't be able to get work there anymore. The problem is, there are so many of us. There are a lot of Afghans here, and we all need money."

Each night, she added more roupees to the pouch hung around her neck. Each night, she was a little bit closer to the sea.

One day, she saw her reflection in a store window. Her hair was getting long. She was starting to look like a girl again.

She went to one of the barbers who set up shop along the edge of the sidewalk. She sat down on the bit of cardboard he'd placed on the cement to make customers more comfortable. Beside him, in a little box, were his scissors, brushes and razors, and a little mirror so people could check out his work when he was done with them.

"I'd like my hair shaved off," Shauzia told him, and they agreed on a price. She wouldn't need to get it cut again for a long time.

While he was working, the barber joked about giving Jasper a shave, too. The jokes were not very funny, but it made Shauzia feel better about losing her hair.

She avoided her reflection after that, but her head was a lot cooler.

When she got to France, she would grow her hair again, she promised herself.

Each evening, she bought food to share with Jasper out of her day's earnings. On hard days, when she didn't earn much money, she bought only bread. On better days, she bought meat patties from a street vendor, after watching him cook the spiced ground meat in huge, round pans over fires.

Sometimes a grocer she worked for gave her fruit along with her pay. That was a special treat. And Jasper's nose often found him things to eat on the street.

Each evening, as the sky was getting dark, she would sit with Jasper in their little space, and she would tell him about the sea until they were both ready to sleep. She was lonely, but she was usually too tired to spend much time thinking about it.

One night, Shauzia was jolted out of her sleep by the sound of Jasper barking. She opened her eyes to see lights shining brightly down into her face.

She tried to sit up, but Jasper was standing right on top of her, barking and snarling.

She could feel something grabbing at her, and she tried to pull away. Men's angry voices reached her ears through Jasper's barking. Every time they tried to get hold of her, they were kept back by his snapping jaws and pointed teeth.

"We'll come back with a gun and kill your dog," the men said. "You wait here for us."

They laughed and then went away. Jasper sniffed at Shauzia, licked her face, then lay down right across her belly.

Shauzia clung to Jasper and struggled to breathe through her panic.

"We have to get out of here," she said, gently nudging him to the ground.

They headed off down the alley. Shauzia was shaking so badly that she could hardly walk, and she clung to Jasper's fur for support.

They kept walking for the rest of that night, and avoided all the people they saw.

FIVE

Shauzia and Jasper walked until the sky got light. Exhausted, they collapsed in the doorway of a gun shop on the modern main street of the Saddar Bazaar. They managed to get a bit of sleep until they were chased away by the owner when he came to open his shop for the day.

Shauzia's head was thick with unslept sleep. She kept bumping into people and stumbling over the uneven places on the pavement. Once she walked right into a newspaper stand, almost tipping over the table full of newspapers

"Watch what you're doing!" the angry newspaper seller spat out at her. He kicked Jasper. Jasper yelped at him.

Shauzia pulled her dog away, and they bumped into an Afghan antiques dealer, setting out his goods outside his shop. He yelled at them, too.

"I don't like it here," Shauzia told Jasper, kneeling to pet him and quiet him down. She pushed her face deep into his soft fur and smelled his good dog smell. The world was full of nasty-tempered adults, and what she really wanted was to never have to see any of them again.

They kept walking. Shauzia just wanted to sit some place and be quiet, but every time they sat down they were told to go away.

She left the main street, wandering through the narrow, dark streets of the older market. Finally she came back into the sunshine where the market ended by the railway tracks.

There were a lot of people here, too, but they were spread out, not so cramped together as they were in the shops. Shauzia felt she could breathe a bit. She and Jasper turned and walked along the tracks.

A small herd of goats and fat-tailed sheep poked their snouts among patches of weeds. Afghan families had set up crude shelters in the dirt beside the tracks. A Pakistani used-clothes peddler displayed torn Mickey Mouse sweaters and tweed skirts on big sheets of plastic for customers to see. The air smelled of exhaust fumes, excrement and smoke from little cook fires dotted here and there.

A group of Afghan children scavenged in a rubbish heap, dragging large blue sacks behind them. Shauzia watched them for awhile from the tracks. Jasper wagged his tail and strained at his leash, so she let him go. He trotted up to the children, wagging his tail and pushing at them with his snout, wanting to be petted.

Shauzia hung back while the children – four

boys and a small girl – greeted Jasper. The little girl was scared at first. Jasper was as tall as she was. But he licked her face, and she giggled, and Shauzia could see she wasn't scared anymore.

"His name is Jasper," she said, leaving the tracks and joining the children. "It's an old Persian name."

"Can he do tricks?" one of the little boys asked.

"Of course he can. He's a very smart dog. Jasper, sit!" Shauzia took him through his tricks. The children left their bags to one side while they played with him, tossing a stick for him to chase and retrieve.

Two of the boys seemed to be around Shauzia's age. The other two were younger, maybe eight or nine years old. Shauzia thought the little girl looked to be around five. She and the smallest of the boys had nothing on their feet. Shauzia wondered how they managed.

She wondered what they were searching for among the garbage, and picked up one of their sacks to take a look.

"That's mine! Are you trying to steal?" One of the older boys pushed her hard away from his bag. Shauzia fell back against the ground, grinding bits of gravel into her palms.

Jasper was beside her in an instant, barking at the boy.

"I wasn't stealing," Shauzia insisted. "I just wanted to see what kinds of things you were collecting." She patted Jasper with long, slow strokes to calm him down.

She got to her feet. Jasper stopped barking. The little girl came up to pet him, and he wagged his tail again.

"You've never picked junk before?" asked the boy who had pushed her.

"Do I look like a junk picker?" Shauzia retorted, brushing herself off. "I work."

"At what?"

"At proper jobs."

"So why don't you go and do your job, and quit trying to steal our stuff?"

Shauzia kicked at the boy's junk bag. "There's nothing in there worth stealing."

"You call this nothing?" He grabbed the bag and pulled out items, waving them under Shauzia's nose. "Three plastic bottles, a whole newspaper, and two empty tin cans. That's better than you could find!"

"We'll see about that," Shauzia replied.

"This is our junk pile," another boy said. "Why should we share it with you?"

"My dog is a watch dog," Shauzia said. "He'll attack anyone who tries to bother us."

The boy who had pushed Shauzia had bruises on his face, as though he had been in other fights recently.

"Some watch dog," he said. "He doesn't look so fierce." He hung back, though.

"If you're not afraid of him, go ahead and pat him," Shauzia said.

"All right, I will." The boy bent down and reached out a hand. Jasper growled, and the boy backed away.

"It's all right, Jasper," Shauzia said, putting her hand on the boy's shoulder. "Go ahead and pat him," she said. "Now that he knows you're my friend, he won't hurt you."

The boy held out his hand. Jasper sniffed it, then pushed at the hand with his snout.

"I was sleeping in the alley last night," Shauzia told them. "Some men tried to get at me. Jasper scared them away."

"Would your dog protect us, too?" the little girl asked.

"Sure he would. He'd love to, wouldn't you, Jasper?" Jasper was already wagging his tail so hard he couldn't wag it any harder.

"My name is Zahir," the boy with the bruised face said. The other boys were Azam, Yousef and Gulam, and the little girl's name was Looli.

"I'm Shafiq," Shauzia said, giving them her boy name.

"A boy I know was taken by men like that," Zahir said. "They kept him and they cut something out of his belly before they let him go."

"Was he still alive?" Shauzia asked.

"He was alive for a little while," Zahir replied.

"Then he died," Yousef added.

"Go ahead," Zahir said. "Look in my bag."

Shauzia looked at the collection of cardboard, newspaper, bottles and cans.

"We sell it to a junk dealer," Zahir said.

"Not all of it," Gulam said. "The things that burn, we take home to cook our meals."

"Do you have families?" Shauzia asked.

"Gulam and Looli live with their uncle's family," Yousef said. "The rest of us are on our own."

"So am I," Shauzia said. "How much money do you make?"

"Maybe five roupees. Maybe ten. You can come with us if you like," Zahir said.

The children drifted back to work. Shauzia realized how lucky she'd been to find the jobs she had. She joined them as they sifted through the junk that other people had thrown away.

She started off rooting through the garbage with her foot.

"Not that way," Looli said. She was munching on some dry cones an ice-cream shop had thrown away. "You have to use your hands." She showed Shauzia how to dig right into the pile of garbage to get at whatever might be buried there.

The trash smelled bad, but the smell didn't bother Shauzia. After all, she had lived with sheep for months. The flies were familiar, too. She dug right into the trash, opening plastic bags and dumping the contents onto the ground. She put the paper and rags she found into the little girl's bag.

She would go back to looking for proper jobs tomorrow, she decided, but for today, she just wanted to stay with other children.

Jasper, with his superb dog nose, was good at sniffing out things to eat in the garbage, but Shauzia didn't do too badly, either. Along with the paper and bits of wood from a broken crate, she found an empty spice jar and a cracker box – with some crackers still in it!

"Hey! I found some food!" she exclaimed.

In the next second, she was flat on her back in the trash.

"All food comes to me," Zahir said, holding the box of cracker bits high in the air.

But Shauzia was hungry, and she was tired of being bullied. She sprang up without thinking and threw herself at the boy. They rolled in the trash, trying to hit each other. Jasper jumped around them, barking. The other children picked the spilled cracker bits off the ground and ate them.

Shauzia and Zahir ran out of fight before there was a clear winner. They sat in the trash, brushed themselves off and glared at each other.

"Don't try taking anything away from me again," Shauzia snarled.

"Just remember who's boss here," Zahir snarled back.

Since the crackers were gone anyway, they called a truce and went back to sorting through the junk pile.

Late in the afternoon, one of the smaller boys found a length of string. He tied it to the handle of a plastic shopping bag and ran through the dump along the wasteland beside the railway tracks. The bag fluttered behind him like a bird, high above the garbage and the people making their homes in the dirt.

To Shauzia, it looked beautiful.

The sun was hanging low in the sky when Looli put her tiny arms around Jasper's neck and gave him a hug.

"We have to go now," she said.

Shauzia watched the little girl take her brother's hand as he slung her junk bag and his own over his shoulder, and the two of them walked away.

The other boys shouldered their junk bags and started walking in another direction.

"Are you coming? Zahir called back. "Or do you have some important job to go to?"

The other boys laughed. Shauzia thought about being offended, but decided not to be. She looked at Jasper, shrugged and jogged to catch up to the boys.

For the first part of the evening, they roamed around Peshawar like a pack of animals, tossing odd bits of junk into their bags. "Give us money!" they yelled at everyone they met, laughing when the people looked scared and ran away. Shauzia hung back a little, not yelling, but still very glad to have the company.

By nightfall they had reached a large modern hotel. It was so beautiful, it took Shauzia's breath away.

"Is that a palace?" she asked. She and the boys were scrunched down among some bushes. Across the street a huge white building gleamed in the spotlights. Cars drove slowly up a long driveway lined with large round flower pots overflowing with color. A man in a splendid uniform guarded the double set of doors at the front.

"It's a hotel," Zahir said. "Don't you know what a hotel is?"

"Of course I do," Shauzia lied. There hadn't been such places in Afghanistan. "What are we doing here?" The gravel she was kneeling on pressed into her flesh.

"See the light in the hall?" Zahir pointed to a long, low building that jutted out the side of the hotel. "That means there's a big party tonight."

"I still don't understand."

Zahir sighed at her stupidity.

"We're here for the leftovers. Aren't you hungry?"

Leaving their junk bags hidden among the trees, they scurried around to the back of the hotel.

Shauzia heard metal and glass banging and water running. She smelled cooking smells from the open door of the kitchen. Her stomach lurched with hunger.

In a little while, the kitchen staff brought bins out through the back door. They carried the bins over to the back fence and piled rocks on top of them.

"Why are they doing that?" Shauzia asked.

"To keep us out of them. But we're smarter than they are."

The kitchen workers went back inside. Shauzia and the boys crept over to the bins. Shauzia limped a bit, her leg sore from kneeling on the pebbles. Jasper was right in the middle of the children, but he was clever enough to keep quiet.

The boys silently lifted the rocks off the lids of the trash bins. Shauzia helped. They gently tipped over the bins. Then they tore through the party leftovers, tossing aside the balled-up paper napkins and other garbage to get to the cold rice and chicken bones with bits of meat sticking to them.

Shauzia stripped the meat from the bones for Jasper, since chicken bones were bad for him. His nose found him lots of other things to eat, too.

She could not stuff food in her mouth fast enough. Chunks of mutton gristle, bits of ground-meat patties, potatoes slick with spiced oil – she shoveled it all into her mouth, eating with one hand while the other spread out the trash, searching for more food. When a cigarette butt got mixed up with a handful of rice and spinach, she separated it from the food with her teeth, spat it out and kept on eating.

All around her was the sound of hungry boys chewing.

"Hey! Get away from there, or we'll call the police!"

The kitchen workers yelled at the children from the back door.

Shauzia started to leave, but the other kids shouted right back. They heaved bones and other garbage at the workers. Jasper barked, and trash flew through the air. Shauzia picked up a handful of old food and joined in. She laughed as the kitchen workers raised their hands to protect themselves from the flying leftovers.

It felt great to be shouting and throwing. Shauzia couldn't remember when she had last yelled like that. She couldn't raise her voice when she was a shepherd because it would have scared the stupid sheep. She couldn't yell in Kabul because it would have been foolish to draw attention to herself – she didn't need the Taliban looking closely enough at her to be able to tell she was a girl.

But she could yell here, and she did, and she had a wonderful time.

The men disappeared for a moment, then came back waving frying pans and pot lids. Shauzia saw security guards heading their way, too, their guns drawn.

The children scattered, and they were away from the area before the grown-ups could reach them. When things were quiet again, they retrieved their bags of junk and went looking for a place to sleep.

Shauzia stayed with the boys that night. They slept, huddled together, in a smelly stairwell. Jasper was their watchdog, and he kept them safe.

SIX

Shauzia stood in the aisle of the rich people's grocery store. She ran her finger lightly along the rows of beautiful packages. The pictures on them promised good things inside. Cakes, biscuits with chocolate on top, meat, cheese – food more wonderful than she had ever seen before.

And there was so much of it! Who could possibly mind if she took a few packages for herself and her dog? They had so many!

Her mouth filled with saliva as her fingers curled around a tin with a picture of a fish on the outside. It could so easily move from the shelf to her bag.

"You again!"

A strong hand gripped her shoulder like a claw. She released the tin of fish and was pushed through the shop.

"This is the fourth time today I've had to kick you out. If you come in here again, I will call the police."

The store clerk shoved Shauzia out the door with such force that she hit the pavement at the same moment that the ferocious Peshawar heat hit her.

The store had been so lovely and cool, like being surrounded by snow.

She picked herself up off the ground, too angry to pay much attention to the raw skin on her hands and ankles. She stood as close as she dared to the door of the fancy store. At least she could catch a blast of refreshing coldness when the rich people went in and out.

Jasper was stretched out in the bit of shade at the side of the store. He was so hot he had barely managed to growl when she was tossed out.

Shauzia couldn't stand in the shade because she would be out of the way of the people she wanted to beg from.

"Spare any roupees?" she asked a man coming out of the shop. He walked right by her outstretched hand. The woman who came out a short time after handed her a rumpled two-roupee note. That made six roupees Shauzia had made all day.

"I hate this," she said to Jasper. "I hate having to be nice to these people who aren't nice to me. I hate having to ask them for anything. The next person who comes by, I'm going to grab their money and run. If they won't give it to me, I'll just take it."

Jasper rolled his eyes, unimpressed. He had heard this speech before.

Inside the store, Shauzia had felt dizzy at the sight of all the pretty packages of food lined up on the shelves. The people who shopped there had to have a lot of money. Surely people with a lot of money wouldn't mind giving her a bit of it.

But rich people weren't any more generous than poor people.

She asked people for a job as well as for money, but no one had a job for her. She would rather be working than begging. Begging made her feel small.

A man and a woman in Western clothes got out of a white van with their two small boys and crossed the parking lot, heading for the grocery store. Shauzia saw them and held out her hand.

"Look at the dog!" The two boys ran over to Jasper. In an instant he was on his feet, wagging his tail.

"Careful, boys. You don't know this dog," the man said.

Shauzia recognized the language they spoke as English, and she dredged up the English words she knew from when she had studied it in school.

"His name is Jasper," she said.

The man and woman tried to get their sons into the store.

"I need work," Shauzia said. She held out her hand for money, in case they preferred to give her that.

"You speak English very well," the woman said slowly. Then she put a ten-roupee note in Shauzia's hand. "Come, boys, let's go inside."

That's more like it, Shauzia thought, putting the money in her pocket. When the family came out again, the little boys headed straight for Jasper.

"Can we take him home with us, Mommy?" one of the boys asked.

"He belongs to this boy," the woman said. The boy stuck out his lower lip and held Jasper so tightly that Jasper had to shake the boy away.

The man gave Shauzia another ten-roupee note. "Buy some food for your dog, too," he said. Then the family piled back into the van and drove away.

Shauzia and Jasper stayed outside the grocery store for the rest of the day, but they earned only a few more roupees. She bought some meat patties to share with Jasper, and some nan. Then she went to meet the other boys.

They were using the old Christian cemetery as a camping place. It was shady and cool during the day, and the weeds were soft to sleep on at night. The gravestones all seemed to mark the graves of British soldiers who had died killing Indians. Shauzia didn't know which war that was. She didn't suppose it mattered.

"How did you do today?" Zahir asked. Shauzia held up the bundle of nan. She didn't say how much money she'd made.

One of the boys had some oranges he'd stolen off an old man's karachi. They ate together. Zahir commanded extra food from some of the children, but he didn't bother Shauzia.

"Hello, can I join you?" A small boy, his blue

junk bag at his feet, stood on the other side of the graveyard fence.

"Sure. Come on over." Zahir went over to him.

Shauzia knew what was coming.

"Swing your bag up first," Zahir suggested. "It will be easier for you to climb over."

The small boy swung his junk bag up into Zahir's waiting arms. Zahir waited until the boy was almost at the top of the fence, then pushed him hard back onto the sidewalk. The boy tried a few more times before he realized that his junk was gone, and there was nothing he could do about it.

Shauzia didn't join in the scramble for the stolen junk, but she didn't do anything to help the boy, either. She wasn't afraid to fight Zahir, but the last thing she needed was someone depending on her, expecting things from her. She would never get to the sea that way.

"I look after myself. He can do the same," she whispered to Jasper as they settled down among the crosses and tombstones and went to sleep.

Each morning, Shauzia would leave the graveyard, sometimes taking Jasper but usually leaving him in the shade with a pan of water poured from a tap outside the old church nearby. She would walk to the Saddar Bazaar or hitch a ride to other parts of the city to look for work.

Moving around Peshawar so much, she quickly

got to know the city. She knew in which neighborhoods she'd most likely find work, which shops gave food away to beggars at the end of the day, and which rich hotels had garbage bins that could be broken into. She learned where there were outdoor water taps, where she could wash a bit and get something to drink. She learned which parks she could nap in during the heat of the day, and which parks had guards who would kick her out before she even got comfortable.

If she was lucky, she worked. If not, she begged. Bit by bit, she kept adding to the roupees in her money pouch.

"We're getting closer to the sea," she told Jasper one evening when they were alone in the graveyard. She showed him the bundle of money. He sniffed at it and wagged his tail. She put the money back in the pouch and hid it under her shirt before any of the boys could return and see it.

"We don't know these boys," Shauzia told Jasper. "All we know is that they're hungry, and you can't trust hungry people. If they knew I had money, they'd steal it from me, just the way I'd steal from them. Well, probably I would."

Boys drifted in and out of the group. Shauzia didn't always learn their names. No one ever said much about themselves. Some things were too hard to talk about.

"Can you spare any roupees?"

By now, Shauzia could ask that question in Dari, Pashtu, Urdu, the Pakistani language and English.

"As much as I hate begging, it's worth coming here every Sunday," she told Jasper.

"Here" was the Chief Burger restaurant on Jamrud Road, near University Town, where most of the foreigners lived. People who wanted food stood out on the street and called their food orders through the windows. After they placed their order, they had nothing to do but watch Jasper do his tricks.

The man who ran the burger stand liked Jasper. He gave him water and bits of ground meat. "I'll make the burgers smaller today. If the customers notice, it will be too late. I'll already have their money!"

Shauzia was happy that her dog was eating. She would have liked some meat herself, but she didn't ask, and it was never offered.

She didn't know whether it was the church, or the pizza, or Jasper's tricks, but she always made a lot of money on Sundays. Sometimes she made more than she did when she was working.

There were many regular customers at the Chief Burger. Shauzia remembered them from week to week, and they remembered her – or, at least, they remembered Jasper, since that was who they greeted first.

Shauzia always hoped they would give her a piece

of pizza along with their roupees, but they never did. Not even the people she saw often, like the couple in the white van that she had first met outside the grocery store. Their two little boys cried when they had to stop playing with Jasper and go home.

"Spare any roupees?" she called out.

"Would you like some money?" a man asked, coming up beside her.

Adults ask such stupid questions, Shauzia thought.

"Yes, I need money," she replied politely, holding out her hand. "I am also looking for work."

The man handed her a hundred-roupee note.

Shauzia thought her eyes would fall out of her head. She had never held such a beautiful thing before.

"Come with me," the man said. "I will give you a job and then I will give you even more money."

"Oh, thank you," said Shauzia. "I will work very hard for you. Come on, Jasper." She bent down to pick up Jasper's leash.

"Leave the dog," the man said. He took hold of Shauzia's arm.

Jasper growled.

Shauzia tried to bend down to reassure him, but the man tightened his grip and began to pull her along the sidewalk toward his car.

"Wait!" she said. "Just let me see to my dog."

The man did not stop. He held her more tightly.

"You're hurting me!" Shauzia cried. Jasper, hearing the panic in her voice, started to bark at the man. But he kept pulling at Shauzia.

"No!" She tried to pull away. "I don't want to go with you!"

A crowd began to gather. The crowd attracted the police.

"What's happening here?" a policeman asked.

"This boy stole from me, one hundred roupees," the man said.

"I didn't steal! He gave me the money!" Shauzia yelled. "He tried to put me in his car, but I didn't want to go."

"Search him," the man said. "You will find my hundred-roupee note in his pocket."

Shauzia didn't want them searching her and taking the rest of her money. She took the bill out of her pocket and held it out to the man.

"Take it back."

One of the policemen took it.

"Evidence," he said.

Then they grabbed hold of her. Jasper barked madly and threw himself at the policemen.

Shauzia screamed and tried to fight back, but the police were bigger, and they threw her into the back of their van.

She looked out of the tiny window of the back door of the van in time to see one of the policemen kick Jasper hard. Then the van pulled away, and she could see nothing more.

SEVEN

"Empty your pockets." The guard at the police station pointed at the counter top. Shauzia looked around at the others in the room. They were all men, sitting behind big desks, drinking soft drinks and watching her while fans whirred overhead. No one moved to rescue her. She was the only child in the room, and she felt very, very small.

"I didn't do anything wrong!" She had been insisting that ever since the police threw her in the van.

"Empty your pockets!" the guard insisted. "Empty them, or we will empty them for you."

With shaking hands, Shauzia took the few roupees she'd earned begging that day out of her pocket and put them on the counter.

The guard unfolded her magazine picture of the lavender field. He looked at it, passed it around, then folded it back up.

"You can keep this," he said. Then he noticed the string around her neck. "What are you wearing?"

Shauzia pretended not to know what he was talking about, but it didn't work. He reached out and pulled up her money pouch, taking it right off her neck. He opened it up and dumped the money on the counter in front of him.

Shauzia stared at all her roupee notes, the ones she had worked so hard to earn, the ones that were going to take her to the sea.

With a sweep of the guard's hand, they disappeared into a drawer.

"That's mine!" she shouted.

"What's yours?"

"The money you took. It's mine!"

"What would a boy like you be doing with so much money? You must be a thief!"

Shauzia tried to leap over the counter to get at her money, but the counter was too high, and the policemen were too big. They picked her up, and in the next instant, she found herself being tossed into a cell.

She landed on something soft, then sprang right back to her feet. She grabbed hold of the cell bars and tried to squeeze through them.

"You can't keep my money!" she yelled. "I earned it! It's mine!"

One of the guards banged his stick against the bars, inches from her clenched fists. Shauzia backed away.

"Quiet down, or nobody gets any supper."

"I want my money!" she yelled at the guard's back as he walked away.

"Stop yelling. You'll only make them angry," a voice behind her said.

Shauzia turned around. The cell was full of boys. Most looked a little older. Some were around her age or a little younger. They were sitting on the floor, staring up at her.

"Well, they made me angry," Shauzia replied, kicking at the bars. "What do I care if they're angry."

"Because they'll take it out on all of us."

"So sit down and shut up, or we'll shut you up."

Shauzia sank to the floor. The other boys had to shift around to make room for her.

"I'm going to get my money back," she said quietly. She hugged her knees to stop trembling and scowled to keep from crying.

"Do you have any proof they took your money?" one boy asked.

"Do you have proof you even had money?" another asked.

"I'll get it back," she repeated. Some of the boys just laughed.

They don't know me, she thought. They laugh because they don't know how determined I am.

Shauzia's panic and rage gave way to discomfort as the afternoon wore on. It was impossible to get comfortable in the cell. The air was hot and didn't move. She longed to lie down or lean her back against something, or stretch her legs out in front of her. There were too many boys on the cement floor of the cell.

Soon her legs were cramped and her back was sore.

The cell stank of unwashed bodies and other foulness. Shauzia found it hard to breathe, and she wondered how the other boys were managing.

Maybe they've been in here so long they've gotten used to it, she thought, just like I got used to the sheep.

She hoped she wouldn't be in the cell that long.

For the first few hours, she jumped at every little noise that came from outside the cell–every time the phone rang in the outer office, every time one of the guards walked past.

"Relax," one of the older boys said. "You're not going anywhere."

"How do you know?"

"Once you're in here, you're in here forever," he replied. "I was only six years old when they locked me up. Look at me now – old enough to grow a beard soon." The other boys laughed.

Shauzia thought they were probably just joking. The shepherds had joked like that. They made fun of how clumsy she was with chores, or laughed at how one sheep liked to butt her in the behind with his head.

Shauzia hadn't minded. There wasn't much else to laugh at. She concentrated now on not letting her fear show on her face. Anger was good. Fear was dangerous.

"If your family can bring in some money, the police might let you go," the boy next to her said in a quiet voice. "You won't be here forever. Don't listen to them."

"What do I care? I've been in jail lots of times."

"You don't look old enough to have done anything lots of times," an older boy said, and they laughed again.

"How long have you been here?" she asked the boy next to her.

He shifted around a little and pointed to a group of scratches on the wall.

"These are my marks, one for every night." His was only one group of scratches. There were other groups, all over the walls.

Shauzia counted the marks. He had been there almost three months. She didn't let on that she could count.

"I have no family," the boy said, looking ashamed. "Not here. They are back in Afghanistan. I came to earn money to get them out, but now I am in jail. The policeman asks me, 'Where are your papers?' I have no papers. My house was bombed. How could I have papers? So I just sit here."

"Are you telling that same story again?" an older boy complained. "How many times do we have to hear it? Our luck is as bad as yours."

In a lower voice, the boy beside Shauzia continued. "We are all Afghans in this cell. The Pakistan boys are kept somewhere else. Is your family with you in Peshawar?"

Shauzia couldn't answer. She was trying too hard not to cry.

She had suddenly realized that whenever the phone rang in the office, it would not be for her. There was no one to pay off the police, no one even to know she was there.

She imagined herself making scratches in the wall – endless scratches that would take up the whole wall, blotting out all the other scratches.

How could she stay in this cramped space, with no way to run, no way to get to the sea? She had been outside too long, moving as she pleased. The ceiling pressed down on her. How could she stay here?

It was too unbearable to think about. She thought about Jasper instead. Worrying about her dog was easier than worrying about herself.

"Is there a toilet?" she asked awhile later.

"Can't you smell it?" A boy jerked his thumb to a partitioned-off area at the back of the cell.

Shauzia stepped through boys as if she were stepping through a flower garden. The partition gave her a small amount of privacy, but the toilet was just a stinking hole in the floor.

Sheep are cleaner, she thought, and she did not linger there.

A guard came by with a tray of metal cups of tea and a stack of nan.

"Here is your supper," he said.

The boys dove at the food like the wild dogs Shauzia had seen in Kabul, pushing each other to get to the bread. The guard laughed.

Shauzia ignored the food. The cell door was still being held open by the guard. In an instant, she was on her feet and halfway out of the cell.

"Where do you think you're going?" The guard grabbed her.

"I shouldn't be here," Shauzia yelled, trying to pull away. "I've done nothing wrong!"

"Get back in there!" The guard shoved her into the cell. She fell across the tea tray, spilling the cups that hadn't been snatched up yet. The cell door banged shut.

One of the boys punched her hard in her side. "That was my tea you spilled," he snarled, "and my buddy's tea. You'll have to give us your tea from now on to make up for it."

"I don't have to give you anything," Shauzia snarled back.

"Keep it up," the boy said. "You can't hide from me."

Shauzia went back to her space on the floor. There was, of course, no bread left, or tea.

"Here," the boy beside her said. "I'll share my bread with you." He tore his nan in half and held it out to her.

Shauzia knew that if she accepted his kindness, she would have to show kindness in return, and that would make her look weak. So she shrugged away his offering. She'd been hungry before. Right now, that was the least of her worries.

The boy next to her made another notch in the wall with the edge of his metal cup. The other boys were adding notches to their own groups of scratches.

"I'll make one for you," the boy said, putting a scratch on a bare spot on the wall.

Shauzia looked at it once, then turned away.

The guard collected the tea cups, then turned off the overhead light.

"Pleasant dreams, boys," he sneered.

The boys stretched out on the floor as best they could in the overcrowded cell. Shauzia did the same, then sat upright again as one of the boys began a low rhythmic moaning.

"That's just the Headbanger," she was told. The moaning boy rocked and banged his head into the wall over and over as he moaned. "He's all right when the lights are on, but he doesn't like the dark. He does this every night. You'll get used to it."

"Soon you'll be like him," another boy said, and several boys laughed.

Shauzia watched the Headbanger for awhile, then lay down again. Fleas bit her ankles and neck. She wrapped her blanket shawl around her to keep them from getting at the rest of her, but was soon so hot that she had to take it off again.

The night went on forever. Some of the boys cried out in their sleep, and the fleas kept biting.

Worry and fear would not let her escape into sleep. She tried to tell herself that things would work out. The police would realize they had made a mistake, and they would let her out in the morning.

But she didn't really believe it. People disappeared in Afghan prisons. Maybe it was the same in Pakistan.

It was awful being separated from Jasper, not having him around to protect her, not being able to reach out and feel him breathing beside her.

Would she go crazy in this terrible place? Would she lose her mind, locked away from the sun? She had seen crazy people in Afghanistan. The craziness took over more and more of their minds until there was nothing left of themselves – just craziness on two legs.

She reached out a hand and put it gently on the chest of the boy sleeping next to her. She could feel his heart beating deep within him. She could feel his lungs take in air and breathe it out again.

She closed her eyes and pretended he was Jasper. And finally, she slept.

EIGHT

Breakfast in prison was more bread and tea. Shauzia grabbed her share of bread and drank her cup of tea before the boy who had punched her could take it. But the tea made just a small dent in her thirst.

"That was mine!" the boy growled.

"Wait awhile and I'll piss it back to you," she said.

The others laughed, and this time they were not laughing at Shauzia.

The boy would have come at her, but just then a guard came to the cell door.

"Get ready for the showers," he said.

The other boys leapt to their feet.

"The water is cold, and it will cool us off," a boy beside Shauzia said. "While we're out, they'll hose down the cell and the toilet. Everything will be better. You'll see."

Shauzia was horrified. There would not be private showers. She could not expose herself as a girl to all these boys.

She was so scared that she could barely think.

The other boys pressed against the bars at the front of the cell, eager to be first into the showers. It was a chance to stretch their legs, and they yelled and pushed and hit out at each other in their excitement. Shauzia let them push her out of the way, until she was alone at the back of the cell. She pressed herself against the cement.

Maybe if she pressed hard enough, she could push herself right through the wall.

There was a bang on the bars as the guard used his stick to make the boys back up.

"Boy who was brought in yesterday, step forward," the guard called out.

"It was me!" the other boys shouted. "I was brought in yesterday!"

Through all of this, Shauzia heard another voice speaking in English, then switching to Dari.

"No, it's not any of these," the voice said. "Is there another boy in there? The one who was arrested at the Chief Burger?

Shauzia leapt forward, shoving her way to the cell door. On the other side of the bars was one of the after-church-pizza Westerners, the father of the two little boys who liked Jasper so much.

The man smiled down at her. "You have a very smart dog."

Shauzia leaned into the bars and motioned for him to crouch down so she could tell him something.

"You have to get me out of here," she pleaded. "It's shower day."

The man looked perplexed, so she pressed her face against the bars.

"I'm a girl!" she whispered.

He looked at her closely, blinked once, then started talking to the guards. They moved away from the cell door. Shauzia couldn't hear what they were saying, but she could see the Western man take out his wallet and exchange arm-waving gestures with the guards while they talked. Her heart sank when she saw him put his wallet back in his pocket, then leapt when he took it out again. They argued some more. Then the man nodded, took some bills out of his wallet and handed them to the guards.

The guards unlocked the cell door, reached in through the throng of boys and pulled Shauzia out. She looked back at the boys in the cell, then wished she hadn't. Even the bully looked small and lost with his face behind bars.

The Westerner took her by the arm and led her toward the police station exit.

"Wait!" she cried. "They have my money!"

He kept shepherding her through the station. "Your money is gone. It never existed," he said quietly. "Let's just get out of here before they change their minds."

Shauzia's anger bounced around inside her, with no way to get out. But she forgot about it as soon as she walked out of the police station compound, and a large, furry creature threw itself at her so hard she almost fell over.

"Jasper!"

He licked her face all over, and she would have happily sat on the pavement for hours hugging him, if the man hadn't bustled them both into his van.

Shauzia and Jasper stuck their heads out the window and let the breeze rush past them as the van wove in and out of the crazy Peshawar traffic. The fresh air felt wonderful, even filled with heat and exhaust fumes.

"What's your name?" the man asked.

"My girl name is Shauzia. My boy name is Shafiq," Shauzia said, pulling her head in. She laughed at the way Jasper looked, fur flying back from his face.

"My name is Tom."

"How did you find me?"

He handed her a plastic bottle of water, and she drank deeply while he told her.

"It was your dog," he said. "When we got to the Chief Burger for our pizza yesterday, Jasper practically threw himself at us. We asked around and found out what had happened. I'm sorry it took so long, but it took all this time to find you and persuade the police to let you go."

"Where are we going now?"

"Barbara, my wife, made me promise to bring

you home if I was able to get you out of jail. She'll be delighted that you're a girl. Why are you pretending to be a boy?"

"I just felt like it," she lied, keeping her privacy out of habit more than a distrust of Tom.

"Is your family still back in Afghanistan?" he asked.

"They're dead," she lied again, then stuck her head back out the window. She couldn't remember the last time she had ridden in such a fast-moving vehicle.

If I had one of these, she thought, I could be at the sea in no time.

They turned into University Town, a neighborhood of big trees, high walls and flowered shrubs spilling their blossoms into the street. The noise of the traffic on Jamrud Road was left behind as the van made several turns, finally stopping before a high metal gate in a wall.

Tom got out, unlocked and opened the gate, then drove the van through.

Shauzia and Jasper stepped out of the van into a whole new world.

"Daddy's home! Daddy's home!" The two small boys rushed along the front porch and ran through the garden to hug their father. Behind them, wiping her hands on a dishcloth, came their mother, Barbara. She put her hands on Shauzia's shoulders.

"So Tom was able to get you out! Welcome to our home."

Shauzia looked up into Barbara's face. Her smile was warm. Shauzia couldn't remember anyone smiling at her like that before, except Parvana.

"You must be hungry," Barbara said. "We have lots of food in the house to feed a hungry boy."

"The hungry boy is a hungry girl," Tom said, swinging his small giggling son in a circle.

Barbara looked down at Shauzia. "A girl! Oh, how wonderful! I'll have some company in this house full of boys. Come inside. We'll get you cleaned up and fed, and you can tell us all about yourself."

Shauzia's eyes almost burned from the bright colors of all the flowers in the courtyard garden. Birds were singing in the trees. The rest of Peshawar, beyond the high walls, might not even have existed.

Her eyes grew wide when Barbara drew her into the house. The entranceway alone was bigger than the room she had shared with her whole family back in Kabul.

"Tom is an engineer," Barbara said as she took Shauzia from room to room. "He builds bridges, mostly in the northern part of Pakistan. We're here on a two-year contract. Our families thought we were nuts to come, especially with the children, but we like a bit of adventure. We're from Toledo, in the United States. There's not much adventure there."

Shauzia was glad of Barbara's chatter. She felt shy amid so much wealth. The house had a living room with big windows that looked out onto the garden. The chairs looked soft, and there were lots of cushions in pretty colors. A television set was showing cartoon characters singing a bouncy English song. Toys littered the floor.

"Here is our dining room," Barbara said as they passed through a room with a long wooden table surrounded by chairs. Shauzia looked at all the dishes stacked in a glass-windowed cupboard. "And this is our kitchen."

They walked into a large sunny room, the source of the good smells Shauzia had been sniffing since she had walked into the house. Tins of food and fancy boxes of cookies and crackers were stacked neatly on shelves. A bowl overflowed with fruit.

Shauzia just wanted to look at everything and smell the good smells, but Barbara kept her moving.

They went upstairs, where there were more rooms and more toys on the floor. Children's clothes were scattered everywhere.

"Please excuse the mess," Barbara said, as Shauzia stepped over a toy truck. "I'm trying to teach the boys to clean up after themselves, but they simply refuse to cooperate." Then she showed Shauzia a lovely blue room with a pattern of little flowers on the wall. There was a Western toilet, gleaming taps and a shower stall with a blue curtain.

My family lived like this once, Shauzia thought, a long, long time ago, before the bombs started falling. The memory of it seemed like another person's life, not her own.

"Into the shower with you," Barbara said. She showed Shauzia how to work the taps. "Use as much soap as you want. Leave your dirty clothes on the floor. I'll find you something clean to wear."

Then she left her alone.

Shauzia was glad for some time to catch her breath. She gently touched her finger to the blue-flowered wallpaper, then felt the smoothness of the tile.

There was a mirror over the sink. She walked over and looked into it.

She didn't recognize the head that stared back at her. It had been years since she had seen her face. The room she had shared with her family in Kabul had no mirror.

In her mind, she was still a schoolgirl in a uniform with long dark hair that curled up at the end. But the face that looked back at her now was older than she remembered. It was longer and the cheeks were hollower. Shauzia wondered who this girl was.

There were noises downstairs as the boys came back into the house. Shauzia heard Jasper's feet running up the stone staircase and whimpering outside the bathroom door. She left her reflection and let him in.

"You don't care what I look like, do you, Jasper?" His wagging tail made her feel better.

She shucked her filthy clothes and got into the shower. She turned on the taps and let the hot water stream over her body. The soap smelled of flowers and spices. She lathered and rinsed, lathered and rinsed, washing the grime and stink off her body.

"Why don't you join the children in the garden?" Barbara suggested when Shauzia appeared in the kitchen dressed in a woman's shalwar kameez. It felt great to be clean and dressed in clean clothes. Her skin smelled good, like the soap. Barbara handed her a glass of cold milk. "Dinner will be ready soon."

Shauzia and Jasper went into the garden where the boys were playing. One boy had a truck the other boy wanted, and they started to argue. Shauzia didn't like to look at them. They were chubby with good health, and their laughter and arguing hurt her ears.

She tasted the milk. It was smooth and good. She poured some into the palm of her hand and held it out to Jasper.

"Let me do that!" one of the boys yelled, and they both crowded in on her, eager and demanding. Shauzia leaned back to get away from them, but they kept pressing in on her.

She was rescued by Tom, who called them all in to supper.

"Shauzia, you sit here." Barbara pulled out a chair for her at the long wooden table. In front of her was a bright yellow plate and shining cutlery. On the table were platters of chicken and bowls of vegetables. Barbara poured her another glass of milk while Tom supervised the boys as they washed their hands.

"Have you used a fork before?" Barbara asked.

Shauzia nodded. Many Afghans ate with their fingers, but her family had been very modern. They had lost all their cutlery in a bombing and ate with their fingers after that, but Shauzia still remembered how to eat with a fork.

She watched Tom and Barbara put napkins on their laps, and she did the same.

Once she started eating, she didn't think she could stop. At first she tried to copy the adults and use her fork properly, but that was too slow, so she used her fingers, too. She ignored everything except the food. Barbara kept refilling her plate, and Shauzia ate it all, without really distinguishing between chicken, rice or vegetables.

When she started to get full, she remembered to save some food for the next day. The napkin came in handy for that.

"Do you still have room for dessert?" Barbara asked, placing a bowl of chocolate ice cream in front of her.

"I want ice cream!" the smaller boy, Jake, whined.

"Eat your carrots first," Barbara said.

"No!"

"Eat just one bite of carrot," Tom said.

Shauzia watched as Jake, frowning, put the tiniest piece of carrot into his mouth. Barbara took his plate away and replaced it with ice cream. Shauzia eyed the food that was still on the plate as Barbara carried it to the kitchen, then turned her attention to her ice cream.

It was so good, she picked up her bowl and licked up the remains of it.

"Paul, put your bowl down," Tom said to the older boy.

"But she got to!"

"Never mind. You know better."

Shauzia felt her cheeks burn. She had made a mistake. Would they throw her out?

"I've made up a bed for you in the spare room," Barbara said. "Do you want to see it now? Then you can go to sleep any time you want to."

Shauzia nodded and got up from the table, holding her napkin full of food down by her side.

"Jasper's sleeping with me tonight," Jake announced.

"No, he's not. He's sleeping with me," insisted Paul.

Shauzia left them to their argument. Jasper trotted along beside her as they went upstairs.

After brushing her teeth with a new red toothbrush, she saw her bedroom. It had a real bed in it, with sheets and blankets and a pillow. Barbara handed her a nightgown to put on. She was suddenly very tired.

Barbara gave her a hug. "Sleep well. We're very glad to have you here."

Shauzia's arms remained at her side. She wasn't sure if she should return the hug. She wasn't sure if she could remember how.

Barbara showed her where to turn off the light, then left her alone.

Shauzia hid the food under the bed. She changed into the nightgown and slid into bed between clean sheets. Her belly was so full it hurt, and her skin still smelled of the soap from the shower.

Jasper hopped up on the bed and stretched out beside her.

"I think they're going to ask us to stay here with them," she whispered. "I could clean for them, and at night, when everyone is asleep, I could play with some of those toys. I could go back to school, and learn to be... anything!"

She leaned on her elbows and looked into Jasper's face. "We'll still go to the sea. We'll still go to France But would it be all right with you if we stayed here for a little while?"

Jasper thumped his tail and licked her hand.

Shauzia put her head back on the very soft pillow. "I wish Mrs. Weera could see me now," she whispered. Then she smiled and fell asleep.

She woke up a few hours later. After listening carefully to make sure everyone was sleeping, she tiptoed downstairs to the kitchen. The garbage was full of perfectly good food. She rescued it, took it upstairs and hid it under her bed.

She could never tell when she would be hungry again.

NINE

The next few days passed by in a haze of eating and sleeping.

Shauzia hadn't realized how tired she was. Inside this walled-in paradise there were birds and flowers and no piles of garbage to search through.

She ate three meals a day at the big table, plus the snacks that Barbara handed out between meals.

"Make yourself at home," she told Shauzia. "We want you to be comfortable."

"Why are you doing this?" Shauzia asked.

"Tom's salary goes a long way over here," Barbara told her. "We like to share what we have. Besides, us girls have to stick together!" She gave Shauzia another hug, and this time, Shauzia hugged her back.

Sometimes beggars would ring the bell outside in the street, and Tom or Barbara would open the door in the gate and hand out oranges or coins. The gate was high and made of thick steel, so Shauzia never saw the people who came to the door, but she was glad they were getting some help.

She kept intending to help out around the house, but she kept dozing off instead. She would sit down for a moment after breakfast or lunch, in the living room or on the porch, and wake up several hours later.

"I'm sorry," she said to Barbara, after sleeping away the afternoon and not helping with dinner.

"You've been tired for a long time," Barbara said, putting her arm around Shauzia's shoulders. "You'll get caught up on your rest soon, and then you'll feel better."

Shauzia liked it when Barbara smiled at her. She liked to watch her and Tom wrestling with their boys, or playing trucks with them, or reading to them at bedtime.

Tom and Barbara spoke Dari to her, but the boys knew only English. Shauzia turned over each new word she heard in her head, and whispered it to Jasper until she felt comfortable saying it out loud. Bit by bit, her English improved.

No one spoke about the future. Shauzia didn't want to ask. Maybe they had forgotten that she was an outsider. Maybe they already thought of her as one of their own children. She didn't want to remind them that she wasn't.

One day, Shauzia woke up in the morning and felt really awake.

"I think I've caught up on my sleep," she said to Jasper. Jasper looked good, too. He'd been eating well, and his coat was soft from lots of washing and brushing.

"You look bright-eyed this morning," Tom said to her at breakfast.

"I'd like to start helping out," Shauzia said, pleased to be noticed. "I'm very good at cleaning."

"We already have a cleaning woman," Jake said, his mouth full of scrambled eggs.

"Waheeda only comes twice a week, which is not enough to keep this place clean," Barbara said. "If you two boys would only pitch in and pick up your toys now and then."

"Talk to the hand," Paul said, stretching his arm, palm out, to his mother.

"You know I don't like that. He got it from a video," Barbara told Shauzia.

"Maybe you shouldn't watch videos for awhile," Tom said. Paul slammed his fork onto the table, scattering bits of egg. He made the loud whining sound that hurt Shauzia's ears.

Shauzia took advantage of the distraction to take more eggs from the platter, and to put them and some toast into her napkin. The pile of food under her bed was getting bigger every day. If Tom and Barbara ever asked her to leave, she'd have food to last for quite awhile. Maybe it would last until she got to the sea.

"I'd like to take the boys swimming this afternoon," Barbara told Shauzia when they were doing the lunch dishes together. "We go to the American Club. I wish I could take you, but it's only for ex-patriots. You know, foreigners? Would you be all right here on your own for a few hours?"

Shauzia found the question funny. After all, she had been looking after herself for a long time.

"I will be all right," she said.

She waved goodbye as they drove away and closed the gate after they left.

She was almost back in the house when the gate buzzer rang.

"Don't answer the doorbell," Barbara had said. "I have a key for the gate, so we'll let ourselves in."

Shauzia was going to do as Barbara said, but the buzzer sounded again. She couldn't just leave some-one out there.

She opened the door in the gate. An Afghan woman was holding a baby, her hand stretched out.

"Can you give me something for my children?"

"Yes, I can. Come into the garden." Shauzia ran into the house and filled a plastic bag with fruit and biscuits from the cupboard. She handed it to the woman, who thanked her many times, then left.

"That was fun," Shauzia said to Jasper. She went into the house and was just settled on the living-room floor, getting ready to play with the toys, when the bell rang again.

This time it was a group of children carrying junk sacks, looking for cardboard or cans to add to their collections.

Shauzia had an idea.

"Come in," she said. "Come in and play."

She got food for everyone and showed them the toys. The children looked like they didn't know what to do with them. Shauzia closed a small hand around a toy car and made it move across the floor.

The bell rang a few times more. She brought a heavily pregnant woman into the house and took her up to one of the beds to sleep in a cool, dark room. An old man drank a glass of milk and fell asleep in the shade of the garden.

More women and children came to the door. Shauzia invited everyone in. "The people who live here like to share," she said. Jasper greeted them and made everyone feel welcome.

Shauzia gave out food until the cupboards and the fridge were empty. When there was no more food to give away, she handed out toys, clothes, blankets – anything the beggars could use.

With everyone eating, the children playing with toys and with Jasper, the house felt like it was having a party.

"Here's a pillow for your back," she said to one woman, handing another a pair of Barbara's sandals to replace the ripped ones she had come in with. She took people up to the bathroom so they could shower, and found a supply of bars of soap in a cupboard. She handed these out, too.

Shauzia was up in the bathroom, helping two little girls shower and wash their hair, when Barbara and the boys came home. The girls were giggling so much at the soap bubbles in their hair, Shauzia almost missed Barbara's shriek. Then Barbara shrieked a second time, and Shauzia definitely heard that.

"What is going on here?" Barbara yelled. "Shauzia!"

Shauzia, her hands full of hair she was rinsing, called down to her. "I'm up here."

Barbara was in the bathroom in seconds.

"Look how clean they are," Shauzia said, wrapping the little girls in towels.

"Who are all these people? What have you been doing?"

Shauzia smiled up at her. "Sharing. Like you shared with me."

"Sharing?"

"They came to the gate. They needed things."

"And you just invited them in?"

Shauzia didn't understand. "I thought you would be pleased. I thought this is what you like to do. You have so much."

"Where are their clothes?" Barbara's face was hard as she looked down at the little girls, dripping water on her bathroom floor.

Shauzia pointed to the sink. She had put the

clothes in water to soak before washing them. She was planning to wrap the girls in sheets while the hot Peshawar sun dried their clothes.

Barbara wrung the excess water out of the clothes and handed them to Shauzia.

"Get the girls dressed," she said, and then she went downstairs. Shauzia heard her telling the other people to get out.

"Mommy! There's a lady sleeping on my bed!" Jake hollered, and soon the pregnant woman was out of the house, too.

Shauzia helped the little girls get dressed in the wet clothes, and she ushered them out the gate.

"I'm sorry," she said to them.

"That was fun," one girl said. "We smell good now." Shauzia watched them walk down the lane, dragging their junk bags behind them.

"Look at this mess," Barbara said, picking up the toys and dishes that littered the room.

"I'll help," Shauzia said, bending down to pick up a plate.

Barbara put a hand on her shoulder. "You've done enough. Please go and sit in the garden." There was no warmth in Barbara's voice or face.

Tom came home an hour later. Shauzia stayed outside, but she could still hear their voices, rising and falling.

"No food left in the house! Things missing – toys, clothes. Strangers in our beds!"

In a little while, Tom came out with the boys.

"We're going to get pizza!" Jake said. "Can Jasper and Shauzia come with us?"

"No, we'll be right back," Tom said, and they drove away.

That evening, Shauzia finally got to taste pizza. She liked it very much, but the atmosphere at the table was too tense for her to really enjoy it.

After supper, Shauzia washed the dishes. Barbara and Tom took the boys upstairs to get them settled for the night. Shauzia heard another shriek, this one from one of the boys.

A moment later, Tom called down the stairs. "Shauzia, could you come up here?"

They were all in her room. A swarm of ants was moving on her floor and under her bed.

"Why were you hiding food?"

"So I'd have something to eat when… " She stopped talking.

"When what?"

"When I didn't have anything else to eat."

"I'll get the broom," Tom said after an awkward silence. He swept up the rotten, ant-infested food. Barbara washed the floor. Shauzia stood in a corner, watching them and feeling small.

Breakfast was delayed the next morning while Tom went out to buy groceries. It was the middle of the morning by the time they ate.

"We'd like to get you some new clothes,"

Barbara said when they were gathered around the table. "We'd like you to have something new to take with you to the refugee camp."

Shauzia put her glass of milk back on the table. She made her face say nothing.

"It's not that we haven't enjoyed having you here," Barbara said, "but we need to just be together as a family."

"I went to see a friend of mine this morning who works for one of the aid agencies," Tom said. "He told me about a special orphans and widows' section of one of the refugee camps. The woman who runs it is used to taking in new children unexpectedly."

"You'll be able to go to school there," Barbara said cheerfully. "Tom's friend says they even have a nurse's training program."

"There are so many Afghan children like you," Tom said. "We can't possibly take care of everyone."

Shauzia straightened her back and raised her chin. She didn't need them to take care of her.

"The children love your dog," Barbara said. "We'd be happy to give him a home here with us. After all, what sort of life will he have in the camp?"

Jasper moved closer to Shauzia and put his paws on her lap.

"Well," said Barbara, stiffly. "Would you like girl clothes or boy clothes?"

"Boy clothes, please," Shauzia replied. She then proceeded to eat everything in sight. Food was food. And she was still a long way from the sea.

She kept her arm around Jasper in the van all the way to the refugee camp. She could still smell the laundry soap on her clothes. In her lap was a bag with a new boy's shalwar kameez, some candies, a toy car with only two wheels that Jake had given her and a small bar of the good-smelling soap.

Barbara and the boys stayed behind at their house while Tom drove Shauzia back along the road that had first brought her to the city. Tom kept his eyes on the traffic and did not speak to her.

I could push him out of the driver's seat, she thought, picturing Tom bouncing and rolling along the highway. She could take his place behind the wheel and drive the van to the sea. How hard could it be to drive? There were a lot of bad drivers in Peshawar. She'd just be one more.

She didn't do it, though. She didn't push Tom out onto the highway, and she was still in the van when it passed through the main gates of the refugee camp and into its maze of mud-walled streets.

"You'll be fine here," Tom said after stopping the van in front of the entrance to the Widows' Compound. "There are lots of other children here, and I'm told that the woman in charge will be happy to have you."

Shauzia and Jasper got out of the van.

"Would you like me to go in with you?" Tom asked.

Shauzia shook her head. It was right to thank Tom, so she said thank you, and she meant it.

But as she watched his van drive away, she couldn't help thinking that all he'd done was take her out of one prison and put her into another.

"Shauzia's back!" Children streamed out of the compound and threw their arms around her and Jasper. Jasper kissed everyone hello, and wagged his tail so fast it was almost a blur.

Shauzia was surrounded by the stinky camp smell again. She could no longer smell the laundry soap on her clothes, and the flowery scent had already left her skin.

She opened the bag and gave away the candies, the car and the shalwar kameez. She kept the little bar of soap.

She'd use it to give Jasper a bath.

When they got to the sea.

TEN

Rows and rows of purple flowers, fields and fields of them. Sun shining down out of a brilliant blue sky. A place where nothing bad ever happened.

Deep creases lined the picture. It had been folded up in Shauzia's pocket for a long time. The edges were frayed.

"I don't understand, Jasper," Shauzia said. They were sitting by a wall in the shade. "I used to be able to look at this picture and imagine myself there, sitting among the flowers. It was so clear in my head. It looked like a magical place. Now it just looks like a picture torn out of a magazine." She showed it to Jasper. He didn't even raise his head. He'd seen it way too often.

"Maybe you're right," she conceded. "Maybe I should forget it. It will take ages to earn the money, and I just don't know if I can face trying to do it again. The thought of starting over is awful. Besides, what's so great about a field of purple flowers? It's probably full of thorns. And snakes."

She started to tear up the paper. Jasper raised his

head and growled low in his throat. So she folded the picture back up instead and put it back in her pocket.

She stared at the mud wall across the alley.

"I can't stay here, though. I can't look at these walls for the rest of my life."

She lay down on the ground so that her head was close to Jasper's. "I'll tell you a secret," she said quietly. "I still want to get to France. I still want to get to the sea. But I just don't want to be alone anymore. What do I do about that?"

Jasper kissed her nose. It was no answer, but she felt better.

No one said anything to Shauzia about her time away. Mrs. Weera must have asked them not to. The little kids hugged her and said they'd missed her, the same way they hugged and said they'd missed Jasper, but no one asked her what had happened and why she was back.

At first she wished someone would, especially one of the boys her age. She felt like fighting someone.

As the days went by, though, the anger drained out of her. She spent most of her time following patches of shade around the compound.

Mrs. Weera was being as annoying as always, but in an entirely new way.

She did not give her any more little jobs.

"You'll be wanting to leave again soon to get to the sea, dear," she said when Shauzia picked up some empty water jugs to get filled at the United Nations water pump outside the compound. "Save your strength for that."

Mrs. Weera took the jugs from Shauzia's hands and called a boy over to fetch the water.

That was two weeks ago. Lazing around while others did all the work was fun for awhile, but now Shauzia was so bored she could hardly stand it.

"Are you still here?" Mrs. Weera asked, striding by Shauzia on her way to another part of the compound. "I thought you'd be long gone by now. An active girl like you must be getting awfully bored just sitting around." She kept walking with those quick, giant steps of hers.

Shauzia leapt to her feet. She wanted to yell something, but she couldn't think of anything to say, so she kicked the wall of the hut instead. Hurting her foot made her angrier, and what made it even worse was that there were two boys nearby who watched the whole thing.

They were playing soccer, using a small rock as a ball, and they paused in their game long enough to laugh at her.

"What are you looking at?" Shauzia yelled at them. "And why are you wasting time with games when there is work to be done around here? See those empty water jugs over there? Go and get them filled. Do what I tell you!"

With each word Shauzia came closer and closer to the boys, until she was yelling right in their faces. She paused to take a breath and they ran off, grabbing the empty jugs on their way to the UN pump.

"That was fun!" Shauzia said to Jasper. She looked around the camp with new eyes. "Mrs. Weera thinks she's so good at running things, but there's a lot around here that's not being done properly. Anything she can do, I can do ten times better. Come on."

She started out, then realized Jasper hadn't moved. He was sitting on his haunches and watching her.

She bent down and scratched his ears. "Don't look at me like that. We are going to the sea. We are going to France, and we'll send Mrs. Weera a letter telling her how happy we are to be away from her. But we'll go when I say, not when Mrs. Weera says we should go. And I just don't feel like going right now."

Shauzia threw herself into activity. Instead of taking orders from Mrs. Weera, she thought up projects on her own.

She organized scrounging parties with the older children. They would go to other parts of the camp and pick up stray boards or bits of pipe and anything else they could find lying around that might be useful.

She started an arithmetic class for the little kids, using stones to teach them how to form their numbers.

"One day you will be working," she told them. "If you don't know how to count, you won't know if your boss is cheating you."

She fetched the compound's ration of flour and cooking oil from the warehouse and took her turn carrying containers of water from the UN pump. She stayed out of Mrs. Weera's way, and Mrs. Weera left her alone.

She even made a friend. Farzana was a few years younger than Shauzia, and she was new in the compound. She had been living in another part of the camp with her aunt. Mrs. Weera brought her to the Widows' Compound when her aunt died and there was no one else to take care of her.

"She wasn't really my aunt," Farzana told Shauzia. "I had a real aunt, but she died. I get passed from person to person. I'm glad to be here, because there are so many people. I won't have to move again when somebody dies."

Farzana and Shauzia often went together when Shauzia had errands to do outside the compound. She liked having a friend again. It was almost like having Parvana back.

Everything in the camp was on the verge of falling apart, including many people. Every day they saw men and women sitting against the walls that lined the streets, staring into space. Others talked to themselves. Many looked so sad, Shauzia wondered if they would ever be able to smile again.

I have to get out of here, she thought. I don't want to end up like them.

The clay streets and walls held onto the summer heat.

"I feel like a loaf of nan baking in the oven," Farzana said one particularly hot afternoon.

The air wasn't moving. They sat in the coolest spot they could find, as far away from the others as possible, but it wasn't very satisfactory. If they wanted privacy, they had to put up with the stink of the open sewers. If they wanted less stink, they had to put up with more people.

The babies fussed in the heat, and many of the children had sore bellies. The compound was always filled with the sound of crying and whining.

"The sea will be cool," Shauzia said without thinking.

"What's the sea?" Farzana asked.

"The Arabian Sea, by the city of Karachi," Shauzia said. "It flows into the Indian Ocean."

"What's an ocean?" Farzana asked.

Shauzia was stunned. "An ocean is, well, it's water, a lot of water, in one place."

Farzana was quiet for a moment. "There is an ocean in this camp. I'll take you there this evening, after the day cools down. It's in the part of the camp where I used to live with my aunt."

They fell asleep in the shade. If Mrs. Weera was yelling out orders anywhere in the camp, they blissfully didn't hear her.

"Here's our ocean," Farzana said later that day. They were standing by a square cement pond, maybe thirty paces long on each side. It was full of water. It was also full of garbage, green scum and sewage. Clouds of mosquitoes and other bugs hovered over it.

Shauzia watched a woman dip a bucket into the slimy mess and haul some water away.

"That's not an ocean," Shauzia said. "An ocean is water as far as a person can see. It's deep and blue and smells good, and I'm going to go there."

"I'd like to see something like that," Farzana said. "Take me with you."

"I can't take you with me to the ocean. It's a very long way, and I'm having enough trouble getting myself there. Besides, I'm not stopping once I get to the sea. I'm going on, and I don't want anyone slowing me down. How could I take you with me?"

Farzana turned her back to Shauzia. "I don't need anyone to take me anywhere. I can get to the sea by myself."

Shauzia watched her walk away. The younger girl's head was held high, but Shauzia knew she'd hurt her feelings.

"Maybe I should say yes," she said to Jasper. "It would be a lie, but it would make her happy for a little while." Sometimes it was hard to know the right thing to do.

Shauzia hurried after her friend.

"All right," she said. "I'll take you with me. We'll go to the sea together."

ELEVEN

Shauzia fanned away the flies that kept collecting on the sweat on her face. All around her, others were doing the same.

"Every time we come here, we wait," a man beside her said. "Do you think we have nothing else to do? I should be looking for a job."

"Are there jobs around here?" Shauzia asked.

"There is work in Peshawar," the man replied.

Shauzia brushed the flies away again and went back to her thoughts. She wasn't ready to return to Peshawar.

She was sitting with hundreds of others in the camp's central warehouse. They were waiting for the flour to be distributed.

"Why don't I just go and get it at the end of the day?" she had asked Mrs. Weera.

"Because by then our allotment could have disappeared. You need to be there to grab our ration when it comes in." The flour was delivered on a big truck by an aid agency.

At the end of the afternoon, one of the warehouse guards announced to the crowd, "No flour today. Go back to your homes."

"What do you mean, no flour?" a man called out. "I can see it through the window. I have children to feed."

"That flour is for other people," the guard said. "There is not enough to give out to you today. Go back to your homes."

There was nothing else to do. Shauzia and the others went back to their homes.

"We can make do without it for a few days," Mrs. Weera said, when Shauzia told her what happened.

"How?" Shauzia demanded. A picture of the full shelves and refrigerator in Tom and Barbara's house came into her head. She pushed it aside. "We should complain to somebody."

"We will manage," Mrs. Weera said, putting an end to the argument. They managed by eating less.

Shauzia went back to the warehouse on the next scheduled day for flour distribution, at the end of the week. The same thing happened again, and Shauzia returned to the Widows' Compound empty handed.

When it happened again the following week, she was fed up. And hungry.

"I should go back to the city," Shauzia grumbled to Mrs. Weera. "I could find a job there and buy something to eat."

"But how would you get the food back here?"

Mrs. Weera asked. "You're not thinking, Shauzia."

"Why would I bring the food back here? I'm not responsible for all these people!"

"Yes, you are. And so am I. We have two good legs, two good arms, two good eyes, and minds that work properly. We have a responsibility to those who don't have what we have."

"Then let's do something," Shauzia yelled. "Everyone in the compound is hungry, and we just sit here on our two good legs and do nothing."

"I've already met with the camp management," Mrs. Weera replied. "There's nothing we can do. The aid agency that sends us flour is dependent on donations. If they don't have the money, how can they buy flour?"

"But there's flour in the warehouse, just sitting there. I saw it through the window."

"That flour must be for some other group of people."

"So we just starve?"

"I've put out a call to other women's organizations, and I'm sure they will help us. Until then, we must be patient."

Shauzia stomped away in frustration.

"We hate being patient, don't we, Jasper?" Jasper wagged his tail in agreement.

Shauzia remembered the raids on the hotel garbage cans. She had an idea.

"The guards only watch the front door," she told

Farzana. "They don't watch the back window. They're too lazy."

They came up with a plan. They needed the help of a dozen of the older children in the compound. They all said yes. Everyone was hungry.

They left the compound early the next morning, just as the sky was getting light. Jasper went with them. None of the adults saw them leave.

Farzana and one of the small boys went to the front of the storehouse. Their job was to keep the guards occupied by talking to them and asking endless questions. The rest of the children went to the back of the storehouse. Shauzia pried open the window with a knife she had borrowed from the compound's kitchen.

They soon had bags of flour making their way out the window and onto the little wagon they had brought with them.

Shauzia never knew how word of what they were doing got out. She didn't recall seeing anyone on their way to the warehouse, but there were a lot of people in the camp with nothing to do but watch other people.

The children's wagon was only half filled with sacks of flour when the first adults started to show up. The larger men pushed the children out of the way and tried to snatch the flour off their wagon. Children had to drape themselves over the sacks of flour to protect them.

The noise the adults made brought the guards, and the noise the guards made brought more people out to the warehouse.

In what seemed to be only moments, a large crowd had gathered. Everyone pushed to the window and tried to break down the front doors to get at the flour. A crowd always draws a bigger crowd, and there was soon a full-fledged riot.

A huge mob of hungry, desperate people swarmed around the storehouse. Shauzia was in a panic about Farzana and the small boy with her, but she couldn't get to them. The crowd of grown-ups was too thick, too crazy with hunger and anger.

There was too much yelling, too much pushing. People beat against the storehouse with sticks, and when they couldn't reach the warehouse, they beat on each other.

Shauzia still had a bag of flour clutched tightly in her arms. She used it to protect her as she pushed toward the crowd.

Someone started pulling on it. Shauzia looked up. A man twice her size was trying to grab her flour.

"I have hungry children to feed!" he yelled.

"What do you think I am?" Shauzia yelled back.

He was bigger and stronger. He raised his arm and slammed his fist into Shauzia's head. She dropped to the ground. Her head hit the dirt with a thud, and she watched the man run off with her flour.

She wanted to get up off the ground and run after him. She wanted to hit him the same way he had hit her, and grab back the flour that she needed to feed herself and her friends. But that message was not making the journey from her brain to her body. All she could do was lie on the ground and watch the legs of the rioters run around and around.

Many of the flour bags broke in the struggle. The ground around Shauzia soon looked like Kabul in the winter, as the flour swirled in the air and settled on the dirt.

The rioters paid no attention to Shauzia. Her body rolled this way and that as people rushed around her and over her, often stepping right on her as if she was a log, rather than a person.

Someone big and heavy stepped on her leg. Shauzia felt a snap. She cried out in pain. Her cries were lost among the yelling of the rioters.

Another blow landed on her head, and then everything went black.

She was unconscious when Jasper finally found her. He stood over her, barking furiously at everyone who came close, protecting her from the raging crowd.

TWELVE

Shauzia's head felt like it was buried under a load of rocks. The noises around her were unfamiliar, and she struggled to open her eyes. The best she could do was open one eye a teeny bit, but not enough to see through. The effort was too much for her, and she dropped into darkness once again.

Some time later, she was able to stay awake long enough to make a sound. Her chest and her head hurt terribly, and what was the matter with her leg? She opened her mouth just wide enough to moan. Then she passed out.

"Shauzia."

Shauzia heard someone calling for her at the end of a long, long tunnel.

"Shauzia."

Bit by bit, the tunnel grew shorter.

"All right, Shauzia. It's time to wake up."

Something was familiar about the voice, but Shauzia's brain was working too slowly to be able to pinpoint what it was.

"Shauzia! Wake up! No more nonsense!"

That did the trick. Some of the darkness lifted from Shauzia's brain. She managed to open one eye long enough to see Mrs. Weera's face hovering over her.

"What… "

"You're in the clinic," Mrs. Weera said. "You've been banged up a bit, but nothing to be frightened of. You'll soon be back in the game."

Mrs. Weera's brash cheerfulness was hard on Shauzia's ears. She waved her arm slightly, telling Mrs. Weera to go.

"No, no need to thank me," Mrs. Weera said, taking hold of Shauzia's hand and putting it between her two strong ones. For a moment Shauzia felt safer than she had ever felt before.

Then Mrs. Weera spoke again.

"And I know you're sorry for causing so much trouble. We'll take care of all that later. Right now, just rest and recover. We'll have you back in shape before you know it."

Shauzia felt the bed shift as Mrs. Weera stood up. She closed her eye. She was glad Mrs. Weera was keeping her visit short.

"Since you have Shauzia for a while, why not get her started on her nurse's training?" Mrs. Weera boomed out to the clinic staff.

Shauzia didn't have the strength to protest. Did Mrs. Weera always get her own way?

The next day, Shauzia's head felt a little better,

and she could open her eye wide enough to see the large cast on her leg.

"You've cracked some ribs," one of the nurses told her. "Your chest will be sore for awhile, but you'll mend. We were worried about your head, but you must have a thick skull. Nothing there seems damaged. You should see your face. It's all bruised."

"I hurt all over," Shauzia said. Since she didn't have a mirror, she didn't care what she looked like. "Can you give me something for the pain?"

"You'll have to live with it," the nurse said. "We're short of painkillers. We're short of everything. The pain will pass with time."

"Is my leg going to be all right?" Shauzia was almost afraid to hear the answer.

"You have a simple fracture. Six weeks in a cast and your leg will be mended."

"Six weeks!"

"Lower your voice, please. Do you have someplace else to be?"

"Of course I do. Do you think I want to be here?"

"I don't think any of us want to be here, yet here we are."

"Well, I don't have to stay here," Shauzia said flatly.

"No one's holding you prisoner," the nurse said, checking the bandages of the woman in the bed next to Shauzia.

"How can I walk with this bad leg?"

"Your leg is merely broken, not blown off. Stop complaining. You are luckier than most."

The nurse walked away then, so Shauzia couldn't talk back without yelling across the clinic. She would have done that if she hadn't felt too weak to shout.

"She must have been trained by Mrs. Weera," she mumbled.

"Try to be patient," the woman in the next bed said. She was more bandages than she was woman. They covered all of her face except for one eye. Her voice was old and raspy. "All things heal with patience."

"Patience just gets you more of what you've already got," replied Shauzia. "Patience never heals anything. All patience does is make you forget you ever wanted anything better. Patience will turn you to stone."

"When all you have to choose between is patience or impatience, you'll find patience much easier on the mind."

"That's fine for you. You're old. You probably wouldn't do anything even if you could. I'm young. I have plans."

"How old are you?"

"Fourteen."

"I'm sixteen," the woman said.

For a long while, Shauzia didn't speak. Then she asked, "What happened to you?"

"A man threw acid in my face."

"Why did he do that?"

"He didn't like what I was doing. I thought I would be safe in a refugee camp, but I don't think there is a safe place for me anywhere."

"What were you doing that he didn't like?"

"I was teaching his daughter how to read."

"Was he Taliban?"

"Does it matter? Not all men with bad ideas belong to the Taliban. It hurts me to talk. Let me rest now."

Shauzia let her rest, and then she fell asleep herself.

When she woke up, the bed beside her was empty.

She grabbed the arm of a passing nurse.

"Where is she?" she asked, nodding at the bed.

"She didn't make it."

"You mean she died?"

"Let go of me."

"You don't care, do you? You don't even look sad that she died. You didn't do anything to help her!"

The nurse yanked herself free. "Do you know how many deaths we see here? How am I supposed to cry over all of them? All you do is lie there and complain. How dare you criticize me!"

"That's enough." An older nurse came over.

"What does she expect of us? There aren't

enough bandages, not enough food, and not enough water." The nurse's voice rose in desperation. "Three more children died today. What sort of place is this? Farm animals are treated better."

"Stop it!" the older woman said sharply. "You're scaring the patients. Take a break and calm down. You're no use to me like this."

The young woman started to cry and ran off. The older nurse headed back to work.

Shauzia turned her head away. She didn't want to look at the empty bed.

The next day, she was given a pair of crutches. "Practice walking with them," the nurse told her, "but don't go far. Several other people have to use them today."

It felt great to be moving again, even though using the crutches was awkward. She walked a little bit away from the clinic and turned around to go back.

Then she stopped and looked at it instead.

The clinic was just one big tent, with the flaps open to allow what little breeze there was to flow through the tent. Cloth screens gave the patients in the beds some privacy, although not much, and kept some of the dust off them. On the edges of the clinic, families of the sick people sat on the ground, waiting for them to get well. Children cried. Nurses and doctors were busy with the line-up of people who had come to see them, cleaning and bandaging wounds and trying to comfort people crying with pain and sorrow.

No one was watching Shauzia to make sure she returned the crutches. She turned into a narrow, mud-walled street, and the clinic slipped out of sight behind her. She was getting out of this place.

First, though, she needed to find Jasper, who hadn't been allowed in the clinic. She'd make one last trip to the Widows' Compound, get her dog, and then leave without speaking to anyone.

No more Mrs. Weera. No more sick, desperate, crazy people. Just her, her dog and the great blue sea.

THIRTEEN

Shauzia made slow progress. Walking with crutches was hard. Sweat ran down the inside of her cast, making her leg itch and hurt at the same time. She half wanted to go back to her bed in the clinic, but she kept on.

"Boy, where are you walking to in this heat?" one of the men sitting at the side of the road called out as she walked by.

"Old man, what are you waiting for in this heat?" she asked in return.

"I am just waiting," the old man replied. "It is what I do. I don't remember what I am waiting for, but still, I wait. One day, you will wait like I do."

"Never!" Shauzia exclaimed.

"Already you are walking in the heat to get somewhere, but where can you go? There is nowhere but here. This street or that street, it is all the same. One day you will know this, and you will sit down and wait."

Shauzia walked away while the man was still talking.

She passed a lot of men like that, sitting and waiting, their eyes following her as she made her slow and awkward way down the road. The crutches were too short for her, and her back hurt as she stooped over to use them. She didn't speak to any more of the men. They didn't speak to her. They just watched, and waited.

Her leg was hurting very badly. She was hot and tired. She needed to get out of the sun and put her leg up.

She turned around to go back to the clinic, and realized she was totally lost.

She had been walking without noticing where she was going. The roads and pathways in the camp went in all sorts of directions. She hadn't been to this section when she'd run errands for Mrs. Weera. She had no idea where she was or how to get back.

She asked one of the sitting-and-waiting men where the Widows' Compound was. The man chewed the question over in his mind while Shauzia leaned impatiently on her crutches.

Another man came along. "What is happening?" he asked the first man.

"Boy wants to get to the Widows' Compound."

"Why do you want to do that, boy?"

The two men talking drew the attention of a third. Three men drew the attention of three more, and soon there were a dozen men in the little dirt street, debating the direction of the Widows'

Compound, and even questioning whether there was a Widows' Compound.

"Why do you want to go there, boy?" someone asked her again. "Don't you know they started the food riot? You keep away from them. Women living together like that, they get up to no good."

The discussion switched to the food riot. The men said the widows had used a bomb to blow open the storehouse doors.

Shauzia used the opportunity to slip down a pathway, away from the men and their crazy stories.

She kept walking, turning this way and that, hoping to come upon something that looked familiar.

The mud walls came to an abrupt end, and Shauzia found herself looking out at an endless sea of tents.

It was the camp for new arrivals. Mrs. Weera had told her about it, but she had never seen it.

"There is no room for them in this camp, but they still come. Where else will they go? They arrive with nothing," Mrs. Weera said. "Some of them wait six months or more for a tent."

Shauzia turned around. This was neither the Widows' Compound, nor the way out of the camp.

The thought of heading back into the maze of mud walls made her turn around again. Maybe she could walk through the camp for new arrivals and find a faster way back to the Widows' Compound. The compass in her head told her that would be the right thing to do.

She waded into the new camp.

There were no roads or pathways that she could see. There was barely room to walk between the tents and, in some places, there was no room at all.

Some people had proper tents made of white canvas with UNHCR stamped on the side in big black letters. Some people had tents made out of rags stitched together. Some people had tents made from sheets of thin plastic stretched over sticks.

Shauzia poked her head into some of the tents. "Do you know where the Widows' Compound is?" she asked.

The people inside stared back at her with vacant eyes. The temperature inside the tents was even hotter than the temperature outside, but people were still crammed inside them. There wasn't really anyplace else to sit.

"Give me your crutches," a voice called out from a tent. Shauzia bent down and saw an old woman sitting inside. She was missing a leg. "Give me your crutches, so I can go away from here. I do not like this terrible place."

Shauzia hurried away. In her rush, she tripped on a tent peg and went sprawling onto the hard ground.

Children standing nearby laughed at her. Shauzia knew they were bored, and she was entertainment, but she was not in the mood to entertain anybody. She struck out at them with one of her crutches.

"That is no way to behave," a man said, helping

her to her feet. "You are older than they are. You should show them how to be kind."

Shauzia hobbled away without thanking him.

She heard the noise of a truck and saw people rushing around carrying jugs and pans. Shauzia followed the crowd.

It was a water truck. The guards around it tried to get the people to line up, to wait their turn, but everyone was too thirsty. They crowded in around the truck.

Shauzia stayed on the edge of the crowd on top of a small rise in the ground and watched the scene below.

People who managed to fill their jugs with the precious water often saw most of it spill to the ground as they tried to get back through the crowd. One man had his whole jug knocked out of his hands, but when he tried to go back to the truck to have it refilled, he couldn't make his way through the mass of people. He waved his jug in frustration, hitting someone on the head. That man hit back, and soon a huge fight was underway.

Shauzia turned and walked away. She didn't want her other leg broken.

She found her way to the edge of the tents, to a rough bit of road. A white van, like the one aid agencies used, was coming toward her, so she stood in the middle of the road to stop it.

"I'm lost," she called out.

The aid worker got out of the van. "Where do you belong?" he asked.

"I belong at the sea!" Shauzia started to cry. "I belong in France! I belong in a field of purple flowers, where nothing smells bad, with no one screaming or pushing around me. That's where I belong."

The aid worker helped Shauzia into the passenger seat of the van and waited until she had stopped crying before he asked, "Where do you live now?"

Shauzia wiped the tears off her cheeks. "The Widows' Compound," she said.

They started to drive. The sea of tents and sad people seemed to go on forever.

"Who are they?" Shauzia asked.

"They've just left Afghanistan," the aid worker told her. "People are rushing to get across the border before the Americans attack."

"The Americans are going to attack?"

"They're angry about what happened in New York City."

"What happened?"

The aid worker kept one hand on the steering wheel while he fished around on the floor with his other.

"Here it is." He handed Shauzia a piece of newspaper he had found.

Shauzia looked at the photograph. Smoke poured out of the mangled remains of a building.

"Looks like Kabul," she said, letting the paper drop back to the floor.

She leaned her head against the window. The people they drove past did not look strong enough to blow up anything.

Then she closed her eyes and didn't open them again until they arrived at the Widows' Compound.

Her bed in the clinic had been given to someone else, Mrs. Weera told her. She set up a charpoy in some shade for Shauzia to rest on. Jasper sat on the ground below her, and the compound's children gathered around begging for stories until they were shooed away by Mrs. Weera so Shauzia could rest.

The next day there was an attack on the Widows' Compound. Half a dozen men tried to get over the walls, yelling that the women inside were immoral and should not be allowed to live together without men to watch over them.

Mrs. Weera and the other women beat the men back over the walls with brooms and anything else they could grab. Shauzia was stuck on the charpoy. Her crutches had been returned to the clinic, so she could do nothing but watch and yell at the men. Jasper, with his bark and his bared teeth, helped scare the intruders away.

Mrs. Weera had to hire extra guards. She didn't say so, but Shauzia knew she was worried about how she was going to pay for them.

Shauzia spent the next few weeks sitting with the women from the embroidery project. She hemmed napkins and tablecloths and waited for her leg to heal.

FOURTEEN

The Red Crescent nurse put down her cast cutters and pulled apart the cast.

Shauzia's leg looked scrawny and weak.

"Try to stand," the nurse said.

Shauzia carefully put some weight on the leg. It twinged a bit, but otherwise it felt all right. Jasper gave her newly freed leg a big sniff and a gentle lick.

"It was a simple break," the nurse said. "You were lucky. Stay away from riots from now on."

Shauzia took some more steps, trying out her mended leg.

"We'll have your first-aid kits ready this afternoon," the nurse said to Mrs. Weera, who had brought Shauzia to the clinic. "When are you leaving?"

"Tomorrow, I think. Or maybe tonight. I can't decide whether it's safer for us to travel after dark, or if we should wait until daylight."

"Both have risks," the nurse agreed.

"Where are you going?" Shauzia asked. Was she really about to be free of Mrs. Weera?

"Mrs. Weera is a very brave woman," the nurse

said. “I hope you treat her with respect. She is taking several nurses back into Afghanistan.”

“You’re going back?” Shauzia almost yelled. “Why would you want to do that?”

“Our people are being bombed,” Mrs. Weera replied quietly. “Thousands have gathered at the border, trying to get out, but the border has been closed. Nurses are needed.”

“If the border is closed, how will you get in?”

“We’ll have to sneak in, probably across the mountains.”

“Just you women? You’ll never get away with it. The Taliban will arrest you.”

“We’ll have to take that chance,” Mrs. Weera told her. “People need us, and they’ll help us as best as they can. We should get back to the compound now. I have lots to do.”

The compound had been full of activity for the past week, but Shauzia hadn’t paid too much attention to it. The embroidery group had switched from fancy needlework to cutting strips of material for bandages and patching the worn spots in old blankets. Shauzia had noticed all the rushing around, but she had not cared to ask about it.

That evening she sat on the ground, her back against the hut where she slept, and where the women’s organization had their office. Women kept going in and coming out again. They paid no attention to her.

Farzana sat down beside her. Jasper thumped his tail and put his head in Farzana's lap.

"It's going to be awfully quiet without Mrs. Weera here," Farzana said.

"We'll still be able to hear her snoring at night. Even if she's on the other side of the world, her snores will reach us. She'll probably shatter the eardrums of all the Taliban soldiers, then take their place as ruler of Afghanistan."

"She'd have a whole country to boss around then," Farzana said with a giggle. "She'd like that."

"You think the Taliban has crazy laws? Mrs. Weera's would be even crazier. She'll force everyone to spend every afternoon playing field hockey."

Farzana laughed again. "She'll even make old people play, and the people on crutches."

"She's crazy!" Shauzia was angry now. She threw a stone across the courtyard, narrowly missing one of the busy women. "She's absolutely crazy to be going back into Afghanistan, especially without a man. She thinks she can make anything happen just because she wants it to happen. She's crazy!"

"What do you care?" Farzana asked. "You're going to the sea."

"That's right," Shauzia said. "Now that my cast is off, I'll be heading out."

"You're not taking me with you, are you?" Farzana asked.

Shauzia didn't reply.

"It's all right," Farzana said. "Mrs. Weera told me you wouldn't, but I already knew."

Shauzia didn't know what to say. She stroked Jasper's soft fur. She didn't like what she was feeling.

"So why do you just sit here?" Farzana asked. "Why don't you go?"

"I am going," Shauzia said. "I'm just resting first. It's a long way to the sea."

"Rest someplace else," Farzana said. "I don't want to be around you right now."

"I was sitting here before you were."

"Do you have to have everything your way? I'm staying right where I am. You leave."

"All right, I'd be glad to." Shauzia got to her feet. "Just about anybody would be better company than you. Come on, Jasper."

Jasper rolled his brown eyes to look at her, but his head stayed in Farzana's lap.

"Stupid dog," Shauzia said, and she stalked off away from them.

She found a place to sit against the compound wall, where she didn't have to look at anyone. Then she took the magazine photo of France out of her pocket.

Maybe it was the dim evening light. Maybe it was her anger at Jasper for choosing Farzana over her. Whatever it was, for some reason the field of purple flowers didn't look so inviting anymore. In fact, it looked a little dull.

Shauzia put the picture back in her pocket and

leaned against the wall. For a long while, she sat and thought.

"They're leaving! Mrs. Weera's leaving!"

Shauzia heard the call and got to her feet. She had to see them leave. She had to make certain Mrs. Weera was well and truly going.

Everyone from the compound gathered in the courtyard to say goodbye. Shauzia hung back, watching, wanting to run away, but feeling compelled to stay.

Mrs. Weera sought her out. She wrapped Shauzia in one of her giant hugs.

"You are a precious, precious child," Mrs. Weera said softly. "I hope you get to the sea. I hope France welcomes you with open arms. They would be lucky to get you."

Mrs. Weera released her and joined her nurses. With one final wave, they left the compound.

The others drifted off to their homes. Shauzia, Farzana and Jasper stood in the doorway and watched the women walk away.

"They'd be so much safer if they had a man with them," Shauzia said.

"Or even a boy," Farzana said.

Without another thought, Shauzia sprang into action. She fetched her shoulder bag and blanket shawl from the hut. She stopped briefly where Farzana and Jasper were standing.

"Take care of Jasper," she said to Farzana. "If the two of you get to the sea, give him a bath in the waves with this." She handed Farzana the bit of flowery soap from Tom and Barbara. Then she reached into her pocket, took out the photo of the lavender field, and gave that to Farzana, too.

Finally she bent down and hugged Jasper hard. She knew he wouldn't mind that she was crying.

Shauzia left the compound then, and headed off to meet Mrs. Weera and the nurses.

She had almost twenty years before she had to meet her friend Parvana at the top of the Eiffel Tower in Paris. She'd get there. But first she had a little job to do.

Mrs. Weera had long legs. Shauzia had to run to catch up to her.

AUTHOR'S NOTE

Afghanistan is a small country that lies between Europe and Asia. It contains mountain ranges, fast-flowing rivers and golden deserts. Its fertile valleys once produced an abundance of fruit, wheat and vegetables.

Throughout history, explorers and traders have passed through Afghanistan and tried to control it for their own interests. The country has been more or less continuously at war since 1978, when American-backed fighters opposed the Soviet-supported government. In 1980, the Soviet Union invaded Afghanistan, and the war escalated, with the United States backing Afghan freedom fighters, many of whom were war lords. The fighting was fierce, cruel and prolonged.

After the Soviets were defeated in 1989, a civil war erupted, as various groups fought for control of the country. Millions of Afghans became refugees, and some still live in huge camps in Pakistan, Iran and Russia. Many people have spent their whole lives in these camps, and millions of Afghans have been killed, maimed or blinded.

The Taliban militia, one of the groups that the US and Pakistan once funded, trained and armed, took control of the capital city of Kabul in September 1996. They imposed extremely restrictive laws on girls and women. Schools for girls were closed down, women were no longer allowed to hold jobs, and strict dress codes were enforced. Books were burned, televisions smashed, and music in any form was forbidden.

In the fall of 2001, al Qaeda, a terrorist group based in Afghanistan and protected by the Taliban, launched attacks on the Pentagon and the World Trade Center in New York City. In response, the United States led a coalition of nations into bombing Afghanistan and drove the Taliban from power. Elections were held and a new government and constitution were set up. A number of schools for boys and girls were opened, and in some parts of the country women were allowed back into the work force.

However, Afghanistan is far from being a nation of peace, for many reasons. The Taliban has returned to fight a very effective guerrilla war against the government and foreign forces. Afghanistan has become a major producer of opium, from which heroin is made. There is a great deal of corruption at all levels of government. Finally, Afghans, like people around the world, are uncomfortable with foreign forces fighting in their country.

Struggles for women's rights continue as well, with girls' schools being burned and women activists being assassinated.

There are no easy answers for the people of Afghanistan as they face such a difficult situation. Learning more about this beautiful, tragic country and its wonderful people is one small way to try to avoid the many mistakes outsiders have made that have brought Afghans to this difficult time in their history.

GLOSSARY

Badakhshan – A province of northeast Afghanistan.

bolani – A kind of dumpling.

burqa – A long, tent-like garment worn by women. It covers the entire body and has a narrow mesh screen over the eyes.

chador – A piece of cloth worn by women and girls to cover their hair and shoulders.

charpoy – A bed consisting of a frame strung with tapes or light rope.

Dari – One of the two main languages spoken in Afghanistan.

Eid – A Muslim festival coming at the end of Ramadan, the month of fasting.

Ghengis Khan – The Mongol conqueror (1162-1227) who formed a vast empire that stretched from China to Persia.

jenazah – A Muslim prayer for the dead.

karachi – A cart on wheels pushed by hand, used to sell things in the market.

kebab – Pieces of meat on a skewer, cooked over a fire.

land mine – A bomb planted in the ground, which explodes if it is stepped on.

mullah – A religious expert and teacher of Islam.

nan – Afghan bread. It can be flat, long or round.

Pashtu – One of the two main languages spoken in Afghanistan.

pattu – A gray or brown woolen blanket shawl worn by Afghan men and boys.

pilaf – A rice dish that usually contains vegetables, meat and spices.

Ramadan – A month of fasting in the Muslim calendar.

Red Crescent – The Muslim equivalent of the Red Cross, an international organization that provides aid to the sick and wounded in times of disaster and war.

roupee – Basic unit of money in Pakistan.

shalwar kameez – Long, loose shirt and trousers, worn by both men and women. A man's shalwar kameez is one color, with pockets in the side and on the chest. A woman's shalwar kameez has different colors and patterns and is sometimes elaborately embroidered or beaded.

Soviets – The Soviet Union before its break-up, including Russia and other Communist countries.

Taliban – An Afghan army that took control of the capital city of Kabul in September 1996, and was forced from power in the fall of 2001.

attress used in many stead of chairs or beds.

ons, an international organization tes peace, security and economic ent.

– United Nations High Commission on ugees.

ek – The language of the Uzbek people of central Asia.

MY NAME IS PARVANA
DEBORAH ELLIS

Whatever became of the brave, resourceful heroine of *The Breadwinner*? At last, readers can find out...

In post-Taliban Afghanistan, American soldiers have just imprisoned a teenaged girl. But who is she? Why was she found wandering alone in a bombed-out school? Could she be a terrorist?

The girl is held on an American military base and interrogated. Yet she does not respond to questions in any language and remains silent, even when she is threatened, harassed and mistreated over several days. The only clue to her identity is a tattered shoulder bag containing papers that refer to people named Shauzia, Nooria, Leila, Asif, Hassan — and Parvana.

In this long-awaited sequel to *The Breadwinner Trilogy*, Parvana, now fifteen, waits for foreign military forces to determine her fate as she remembers the past four years of her life. Reunited with her mother and sisters, she has been living in a village where her mother has finally managed to open a school for girls. It's the life Parvana has been dreaming of.

But this is Afghanistan, the war is far from over, and many continue to view the education and freedom of girls and women with suspicion and fear.

And that means Parvana — and her family — are in danger.

Hardcover with jacket • 978-1-55498-297-4 • $16.95 CDN / US
EPUB • 978-1-55498-299-8 • $14.95 CDN / US

ABOUT THE AUTHOR

DEBORAH ELLIS has achieved international acclaim with her courageous and dramatic books that give Western readers a glimpse into the plight of children in developing countries. She has won the Governor General's Award, Sweden's Peter Pan Prize, the Ruth Schwartz Award, the University of California's Middle East Book Award, the Jane Addams Children's Book Award and the Vicky Metcalf Award. A long-time feminist and anti-war activist, she is best known for her Breadwinner Trilogy — a series that has been published around the world in twenty-five languages, with more than one million dollars in royalties donated to Street Kids International and to Canadian Women for Women in Afghanistan. She recently received the Ontario Library Association's President's Award for Exceptional Achievement, and she has also been named to the Order of Ontario.

Deb lives in Simcoe, Ontario.